REGARDING REBECCA

❖

Hearts of Cornwall

K. LYN SMITH

Copyright © 2026 by K. Lyn Smith
All rights reserved. No part of this publication may be reproduced, stored or transmitted in any form or by any means without the prior written permission of the author. The only exception is by a reviewer, who may quote short excerpts in a review.

Regarding Rebecca is a work of fiction. Unless otherwise indicated, names, characters, places and incidents are products of the author's imagination or are used fictitiously. Any resemblance to actual events, locales or persons, living or dead, is entirely coincidental.

Davenwood Press, USA
Paperback ISBN: 979-8-9911573-4-6

GET A FREE BOOK

Subscribe to K. Lyn Smith's newsletter at klynsmithauthor.com and receive a free copy of the Hearts of Cornwall prequel novella, *Discovering Wynne*.

"[Miss Bing] writes me word that Miss Blackford is married, but I have never seen it in the papers, and one may as well be single if the wedding is not to be in print."

— Jane Austen,
in a letter to niece Anna Lefroy

CHAPTER 1

NEWFORD, CORNWALL—SUMMER, 1821

Merryn Kimbrell stood in his cousin's bank office, one hand bracketing his jaw as he studied the anonymous draft. It had been issued by a London bank and drawn on the account of an intermediary, so there was little chance of identifying its origin.

"I cannot like it," he said, replacing the paper on James's broad desk.

Several of their relations had joined them in the office and now watched him, waiting. Sunlight came through a pair of windows that commanded a view of Newford from the top of the high street. Merryn pressed a loose board in the oak floor with his boot. He'd send someone with nails soon to repair it, but for now, the question of his anonymous subscription was the more pressing matter.

"'Tis a generous investment," James said, and the others indicated their agreement.

Merryn couldn't argue the point. "You say it came with assurances of more?"

James leaned back in his chair behind the desk and lifted a letter bearing a London postmark. "Aye. According to the bank, the draft is only the first payment, with more funds to follow as the work progresses. They've undertaken to manage the investment on behalf of their client, whoever that may be."

"You've no notion who might have sent it?" Gavin asked. He stood near the door, feet braced for trouble.

Merryn shook his head. "I've corresponded with a number of London gentlemen in the past weeks, but I can't imagine any would desire to keep his involvement in the project secret."

"Per'aps 'tis a gentleman accustomed to doing business with Sir Felix, and he doesn't want his investment with another known?" This came from Alfie, who was at the windows with his arms crossed. "There are many who wouldn't look favorably on a man's support of their rival—and certainly not where royal favor is at stake."

"Per'aps," Merryn agreed. "But though I enjoy the sentiment, I doubt Sir Felix considers me a rival so much as a flea on his dog." With a title to his name, Sir Felix had no reason to concern himself with a builder who had nothing but his reputation and the quality of his work to recommend him.

"'Tis only a matter of time before His Majesty sees your superior work," Jory said. "His favor will open all manner of doors throughout Cornwall. Britain, even."

While Merryn appreciated his cousins' trust in him, they couldn't afford to risk their own investments. Jory and his wife had a young daughter to consider—a pretty lass with blue eyes and a head of gold curls. Indeed, a number of Merryn's cousins had recently found their way to newly-wedded bliss. A failed investment—and royal disfavor—would hardly be a fitting start to their marriages.

The thought allowed a memory of coppery locks to slip through the stout barrier in his mind before he muscled it back out. Five years of practice had made him an expert at such discipline. He put his attention back to the matter at hand.

He had a decision to make. Accept his unknown benefactor's investment in Newford's royal preparations or return the funds. The anonymous amount neatly filled the gap between what he'd already secured and what he needed to complete the harbor improvements... and the bridge and the road works and an ambitious pavilion in which to receive His Majesty. A gap that had been steadily growing as the costs of the work continued to climb. With the assurance of more funds to follow, he would be foolish not to consider it.

There was another option, of course. The bank book in his desk at home held funds enough to solve this dilemma and more besides. For five years that money had sat untouched. He'd told himself it was a matter of principle, but lately, he'd begun to wonder if his refusal was honorable as much as it was stupid.

Still, he would not. Could not.

Which left him with little choice but to accept the anonymous amount.

Aside from his cousins, Merryn had other investors who eagerly awaited progress on the work that would earn Newford the King's favor, and discontent was already brewing. Trewyck, who maintained an estate near Weirmouth, had been making noises about putting his funds elsewhere. Perhaps with Sir Felix in Truro. The sooner Merryn could complete the harbor improvements, the easier they all would be.

"An investment like this might put a halt to Trewyck's retreat," Alfie said in echo of Merryn's thoughts.

"Per'aps you could put it to the other investors," Jory suggested. "They should know what funds are backing their own."

Merryn rubbed his jaw. "And hear ten opinions from ten men? We've no time for that manner of debate." He looked to James. "The bank says the account is in good standing?"

James nodded. "The draft wants only your endorsement."

"'Tis nothing short of suspicious," Gavin said, and his skepticism was nothing less than Merryn expected from his constable cousin.

"You think I should return it then?"

"I think you shouldn't depend upon it."

Merryn released a breath. "I'll give it more thought before I decide," he said. It was the only assurance he could give them at this point. He collected the draft from James's desk and resettled his hat on his head.

After leaving his cousins, Merryn returned to his office at the other end of the high street. Situated near Newford's small harbor, it overlooked the river that emptied into the sea.

Merryn still thought of the building firm as his father's, though Pedrek Kimbrell had been gone for more than a decade.

His father's office. His father's massive oak desk and worn-in leather chair.

His father's worktable near the windows, though it was now papered with designs for reinforcing the bridge to Truro, and plans for renovations at the squire's Abbey, where George IV would be entertained with a grand ball.

Merryn leaned back in the chair behind the desk and spied a letter bearing Trewyck's seal atop his afternoon post. With resignation, he opened it.

The man, as he feared, had grown tired of waiting. Trewyck threatened to withdraw his investment if more funds weren't found. To add insult to injury, he'd decided to support the preparations at Truro instead.

If Trewyck carried through with his threat, more withdrawals would follow. Merryn might be forced to abandon the project altogether, and Newford would lose any chance of hosting His Majesty. His jaw tightened against a sigh, and he considered the dilemma of his anonymous investor. He took the bank draft from his coat and read the amount once more. Then, with a bit of uneasiness still twisting through him, he endorsed it with a firm stroke of his pen.

The King would come, and Merryn would see that Newford was ready to receive him properly.

CHAPTER 2

PARIS

THE SOUNDS OF merriment coming from the salon were loud and unceasing, and Rebecca escaped to her darkened sitting room with a sigh. She loved her aunt dearly, but Tante Eugénie's friends could be a trifle exhausting, even at the best of times. And with her solicitor's letter weighing on her mind, this was decidedly *not* the best of times.

She pressed the door closed and leaned against it as Monsieur Dupont's rumbling laughter sounded again. Mrs. Pemberton must have made another droll jest. Straightening from the door, Rebecca lit a candle from the fire in the grate then moved to the writing desk.

The window above it overlooked her aunt's garden, which was bright with torchlight. The paths held no fewer than a dozen statues of masculine figures, some with less draping than others, and all carved of smooth alabaster. Five years before, as an innocent newly arrived from England, she'd made herself look at them until she could do so without blushing.

The effect of all this study had only prompted thoughts of the husband she'd left behind. Was he formed in the same manner? She couldn't imagine that any man of flesh and blood could be so nicely shaped, although her husband's arm had felt pleasantly firm beneath her hand the few times they'd walked out together before their marriage.

Thoughts of her husband put her in mind of her solicitor's letter, which put her stomach in an uncomfortable knot. She needed something to distract her thoughts, and her ledgers never failed to do it.

She unlocked a drawer and withdrew the topmost book from the desk. Opening it to the current month, she studied the tidy list of accounts.

Amelie, Mrs. Pemberton's lady's maid... 1,785 francs.

Lisette, governess to the neighbor's children... 12,750.

Georgiana, seamstress... 8,670.

Sarah, her own lady's companion... 58,000 francs—nearly three *thousand* pounds. Soon, her companion would achieve her goal.

The list went on for a dozen ladies.

The investments had done well, and the ladies' balances were growing. The amounts weren't large by Rebecca's standards, but they were everything to the ladies on the list. They were the beginnings of independence. Not enough to keep a carriage or enter high society, but certainly enough to rent a small house and dress neatly.

It was improper to feel so much satisfaction for the figures, but that was precisely the sentiment that coursed through her whenever she reviewed them. She'd fought for her own independence—she understood its value better than most. Which made her solicitor's latest communication all the more troubling.

No longer able to ignore her unease, she withdrew Nathaniel Cross's letter from the desk. Though she'd never met him, he had served as her solicitor these past years with the same dedication his father had previously shown her uncle. She had no reason to doubt his report, but that didn't make it any more palatable.

He wrote of Rebecca's cousin, Mr. Gregory Pearce, a man she'd not seen since he sailed for the West Indies a decade before. But accounts had it that Gregory was now returning to England. Though his father—Rebecca's Uncle William—had left him well situated, he'd suffered a number of reversals.

Rumor indicated the sinking of an expensive sugar cargo was among the most recent. Under normal circumstances, her cousin's financial woes wouldn't have been any concern of Rebecca's, but Mr. Cross's letter suggested that might soon change.

The sound of breaking glass came from the salon, followed by her aunt's melodious laughter. Monsieur Dupont must have dropped something again—the man was a hazard to fine crystal. Rebecca ought to return, if only to guard her aunt's remaining goblets, but the solicitor's letter kept her rooted in place.

Mr. Cross went on to say Gregory's agents had made inquiries at the parish church at St. Marylebone—the same church where Rebecca had wed some years before. It seemed her cousin meant to find some flaw in the arrangement.

Her marriage had been hastily done only hours before her uncle's passing. She'd long known that the terms of her father's trust placed her inheritance under her uncle's guardianship until she married or reached the age of thirty. It had been her uncle William who pointed out that on his death, the control of her funds would pass to Gregory. Given her cousin's imprudence, it was doubtful there would have been any funds remaining when it came to her.

Instead, the management of her funds had

passed to her new husband—an imperfect solution, to be sure, but the only one available to her.

The arrangement had been her idea. In exchange for securing her inheritance, she offered him a modest amount to fund his ambitions. He would have capital to build his business, and she would live as she pleased. Theirs would be a marriage in name only.

Her reasons had been simple enough. As a girl, she'd seen her mother's unhappiness in a marriage where her father controlled every expenditure, doling out meager allowances for even the smallest purchases when there'd been no need for such parsimony. Her mother had possessed few freedoms, and Rebecca was determined to avoid the same fate. When she'd explained this to Merryn, he hadn't scoffed at her desire for independence. He'd simply agreed to her terms.

Such an arrangement, of course, required a man as honorable as he was willing. In Merryn Kimbrell, she'd found both. It was a great irony that to secure her independence, she'd had to bind herself to another.

Now, Mr. Cross advised her to return to England "forthwith," so they might put her cousin's inquiries to rest. She was tempted to decline his summons. Gregory could make all the inquiries he wished, but he'd find only the truth. Her marriage was well and duly recorded in the parish register, and nothing would alter the fact. As her guardian, Gregory's own father had given his approval for the match. It ought to have been enough.

But Mr. Cross's words carried a bit of urgency to them, which was unusual for the normally unflappable retainer. And Rebecca, who'd grown rather fond of her independence, felt uneasy for it.

She refolded the solicitor's missive and slid it back into her desk. As she closed the drawer, it caught on a stack of letters bound with a crimson ribbon. She loosened them and squared the edges.

The pile had grown steadily over the years, quarter by quarter. Her husband was nothing if not regular in his correspondence. He'd written without fail, always to inquire after her well-being and whether she required anything.

Though he was the legal trustee of her inheritance, he'd held to his end of their bargain. He never questioned her management of her funds—only offered his support should she need it. Indeed, his letters were each accompanied by a draft drawn on Coutts Bank of London. It was sweet. She had no need for his funds, of course, but she appreciated his consideration.

She toyed with the end of the ribbon but jerked her hand back when a light knock sounded at the door. Shoving the drawer closed, she locked it before responding. "Yes?"

"It is only I," Sarah said as she looked around the door.

Fine threads of silver streaked her dark, neatly coiled hair. Rebecca's governess-turned-companion glanced around the dim room before returning her gaze to Rebecca.

"Are you well?" she asked.

"I am." Then, acknowledging the oddity of sitting in the dark while her aunt's friends gathered down the hall, Rebecca added, "Merely a bit fatigued is all."

"That's understandable. Your aunt has rather outdone herself this year." Sarah's tone was crisp and dry.

She wasn't wrong. What Tante Eugénie had assured Rebecca would be "only a small gathering" for Rebecca's twenty-sixth birthday had blossomed into a week-long celebration: impromptu suppers and salons, outings to the opera and the ballet at the Théâtre des Tuileries and just today, a grand breakfast that had somehow continued well into the night.

Sarah looked to the ledger on the desk. "You've been reviewing the accounts again. Have you worked more of your magic then on our balances?"

Rebecca rose and smoothed her skirt. "Have I taught you nothing?" she teased. "You know very well it is not magic so much as diligence and a judicious management of the risk."

Management of the risk. That brought Mr. Cross's report to mind once more. Returning to England would be an inconvenience, certainly, but it was one she shouldn't avoid if she meant to keep her independence.

Smiling brightly, she said, "Now, what do you say to a journey?"

CHAPTER 3

LONDON

Though Rebecca had grown up in London, the city's streets felt foreign to her after so much time in Paris. They were narrower than the grand boulevards to which she'd become accustomed and lined with buildings of Georgian style and English symmetry. Even the air was different—heavy with damp coal smoke rather than perfumes and warm pastries.

As the carriage rattled over the cobbles toward Mr. Cross's office, she wondered how long she must remain this side of the Channel. The more she thought about it, the more she believed her solicitor's fears were unfounded. Her cousin could have no grounds on which to challenge her marriage. She'd sort this matter quickly and return to Paris—

perhaps in time for the opening of Rossini's latest opera.

"It is nice to be back in England," Sarah said with a sigh. Rebecca couldn't miss the brightness in her companion's features as they watched the city pass beyond the small window.

"Have you been very unhappy in Paris?" she asked.

Sarah turned her attention from the bustling market to Rebecca. "Unhappy? No, but you must admit there's a certain satisfaction in returning to the land of one's family. Do you not agree?"

"I no longer have family in England," Rebecca said. Too late, she realized her error, if one counted one's husband as family.

"Do you not?"

Rebecca gave her companion a quelling look that ended the conversation. It was a relief when they passed through the towered gatehouse at Chancery Lane. A clerk met them at the entrance to a modest building nestled within Lincoln's Inn. The outer chamber was dimly lit, and the soft glow of oil lamps cast faint shadows on the furnishings. The clerk showed Sarah to a comfortable chair where she might wait before leading Rebecca down a narrow corridor.

She found the younger Mr. Cross to be an even-featured man of about thirty, with a straight nose and firm chin that put her in mind of his late father. He rose from behind the desk to offer Rebecca a courteous bow.

"Please, have a seat," he said with a nod for the chair before the desk. "I trust your journey was a pleasant one."

"It was pleasant enough, though I must say I'd rather not have made it at all."

He frowned behind his spectacles. "I assure you, I would not have suggested your return if I didn't think the situation warranted it. But I do believe it will be best if you meet personally with Mr. Pearce once he reaches England. Only then do I think his questions will be satisfied."

"I trust your judgment," Rebecca assured him, "so I must ask: what is it about my cousin's inquiries that give you cause for worry?"

He pulled a file toward him on the desk and opened it. Rifling the pages there, he pulled out one with copious notations made in a strong hand.

"It wouldn't be a matter for concern if your cousin had only inquired at the church, but his solicitors have also made it a point to approach your bank."

Rebecca's eyes widened. "My bank? To what end?"

"To ascertain the balance of your trust, one can only assume." Rebecca scowled, and he lifted a hand to stem her protest. "I have put a stop to that line of inquiry, you may be assured. But it's clear your cousin believes your marriage is invalid. He seems quite confident in his ability to challenge it."

"But my marriage was very properly done. Your father was even a witness to it." An unwelcome thought came to her and she leaned forward. "Was there some problem with the license?"

"No, no, it's nothing like that." Mr. Cross steepled his hands before him. A heavy silence passed before he spoke again.

"When I took on my father's cases, I reviewed his notes. I understand he advised that an unconsummated marriage could be contested, if an interested party was of a mind to do such a thing." He looked at her over the rim of his spectacles. "You and your husband have lived apart these five years."

Rebecca swallowed as heat warmed her face. "Your father's counsel was duly considered."

Mr. Cross busied himself dipping his pen. His mouth twisted as he made a notation on the paper before him.

Rebecca ignored her English sensibilities to add, "Your father also advised that proving such a claim would be problematic. So what legal argument is then left to my cousin?"

"Fraud," he said simply.

"Fraud?" she repeated, the word tight in her throat.

He set the pen back in the stand and steepled his fingers once more. "Your cousin could argue that Mr. Kimbrell manipulated your uncle into approving the match, thereby preventing your cousin from assuming his rightful place as trustee. If your marriage were dissolved, your trust would return to Mr. Pearce's management until you reach thirty years of age." He cleared his throat. "The trustee fees to which he would be entitled on such an amount are... considerable."

That understated the matter, for the trustee fees were not the problem. If her cousin had the management of her inheritance, Rebecca did not doubt it would fall the way of his own funds, and with it, her independence.

"But your father—"

"Is no longer here," Mr. Cross said gently. "I do apologize," he said in a low voice, "but perhaps he didn't lay out the risks for you as clearly as he might have done."

Rebecca's throat tightened. "But surely there must be some evidence to support the legitimacy of my marriage. It was quickly done, it's true, but that doesn't make it fraudulent. Your father must have kept records of the settlement negotiations. There would have been correspondence with my uncle—"

Mr. Cross's expression turned regretful. "There were records, yes. Unfortunately, my office suffered a fire some months ago, and my father's papers were destroyed."

"All of them?"

He shook his head. "I salvaged what I could, but I'm afraid there's nothing that proves your intent five years ago." He adjusted his spectacles. "I'm sorry."

The room seemed to tilt, and Rebecca clasped her hands more tightly. "Then I must ask—why now? My cousin has known of my marriage these five years. What has prompted his inquiries?"

The solicitor's discomfort was plain. "I confess, that may be my fault. When I inventoried what remained of my father's papers, I discovered certain documents. They appeared to have been overlooked when settling your uncle's affairs, so I sent them on to Mr. Pearce." He met her eyes. "They contained a rather thorough accounting of your trust."

"I don't understand."

"At the time, I thought the omission nothing more than oversight. Now, I suspect my father and your uncle may have withheld those particulars deliberately."

"Ah." Understanding settled over her. "My cousin was previously unaware of the full extent of my fortune."

"It would appear so."

Rebecca drew a breath and tried to think. The loss of evidence was certainly a blow, but marriages like hers were common enough.

"Fraud," she said, returning to his earlier assertion. "How could my cousin prove such a thing? Marriages are contracted for the sake of convenience all the time. Alliances are made for money or position, and husbands and wives go their separate ways. It's how things are done."

Mr. Cross nodded. "Normally, a case like this would be hard to win," he admitted.

"Normally…?"

Mr. Cross's jaw tightened, and she knew she wouldn't like his answer. "If either party to the marriage views the union as a sham… Well. Perhaps it's best if I simply show you."

Leaning back, he withdrew a small pamphlet from his desk. He slid it across the polished surface, and confusion pulled at her brow as she took it. The pamphlet was a recent publication: *The Newford Inventory*.

Newford. Her stomach made a small turn behind her rib cage.

She opened the pamphlet. It appeared to be an inventory of… bachelors. Page after page of eligible gentlemen and their attributes. Height, family status, prospects… It was a rather pragmatic ac–

counting, much like a fashion periodical detailing the finest features of the latest pelisse.

Indeed, she thought it would have been amusing to get a husband in such a fashion, were she in the market for one. Then, with Mr. Cross looking on and a weight falling in her midsection, she knew.

She turned the pages more quickly until she found what she sought. An uncomfortable, twisty warmth filled her as she stared at her husband's entry.

She laid the inventory aside. "Well. This certainly puts a wrinkle in things."

"WE'RE GOING TO Cornwall?" Sarah said when they were back in the carriage. "When?"

"As soon as Marie can have us packed again," Rebecca said tightly.

"You're going to see him, aren't you?" Her companion's voice carried a bit of smug satisfaction that Rebecca ignored.

She said only, "I've a rather urgent need to speak with my husband." *My husband*. The words sounded odd coming from her, so rarely did she say them aloud. Then she considered Sarah's earlier wistfulness about her own family. "You've a sister near Taunton haven't you?"

Her companion pulled her head back at the change in topic. "Yes," she said slowly. "Alice is married to a surgeon there."

"Very well. Accompany me to Newford. When I return to London, you may travel on to your sister. I will cover the fare."

"Thank you," Sarah said.

Rebecca thought again of her cousin's challenge and wondered if she'd been too hasty in offering to pay Sarah's fare. There was a very real possibility she wouldn't have the funds to pay for her own fare soon, much less that of a companion. It was a sobering thought.

No, she told herself. It was too early to think about economizing, although Rebecca did have a number of things to consider. Not the least of which was the stark and unexpected fact that her husband hadn't told anyone of their marriage. He could not have, if he was putting himself out as a bachelor.

Hadn't told anyone. Disbelief caused the refrain to play over and over in her mind. How would her cousin ever be convinced their marriage wasn't a sham, with her husband advertising his eligibility in such a manner?

As the carriage neared their lodgings at Mivart's, her initial shock gave way to muddled confusion and... hurt. And anger, but mostly... hurt. Which made no sense, really. Theirs was a marriage of convenience, after all. A marriage that was becoming decidedly *in*convenient. Clearly, her husband must have thought so as well.

She couldn't—she *wouldn't*—lose her independence. But in order to keep it, she required the funds left to her by her father.

Mr. Cross was right—the best way to defend against her cousin's suspicions was to meet them directly. An audience with Gregory, face to face, was paramount. But Gregory and his solicitors wouldn't be content to meet solely with her. To meet him without her husband at her side would only strengthen his position.

No, she must find Merryn and bring him back to London. Forcibly, if need be.

By Mr. Cross's estimation, her cousin would land in England in six weeks. And in six weeks, she and her husband must present themselves as properly married.

CHAPTER 4

THE *CONCORDIA* ROUNDED the headland, and Rebecca pressed closer to the rail as Newford came into view. After three days at sea, she was eager to reach their destination.

Her stomach fluttered with more than just the ship's motion, for in a matter of hours, she might meet her husband again.

Sarah joined her and placed a shaky hand on the rail. She had spent most of the rolling voyage in their small quarters, and Rebecca hoped the feel of steady land beneath their feet would put some color back in her cheeks.

Ahead of them, Newford nestled in a protected cove, with cottages climbing the hillside from the water's edge. They were bright against the verdant landscape as if they'd been freshly whitewashed. Even the quay looked newly constructed, its stones unmarked by years of tide and weather.

She wondered about Merryn's home—was it nearby or tucked up in the surrounding hills?

The harbor bustled with activity while an ancient stone church anchored the other end of the little hamlet. It was all very quaint, but what struck her most was the amount of scaffolding. Wooden supports rose around several buildings, workers swarmed over what appeared to be a new structure near the harbor, and piles of more timbers and stone dotted the waterfront.

She knew her husband's latest improvement venture was larger than the ones he'd previously undertaken, but the sheer scale of it was unexpected.

"Newford is busier than I thought it would be," Sarah said slowly, and Rebecca nodded her agreement. She'd never been to her husband's home, but she had imagined something quiet and… poky.

"What on earth is he building?" she murmured.

"Perhaps the town is merely growing," Sarah offered, though her tone held doubt.

Rebecca's gaze was drawn to movement at the structure above the harbor. She watched as a team of men maneuvered a massive post into place. At their center, directing the operation, stood a figure whose tall frame and confident bearing was still familiar to her, even at a distance of five years. Her heart gave an uncomfortable skip. Merryn.

The ship's captain called out orders as the packet anchored in the deeper water offshore.

A sailor appeared at her elbow. "Miss Pearce? I can help you ashore, ma'am, if you're ready." Her maiden name sounded odd to her ears after so long abroad, but Rebecca had thought it prudent to use. Whatever Merryn had told the people of Newford — or *not* told them, as the case were — she had no wish to cause a stir by arriving as Mrs. Merryn Kimbrell.

She allowed herself to be handed down to a small boat. Her maid Marie followed with Sarah, and their trunks were lowered after them. The oarsmen ferried them toward the quay, which was ripe with the smell of fish. Soon, lines were thrown to waiting dock workers.

Rebecca turned on the seat, but her husband's form was nowhere to be seen. He'd moved on already to some other task.

After they'd stepped onto solid ground, she offered the sailor a coin for his trouble. "Can you direct us to suitable accommodations, sir?"

The man removed his hat to scratch his forehead, clearly waiting to see if more coin would follow. She lifted her brows, but just when another coin seemed inevitable, a small voice spoke from behind her.

"Oi, mum. Ye'll be wantin' the Feather."

Rebecca turned to find a slight lad trailing a handcart behind him.

"Aye," the sailor relented with a scowl. "The lad's the right of it."

"Is it close?" Sarah inquired of the boy as the sailor loped off.

He gave a nod for the hill leading up from the harbor. "We're nearly there, mum, right up the high street. The Fin and Feather be the tallest building in Newford," he added with pride, "wot with a new floor added just last month." He doffed his cap. "Leo's me name. I'll be seein' yer things up right and proper."

Rebecca eyed the boy and his handcart. Her trunk was nearly as long as he was tall. That he thought to lift it onto the cart without tipping it into the sea showed an admirable optimism.

"That is very kind," she said gently, "but I do not think—"

She broke off when he gave her a wink.

"Oi!" he called to a man across the pavement. The broad fellow had shoulders capable of lifting a lady's trunk. Rebecca's uncertainty eased when he hoisted their trunks onto the cart as if they weighed no more than her reticule.

Leo leaned toward her. "Mrs. Teague allus says to use yer wits afore yer back, but she ain't said nofink 'bout usin' another's back."

And on that piece of wisdom, their small porter led the way up from the harbor towing the handcart behind him. The bustling construction activity was even more impressive at close range. New timber framing rose from existing stone foundations, and the scent of fresh sawdust mingled with the salt air. Carts loaded with supplies rumbled past.

Her husband's "improvements project" was more ambitious than she had ever supposed. The scale of the work around them made her chest tighten with unease.

"Rebecca?" Sarah said when she slowed her steps. "Is anything amiss?"

Yes. Things were very much amiss. If Gregory were successful in contesting her marriage, not only would her trust revert to his control, but all she had earned from it as well. Including the funds she'd put into Merryn's latest work.

Rebecca shook her head in reply and resumed her pace. "My husband has been very busy," she murmured.

They found the inn easily enough. The Fin and Feather sat a short distance up the high street, its red signboard creaking in the breeze. It was a broad stone building with mullioned windows that shone like mirrors in the afternoon sun. Flower boxes added cheerful color to the front, and the doorway looked freshly painted.

Rebecca paused at the entrance, suddenly uncertain. She and Merryn had agreed to pursue their own interests separate and apart from one another — an agreement she was now turning on its head. That he would be surprised to see her now was an understatement.

"Shall we?" Sarah prompted gently.

Drawing a breath, Rebecca nodded, and Sarah pushed the door open. Rebecca followed her through. The interior of the inn smelled warmly of beeswax, ale, and pie, and the slate floors were still damp from a recent scrubbing.

A woman looked up from a ledger atop a small desk. She had clear blue eyes, and her hair, drawn back in a simple style, was a brighter shade of red than Rebecca's own auburn tresses. Nearby, a babe cooed happily in a straw basket.

Leo wrestled his handcart through the door behind them.

"Good afternoon," the woman said before introducing herself as Mrs. Teague. Leo's sage adviser, Rebecca gathered — an assumption which resolved itself into fact when the boy called out to her.

"Mrs. Teague! I've brung you some lady customers."

The innkeeper ruffled the boy's hair as her lips quirked. "Apologies," she murmured to Rebecca. "Leo's discretion doesn't quite match his enthusiasm."

The boy bent toward the basket and teased the baby with one finger beneath her chin. Two charmingly plump fists waved the air, and the sound of infant giggles filled the room.

Rebecca ignored them to assure the woman, "I find candor far more useful than discretion." The words left an unpleasant taste in her mouth as she then proceeded to give the innkeeper her maiden name—an act of less candor than she would have liked.

Mrs. Teague inclined her head. "Now, where am I to put you?" She gave Rebecca's finely cut silk a swift but measured glance before considering her ledger.

"We require only clean and quiet accommodations."

"My rooms are the cleanest you'll find from here to Truro," Mrs. Teague promised, "but quiet I cannot guarantee." This statement was punctuated by a hammer pounding somewhere nearby.

The innkeeper tapped her chin with one slender finger. "Room twelve, I should think. You won't hear the commotion from the stables there, though I cannot do anything about the infernal hammering. But room twelve—'tis adjacent to another that will suit your maid and companion nicely."

"I'm certain it will serve."

"You are fortunate," Mrs. Teague said as she made a note in her book. "My rooms are usually full—on account of the Inventory and now with all the building, but a group of ladies left only this morning."

Rebecca had been adjusting her reticule on her wrist, but at the innkeeper's words, she stopped. "You refer to *The Newford Inventory*?"

"Gracious, is there another?"

"I am not aware of one." Rebecca hesitated before asking, "But you've had guests on account of it—to what purpose?"

"Why else but to inspect the bachelors on offer?"

Rebecca's brows climbed. Mrs. Teague was not averse to a bit of candor herself. "Were their visits... pleasant?" she asked, trying with effort to keep an edge from her tone.

Mrs. Teague snorted softly. "If you're asking if they found success in their aim, then the answer is no." Her eyes met Rebecca's and held. "And I doubt that will change anytime soon."

The innkeeper's pointed gaze drew a frown of confusion across Rebecca's brow until she realized the lady's implication. "Oh! But I've not come to—that is, I'm not looking for a husband," she said. She wasn't sure what to do with the one she had.

Mrs. Teague's smile was wry. "'Tis precisely what the others have said."

The sound of boots on the inn's cellar stairs made the woman turn. A deep voice said, "I'll send one of my men shortly to repair the leak—"

Rebecca's breath caught in her throat as her husband's figure came into view. Merryn looked much as he had five years before, though his shoulders seemed broader and his face more mature than she recalled. His dark hair held the impression from his hat, and there was a sprinkling of something—dust or plaster perhaps—on his sleeve.

He stopped speaking when his gaze found her, and his blue eyes widened. The noise of the inn and the street beyond faded until Mrs. Teague called, "Merryn! Come and meet my new guests, Miss Pearce and her companion, Miss Denning."

Merryn's gaze never left Rebecca's face. She watched as he composed himself, his mouth tightening before he managed a polite nod.

"Miss… Pearce," he said carefully. "Welcome to Newford."

The sound of her maiden name on his lips sent a strange and unwelcome shiver through her. Did he think that she, too, had forgotten their vows—or was he merely relieved he didn't have to explain the appearance of a wife?

"Mr. Kimbrell," she replied, proud that her voice remained steady. "How nice it is to see you again." She felt a twinge of satisfaction for the hint of uneasiness her words brought to her husband's countenance.

The innkeeper looked between them with confusion and no little amount of interest. "Are you already acquainted?"

"I encountered Mr. Kimbrell some years ago in London," Rebecca said, marveling at how easily the partial truth fell from her lips.

Merryn recovered and turned to Sarah with a kind smile—the one that creased the corners of his eyes and always produced a flutter low in Rebecca's stomach. "Miss Denning," he said. "'Tis a pleasure to make your acquaintance once again."

Sarah returned his greeting with a polite nod. "The pleasure is mine, Mr. Kimbrell."

"I trust your journey was not too taxing?"

"The packet was comfortable," Sarah replied, though her pallor belied her words.

"I am glad to hear it." He inclined his head courteously, and Rebecca nearly scoffed aloud at this bit of nonsense. The pair of them exchanged pleasantries as if they'd met during a leisurely walk in Hyde Park.

Straightening, Mrs. Teague turned to gather keys from the wall behind her desk.

Rebecca caught Merryn's eye. The look he gave her was unreadable, but she detected a hint of challenge beneath his composed exterior.

Mrs. Teague passed a pair of brass keys across the desk, her eyes going from Merryn to Rebecca and back again. "Mr. Kimbrell's building firm is responsible for all the improvements you see about you." To Merryn, she added, "I was just about to suggest to Miss Pearce that she have a tour of your new pavilion."

"I believe Miss Pearce has lately been in France," Merryn said. "I'm certain she would not be interested in such a provincial endeavor."

With a lift of her chin, she said, "Actually, I find myself quite interested in improvement projects. Perhaps you might show me your work sometime, Mr. Kimbrell."

His jaw firmed at her boldness. "Per'aps," he replied evenly. "Though building sites can be dangerous for the casual visitor."

Before she could offer a reply to that, the inn's door opened to admit a young woman with a dark-haired girl at her side. The woman's features were similar to Merryn's, though her expression was considerably more animated.

"Wynne!" she called cheerfully. "Emilia and I find ourselves in need of sustenance. Please say you've a fresh batch of tarts." The pair stopped then and took in the small gathering at the inn's desk.

"Bronwyn," Mrs. Teague said, "you are just in time to meet your brother's acquaintance from London, though Miss Pearce has lately been in France."

Rebecca studied the newcomer with interest. *Bronwyn.* This was her sister-in-law then.

Bronwyn's brows lifted at Mrs. Teague's pronouncement. "France! How lovely."

She looked expectantly at her brother. The silence stretched just long enough to become uncomfortable before Merryn conceded and made the introductions.

"Miss Pearce," he said stiffly, "Miss Denning, allow me to present my sister, Mrs. Marsh, and her daughter, Miss Emilia Marsh."

"It is a pleasure to make your acquaintance, ladies," Rebecca said.

Bronwyn smiled broadly. She had the sort of energy that filled a room. "I have never met one of my brother's London acquaintances," she said. "Per'aps we might have tea together while you're here. I'd love to hear more about your time in France."

Merryn cleared his throat. "I'm certain Rebecca—Miss Pearce—has other interests to occupy her in Newford."

Rebecca ignored him to reply to Bronwyn, "I should like that very much." She was surprised to find she meant it, not because Bronwyn was her husband's sister, but because the woman's manner seemed warm and engaging. She had a direct gaze that Rebecca found intriguing.

"Splendid!" Bronwyn said, then she glanced

with concern at Sarah, who'd taken a seat on a nearby bench. "I hope the journey wasn't too arduous for you, Miss Denning. If you don't mind me saying it, you're looking a bit whisht."

Rebecca was sorry to see her companion's color had not yet returned. Sarah managed a wan smile. "The sea and I have never been the best of friends, I'm afraid, but a good rest will set me right."

"You poor dear," Mrs. Teague clucked sympathetically. "You'll want something to settle your stomach properly, and our apothecary has just the thing."

"Of course!" Bronwyn said. "You must go there straight away. Merryn, per'aps you can escort Miss Pearce and her companion on your way to... wherever 'tis you go."

Merryn's expression tightened almost imperceptibly before he replied, "It would be my pleasure."

When Sarah stood and retied her bonnet strings as if she meant to accompany them, Rebecca was moved to protest. "You must rest, Sarah. Allow Mrs. Teague to show you to our rooms, and Marie can see you settled. Leave me to manage this simple errand for you."

"Miss Pearce," Sarah murmured, "this is not Paris. To walk unaccompanied with a gentleman—people notice such things in a place like this."

Rebecca strove to maintain her expression, though the absurdity of requiring a chaperone while walking with her own husband was not lost on her.

Merryn's gaze narrowed as he looked between them. "Your companion is right," he said. "This is not Paris."

There was just enough censure in his tone to raise an uncomfortable warmth in Rebecca's cheeks. "Very well," she said. "Let us go."

CHAPTER 5

REBECCA SMOOTHED HER gloves as she left the inn ahead of her husband with Sarah trailing behind. The afternoon sun slanted across Newford's high street, casting long shadows between the buildings. Construction sounds echoed from all directions—hammering, the scrape of stone against stone, and the rumble of cart wheels over cobblestones.

As Merryn joined her side, hands clasped behind him, she considered his tall form from the corner of her eye. His jaw was tight above the folds of a dark neckcloth. It seemed firmer than she recalled. Older and more defined, as though it had been chiseled from one of the cliffs that edged the sea.

Two gentlemen entered the inn behind them, casting curious glances toward Merryn and his unfamiliar companion. Rebecca opted for a polite topic as they began walking.

"Your sister is very pleasant," she said. Were the situation different—were her marriage a real one—she thought she might have enjoyed getting to know her sister-in-law.

Merryn's reply was a discouraging, "In her way."

The high street bustled, and Rebecca felt the curious gazes of more than one person as they passed. That the sight of her husband in company with a female occasioned so much interest ought to have given her some comfort. As it was, she felt unaccountably awkward beneath their scrutiny, as if she were a girl fresh from the schoolroom rather than a wife of six and twenty.

But she had lived these last five years as an Englishwoman in Paris. She was accustomed to being a foreigner.

She put on a smile. They passed a dressmaker and a bakery, then a chandler's shop and a foundry of some sort. Ahead of them, at the far end of the high street, lay the church with its square tower and low stone wall.

"Newford is quite charming," she said, taking in the whitewashed buildings with their slate roofs and flower boxes. "Shockingly so, given the sparse descriptions in your letters."

"I was unaware you required a detailed accounting."

She quirked a brow at him. "Yes, your quarterly

missives have always been rather direct and to the point. Very business-like."

"I thought that was the nature of our arrangement," he said. Then, with a visible effort, he collected himself. Drawing a breath through his nose, he said, "You are well?"

She set her mouth in a grim line, but she could hardly blurt the news of Gregory's return on the high street. She said simply, "I am well enough. And you?"

"Aye," was his response. "Well enough."

He stopped, drawing her to a halt, and nodded toward a narrow building nestled near the end of the street. "The apothecary... 'tis just there."

He stood with his hands still clasped behind his back like a ship's captain directing a fleet. His self-possession was one of the things that had drawn her to him five years before. Even at three and twenty, he'd conducted himself with a quiet, unshakable steadiness that convinced her he could be trusted to abide by their terms.

With a glance to assure they were not overheard, he said, "Have you come on a matter of money? Surely, 'tis something Mr. Cross could have addressed without your coming all this way."

"It is not a matter of money. I manage my portion very well, thank you."

He tipped his head. "Then to what do I owe the

honor of this visit?"

Rebecca swallowed at the bite in his tone. "I haven't come to upset your life," she assured him. "I've come to speak with you about our arrangement. There's been a… development."

A small tick in Merryn's jaw was the only indication he heard her.

Rebecca considered how best to present the matter of her cousin's return to England, but before she could organize her thoughts, a man in rough laborer's garb hurried across the cobbles toward them. Gripping a knit cap firmly in both hands, he paused to give Rebecca a respectful nod before turning to Merryn.

"Sir."

"What is't?"

"An accident. Us were movin' one of the beams as ye asked, but then it shifted and… well, 'tis come down on Dickey's leg."

"I'll be there directly," Merryn said. "Has Rowe been summoned?"

"Aye, the sawbones be on 'is way there now." The man hurried away, and Merryn turned to Rebecca.

"I hope your man's injuries aren't too severe," she said.

Merryn nodded. "As you can see, I'm very busy. If you wish to discuss our arrangement, per'aps 'twould be best if you made an appointment."

"But—"

Merryn touched his brim in a gesture that was more dismissal than courtesy then turned on his heel. She watched his retreating figure as he followed his employee back toward the harbor.

Sarah joined her, brows lifted in question.

Rebecca only shook her head. Make an appointment, indeed!

———

MR. DICKEY'S INJURIES weren't as serious as they might have been. The man had suffered some scrapes and bruises from the pavilion's falling beam but no broken bones that Rowe could find. The fact eased Merryn's guilt over the relief he'd felt at the interruption, but it couldn't have been timed any better to stop the flow of Rebecca's words.

There's been a development.

Her statement wouldn't stop circling his mind. What could she have meant by it? No matter how he tried to discern a different answer, there was only one that made sense: Rebecca wanted an end to their arrangement. Perhaps she'd met someone in Paris.

His heart gave an uncomfortable lurch. If he thought his secret marriage would set tongues to wagging, he could only imagine what a divorce would do. He might as well hang up his hammer, for no one would hire him to fix a broken door, much less invest in anything on the scale of his royal project. Not even the King, with his own marriage laid bare before Parliament, had been able to escape such scandal.

He released a long and creative string of curses but didn't feel any better for it.

At day's end, he rode out to Dickey's home to ensure the man was resting his leg as Rowe instructed. He sent someone for pies and stew to feed Dickey's family—the man's oldest boy had lately begun to grow like the hedges in spring.

Dusk had nearly fallen to full dark by the time he returned to Newford's high street. Lanterns lit the cobbles, and candlelight spilled out of the Feather's front window. Through the glass, his cousins gathered at their usual table. He would join them, but he didn't wish to encounter his wife. Not yet, at any rate.

With a bit of guilt pinching him, he wondered how she found the Feather's accommodations. Wynne and her husband ran a tidy and respectable establishment. She would have all the benefits of their hospitality, but he couldn't escape the thought that his wife should not be obliged to put up at an *inn*. He tried to picture her in his home instead, but the image wouldn't come as it once had.

A curtain moved in one of the Feather's upstairs rooms, and a figure appeared at the window. He stilled, his breath tight in his lungs as his horse stood motionless in the shadows, but it was only another guest. The curtain dropped, and he rode on toward home.

CHAPTER 6

REBECCA PASSED A fitful first night at the inn. Though the mattress was clean and firm, she tossed and twisted about for hours. It wasn't every day one met one's estranged husband, and she imagined some upset to her nerves was to be expected.

The next morning, she woke with puffy eyes and an uneasiness about the day ahead. Her confidence in her own resourcefulness had only grown during her years abroad, and she was unaccustomed to uncertainty. But this situation with Merryn, to say nothing of her cousin's impending return, caused her pulse to beat a little too strongly whenever she allowed herself a moment to think.

She shoved her uncertainties aside and pulled her wrapper tight as she eyed the garments Marie had hung in the wardrobe. She fingered a blue round gown before dropping it in favor of a dress in raspberry-red muslin. The pretty color never failed to lift her mood and bolster her courage, and certainly, her reluctant husband put her in need of bolstering.

After Marie finished pinning her hair, Rebecca collected her hat and gloves. Sarah soon joined her, looking much improved. When Rebecca said as much, her companion replied, "The apothecary's draught worked wonders, as did Mrs. Teague's fine mattress. What is your aim for the day?"

Rebecca drew herself up. "I aim to find my husband. As soon as he agrees to return to London with me, you may continue on to your sister. With any luck, I should think you'll be on your way by nightfall."

Sarah's answering look was both wry and indulgent. "I will wait to pack my things."

Her doubt increased Rebecca's uncertainty even as it stiffened her resolve.

They descended the inn's wide staircase to find Mrs. Teague at her desk with the infant sleeping peacefully in her basket.

"Miss Pearce," the innkeeper said. "I trust you slept well."

"I did," Rebecca lied and hoped the truth wasn't evident in the shadows beneath her eyes.

Mrs. Teague offered breakfast, and as the lady led them to the inn's private parlor, Rebecca asked where she might find Mr. Kimbrell.

Mrs. Teague smiled. "In Newford, you will have to be more specific. We've more than a few Mr. Kimbrells running about, but I imagine you refer to Merryn."

"Yes," Rebecca said, and at the faint lift of the woman's brow, she added, "I wish to thank him for his assistance yesterday with... with the apothecary."

"Well then, he's likely tucked away in his office near the harbor. And if not, then he'll be away to somewhere supervising one of his projects."

"In his office at this hour—truly?" Rebecca said.

"Merryn is always working, except on Sundays, o' course. 'Twould be easiest to give him your thanks at the church."

"But certainly, he cannot work *always*."

The innkeeper drew open the door to the parlor. "Very nearly so, unless he's warming a seat in my coffee room. My cousin has a liking for my raspberry tarts."

"Your cousin? Mr. Kimbrell is your relation?"

"Oh, aye. I was a Kimbrell afore I was a Teague."

Rebecca blinked and absently accepted a serviette from the woman. Cousin. Wynne Teague was Rebecca's cousin by marriage. The lady offered hospitality, and Rebecca returned it with lies and secrets. She silently cursed her husband for not telling his family he had married.

What had he been thinking?

Any appetite she might have had, fled, and she knew only a pressing urge to find Merryn. When the innkeeper left them, she turned to Sarah. "You must dine without me."

Sarah's brows lifted. "You're going to find him now?"

"This matter cannot wait."

"But you cannot mean to go to his office!"

"It seems the only time the man stops moving is to sleep, and I can hardly call at his home." The irony that she couldn't call on her own husband dug a little deeper at her annoyance with him.

"Then I will accompany you," Sarah said as a maid brought in a tray bearing eggs and toast and tea things. Rebecca sighed, wishing there was chocolate. She adored chocolate, and there was none so fine as what she'd had in Paris.

"You will do no such thing," she said when the maid had gone. "I am a married lady and certainly capable of walking about on my own."

"To all appearances, you are *not* a married lady," Sarah reminded her with irritating accuracy. "The people of Newford will see only Miss Pearce being so bold as to approach a man in his office, alone."

Rebecca pulled on her gloves and settled her bonnet atop her curls.

"I shan't be here long enough for their opinions

to matter. Stay. Enjoy your breakfast."

Sarah tucked her chin and eyed the steaming cup of tea before her. "If you're certain…"

"I am." The sooner she could address matters with Merryn, the better.

She left Sarah sipping her tea. Standing at the entrance to the Feather, she assessed the high street. When a timber cart lumbered away from a narrow building near the harbor's edge, she turned in that direction.

A man in a tailored coat and dark neckcloth was leaving the building when she reached it.

Rebecca stopped him with a smile. When his gaze met hers, she recognized the Kimbrell features. The likeness was faint, but she could see it now in his blue eyes and the sharp line of his nose. Another relation, then.

"I beg your pardon, sir. Can you tell me, what is this place?"

"'Tis the office of Merryn Kimbrell," he said.

"And is Mr. Kimbrell in?"

"I'm afraid he's away to Truro. I'm Mr. James Kimbrell—per'aps I can be of assistance?"

Rebecca's smile felt tight. "You are kind to offer, sir, but I'm afraid my business is rather… particular to Mr. Merryn Kimbrell."

His brows lifted in an expression of comprehension, and she wondered if he, too, assumed she'd traveled to Newford on account of the blasted Inventory. With an effort, she ignored the flush that warmed her cheeks.

He tipped his hat and left, and she surveyed the high street once more. Devil and blast! Merryn knew she wished to speak with him. She might assume he was avoiding her, but then she acknowledged to herself that his wife probably didn't warrant much space in his thoughts these days.

The breeze caught the ribbons of her bonnet as she tapped a finger against her skirts. Across the way lay the chandler's and next to that, a dressmaker's shop with a colorful display of cloth in the window. As she considered her next steps, Merryn's sister approached the establishment.

Curiosity about her husband's family—and the fact that she couldn't stand about on the street—had her soon crossing to the shop. She followed Bronwyn inside where the shadows were cool and the air perfumed with the scents of cotton and silk. A few customers already browsed large bolts of cloth on one wall while Bronwyn and the shop owner conferred over a glass case with neat spools of ribbon.

She studied her sister-in-law in the moments before Bronwyn saw her.

What, she wondered, would Bronwyn make of her brother's secret marriage? And would that tidbit, dropped in the ear of her husband's sister, not gain his attention?

"Miss Pearce!" Bronwyn said. She dropped a ribbon and turned more fully toward Rebecca. "How lovely to see you again! I do hope you and Miss Denning are settling in at the Feather."

"We are indeed, thank you. Mrs. Teague and her husband keep a fine establishment."

Bronwyn nodded as if this was a statement of fact rather than opinion. "And our apothecary's remedy—did your companion find it effective?"

"She is much improved this morning and enjoying your cousin's breakfast."

Bronwyn grinned, and the slightly off-center tilt of her smile was not unlike her brother's when he dared to show it. To learn her brother had been married these last five years would likely dampen it.

Any thoughts Rebecca had of revealing her relationship to Merryn evaporated like mist. Now was not the time.

Bronwyn introduced the shop owner, another cousin by the name of Morwenna Williams. Merryn had told her his family was large, but she'd never quite anticipated it would span the length and breadth of Newford. For someone with little family of her own, save an aunt across the Channel and a cousin intent on having her inheritance, it was a trifle overwhelming.

"Morwenna and I were just discussing Newford's next theatrical," Bronwyn said.

"Oh? Does Newford have a theater?"

"Ha!" Bronwyn said without taking offense. "'Tis true, we're not London or Bath, but I'll have you know we can manage a proper production. Why, just last year, we performed *Much Ado About Nothing*. I played the part of Beatrice, and my cousin Ben was Benedick—which is amusing as his given name truly is Benedick."

"What of your brother?" Rebecca said with careful indifference. "Did he also have a part?"

Bronwyn tilted her head to one side, and the cousins eyed Rebecca for a second longer than the question warranted. Rebecca thought she'd pried too much until her sister-in-law released a soft snort of laughter.

"If you knew my brother, you'd understand why that question is so amusing. Merryn is overly fond of his work, so while his firm was engaged to build the sets for our production, he did not play a role in it." She snorted again as if the very notion was ludicrous.

"But this summer's production," she continued, "will be something grander altogether. If you intend to remain in Newford, you will have to secure your ticket before 'tis too late."

Rebecca inclined her head. She enjoyed a good

theatrical, but she had no intention of remaining in Newford any longer than necessary. She couldn't help a smile for Bronwyn's enthusiasm, however.

Fingering a length of cream-colored silk, she asked, "Will you have a part in this one as well?"

With a look for the faint roundness beneath her dress, Bronwyn gave an actress's sigh. "Alas, no. Morwenna and I are merely the committee to ensure it all goes off."

At Rebecca's questioning look, she leaned closer to confide, "I daresay this one will be quite different from our usual efforts, for we're to have a whole troop of London actors—actresses, even!—to put on a proper performance. Newford's matrons will go into fits at such a fast lot running about, but there you have it."

Rebecca smiled. "The ladies are a stiff sort?"

"Dreadfully so," Morwenna said with a laugh, and Bronwyn nodded her agreement.

"Mrs. Pentreath is their leader, but that doesn't mean Mrs. Clifton and Mrs. Tretheway are to be disregarded. The three of them are frightful indeed when they scent an impropriety." She straightened. "Now, Miss Pearce, have you had occasion to try the Feather's raspberry tarts yet?"

Rebecca replied that she had not, though she hesitated when Bronwyn extended an invitation to join her there later.

Rebecca had always collected acquaintances easily, but few whom she considered friends. Bronwyn, however, seemed different. She reminded Rebecca somewhat of her younger self. Or perhaps, what her younger self might have been, had she followed the usual path of a wife.

She would not be long in Newford, but what harm could come of an afternoon of tea and tarts?

Bronwyn waited, a smile lighting her eyes, until Rebecca accepted her invitation. "I think I must sample these tarts for myself."

———

THAT AFTERNOON, MERRYN returned from Truro to find his sister enjoying a repast in the Feather's coffee room. With his wife.

He stopped in the entrance, his heart stuttering in his chest. The thought occurred to him to leave before they saw him. Rebecca's conversation with his sister looked rather intent. What had she said of their acquaintance?

But no—Rebecca had come to Newford as Miss Pearce. Had she arrived as Mrs. Kimbrell, he would have been in the suds entirely, but as Miss Pearce, she'd given him a reprieve he hadn't expected and likely didn't deserve. Unaccountably, the notion put him even more on edge.

Bronwyn looked up then and spied him. When she gave him her usual grin instead of an angry scowl, his pulse resumed its normal pace. His sister wouldn't hesitate to let him know what she thought of him keeping a secret like this. Rebecca hadn't told her of their marriage, but what, precisely, was she up to?

He strode to their table, keeping his attention on his sister and ignoring how the sight of his wife caused his chest to tighten. He greeted them politely then said, "Bronwyn, you're needed at the theater."

She looked at him in surprise. "But I've just come from there."

He should have devised a better ruse, but Newford's theater production had been the first thing to come to his mind. "I believe there's some question about the actors' accommodations."

"Aye," she said as she put her tea aside. "Morwenna and I were just discussing them." She looked to Rebecca. "Would you like to accompany me?"

Merryn ground his teeth. He'd meant to separate his sister and his wife, not send them on an errand together. He relaxed his jaw, though, when Rebecca demurred.

"I thank you for the tea," she said, "but I've some correspondence that requires my attention."

She cast a glance at Merryn, and he detected a flash of determination in her gaze. Or perhaps it was merely triumph that, with his sister dispatched, she might finally have his attention.

He offered an arm for his sister when she stood. "I will accompany you."

"Across the street?" she said with surprise.

"Aye. Across the street."

He knew it was childish to avoid his wife, just as he knew he couldn't do so indefinitely. But when she narrowed her eyes the tiniest bit at his escape, he couldn't deny a perverse twinge of satisfaction. She might have upset his composure with her arrival, and her talk of *developments*, but he would wrest some control of the situation.

She'd have her discussion, but not today.

"Well," Bronwyn said when they'd left the Feather, "'twas a bit rude, leaving Miss Pearce to take her tea alone. Per'aps you ought to have stayed to keep her company."

"Miss Pearce is a grown female perfectly capable of managing tea."

His tone must have been sharper than he'd intended, because his sister gave him a swift sideways glance. He gentled his voice to say, "I don't think 'tis wise for you to spend time in her company."

Bronwyn frowned, which was not unexpected. Though he'd long been the head of his family, his sister had always followed her own inclination with little heed for his counsel. And now that she was married with a family of her own, she had even less need of his advice. It was a fact that caused him relief and resignation in equal measure.

"I find her rather charming," she said.

"You know nothing about her."

"A situation I am attempting to remedy by spending time in her company. You ought to be thanking me, not playing the part of fierce male relation."

"Thanking you? What logic has brought you to that conclusion?"

"Why, 'tis clear enough why the lady's come to Newford."

Merryn tensed, and he forced his arm to relax beneath her hand. "Why? What has she said?"

Bronwyn pulled her head back to look at him. "Well nothing, really. But 'tis clear she's come on account of the Inventory." At the doubting lift of his brow, she added, "You know as well as I do that no unattached lady just happens by Newford. She is here with a purpose, and what else could it be? To be sure, 'tis in everyone's interest for *someone* to ascertain her character before she makes off with one of our cousins." The sideways glance returned as she added, "Or with you. How, precisely, are you acquainted?"

Merryn snorted. "She is not making off with anyone." Himself, least of all.

Bronwyn gave a put-upon sigh. "And that, dear brother, is rather the problem. You ought to at least entertain the notion. I thought the widow who came through last year might have succeeded where others have failed, but alas, she left and here you remain."

"Mrs. Matthews?" he said with incredulity. The widow had been pretty and charming, but she'd stirred no sentiment in him. "She had even less interest in marriage than I do. She confessed to me she'd only come on a lark to see what the Inventory was all about."

"But you walked with her on more than one occasion!"

"Aye," he said slowly. "But not because I was interested in courting her. I merely wished to keep her from walking with *Ben*. Our cousin was being daft, you'll recall, and painfully slow in his addresses to Miss Parker."

"Hmm," she said. "Daft and painfully slow. 'Twould seem to be a family trait. Inherited, no doubt, through the males of our line."

Merryn took a steadying breath and offered a silent prayer for patience. "Speak plainly," he said. "I thought your aim was to *prevent* Miss Pearce from making off with me."

"Making off with you, yes. I should be very put out with anyone who attempted such a thing. But

I've spent the afternoon with her, and I find her quite unobjectionable. There's nothing to say she cannot remain happily here in Newford, if you would only consider the notion of marrying. You are not getting any younger, you know, and she is rather charming."

Bronwyn went on, and Merryn resisted the urge to scrub a hand over his face. His meddlesome sister was trying to match him with his own wife. The situation was laughable, but she was wrong on one very important point. Rebecca would never be content to remain in Newford.

CHAPTER 7

On Sunday, Rebecca woke with renewed determination. Today, she would have her husband's attention. He wouldn't be working, nor would he need to rush off to the aid of injured employees. And if he avoided her on flimsy pretenses like escorting his sister twenty paces across the street, well… she'd walk with them. One way or another, they'd have their discussion.

She had built her independence carefully over these five years. Now she must persuade Merryn to help her guard it.

Marie came in to help her dress, humming softly as she laid out the morning's garments. The maid, who'd been in her employ for six months, had an irrepressible cheeriness to her demeanor. Despite that, she couldn't wish to be a lady's maid forever. Surely not.

"Marie," Rebecca said as the maid began fastening her buttons, "are you absolutely certain you don't wish to invest some of your wages? You know I should be happy to help you."

"Madame is kind, but *non*." The maid's tone was matter-of-fact as her fingers worked the fastenings on Rebecca's morning gown. Their conversation was a worn one, for Rebecca had offered to add Marie's investment to her ladies' funds many times, but the maid was content with her lot in the world. It confounded Rebecca to no end.

"But do you not wish for more independence? A bit more freedom?"

Marie lifted a shoulder. "What is freedom? I am free so long as I think I am." She smoothed the fabric at Rebecca's shoulders before stepping back.

Rebecca shook her head at such Gallic reasoning. She might envy Marie's easy notion of liberty, but her own English habits—an unwelcome legacy from her father—would never let her rest in it. Freedom was far more complicated than a turn of the mind.

When the maid had gone, she collected Sarah for the walk to the church.

The day was a fine one with sun and blue skies and the scents of summer wildflowers heavy in the air. Newford's church was a small structure—much smaller than the church she attended in Paris—but there was a rustic charm to its sturdy stone facade. A square bell tower anchored one side, and a low stone wall surrounded the churchyard. They passed through the lychgate to where the rest of Newford waited for the doors to be opened.

The churchyard hummed with conversation. Sarah, who'd made the acquaintance of a local governess the day before, greeted her new friend. Rebecca left them to their conversation and quickly spied her tall husband in the crowd.

He stood beside a young woman with dark hair and lively features. The lady was pretty in a dress of pink striped muslin, and Rebecca felt an uncomfortable pinch behind her ribs when Merryn smiled at the woman.

Who was this female who commanded his attention? One of the Newford Inventory ladies, perhaps?

With determined steps, she approached the pair and called up her most charming smile. "Mr. Kimbrell, good morning."

Merryn's smile faded. "Miss Pearce." Then, clearing his throat, he indicated his companion. "May I present Mrs. Gryffyn Kimbrell, my cousin's wife. Keren, this is Miss Pearce."

His cousin's wife. The uncomfortable tension in Rebecca's chest eased.

Of course she wasn't jealous. She'd been thinking only of Gregory's challenge. Merryn's participation in the Inventory already had them at a disadvantage without him paying court to ladies left and right. But his cousin's wife... Her relief was unmistakable.

"How lovely to meet you," she said, though she feared her smile was rather too broad.

"Miss Pearce," Keren said warmly. "I hear that you have spent some time in Paris. I'm certain the ladies would love to hear about the latest fashions. Would you like to join us at the gate?"

Rebecca looked beyond Keren to where a small group of women had gathered. More than one cast her a curious glance.

"I should enjoy that," Rebecca said, "but I was actually hoping to have a word with Mr. Kimbrell." Keren's gaze shifted between them, and Rebecca felt compelled to add, "That is, I've a question to put to him about a... a renovation matter."

Keren's smile widened. "Oh! Of course! Merryn is quite sought after for his... building expertise. I wish you good fortune in your endeavor."

She left them with a small wave, and a ridiculous flush filled Rebecca's cheeks that the woman thought she pursued her own husband.

She turned back to Merryn. The look he gave her, shadowed beneath the brim of his hat, was hard to decipher. There was a hint of irritation in it, to be sure, and perhaps a bit of resignation. But also... uncertainty. If there was anything Rebecca knew of her husband, it was that he was rarely uncertain, but she supposed the unexpected arrival of one's wife after five years might give one pause.

"You, husband, are hard to run to ground," she said softly.

Merryn's slow inhale was audible. "I gather you do not have a renovation matter."

"Not at present."

He nodded then led them a few paces away to the shelter of a giant spreading beech.

"The doors will open soon," he said, "so if you've something you wish to discuss, I suggest we do it quickly."

He stood with his arms crossed, feet braced as though he awaited an assault. Rebecca supposed he wasn't too far off the mark in that regard, though the impending attack wasn't from her but her cousin Gregory. She swiftly explained what she'd learned from Mr. Cross.

"Your cousin's return to England... *that* is why you've come all the way to Newford?"

"Well, yes. That, and his solicitor's questions." His stance relaxed a fraction and she wondered what conclusion he'd drawn about her purpose in Newford. "What did you think?" she asked.

He shook his head. "'Tis nothing." Then, uncrossing his arms to clasp his hands behind his back, he added, "I don't think your cousin's return is anything to worry about."

"And if he learns of our arrangement and deems our marriage a sham?"

He leaned toward her, keeping his voice low. "Our marriage is not a sham. 'Twas properly done at St. Marylebone, with the elder Mr. Cross and your companion as witnesses. Your uncle approved the match. 'Twas all recorded in the parish register, or have you forgotten?"

She frowned. "*I* have not forgotten. But we both know the terms under which we married."

"Terms to which we both agreed and have fulfilled."

"Terms," she said, "which did not include…" She waved a vague hand between them, acutely aware they were standing in a churchyard as she spoke of marital congress. "That is, we have not conducted ourselves as most married couples do."

Something flickered in his expression—understanding, perhaps, or discomfort.

"No," he said quietly. "We have not. Those were our terms." He studied the ground for a long moment, and when he spoke again, his voice was more measured. "What is your plan then? You've presented yourself in Newford as Miss Pearce, so 'tis clear you don't mean to acknowledge our marriage here."

"Would you prefer I arrived as Mrs. Kimbrell?"

He pulled in a long breath then released it. "No."

"Precisely," she said.

"What d'you suggest then?"

"I suggest we meet with my cousin when he returns to England and put his suspicions to rest. You must come to London. No one in Newford need know the reason for your travels, if that is your wish."

Merryn's eyes narrowed at that, but just then, the church bells began their peal. The vicar and his curate appeared to push open the heavy wooden doors, and the rest of Newford crowded past to go in. Rebecca's opportunity for conversation with her husband went with them. She wanted to groan with the frustration of it.

Merryn lifted his arm, and Rebecca took it. Her husband's muscles were tense beneath her hand as they entered a church together for the second time.

THE DAY'S BRIGHTNESS yielded to the hushed shadows of the church as Merryn entered with his wife on his arm. His pulse pounded in his ears, muffling the conversations around him. She hadn't come about a divorce. Her *development* wasn't another man, unless one counted her cousin. His relief at that knowledge had been swift, for his royal project never would have withstood the scandal.

He saw her seated with her companion before joining his cousins at the front. James slid over to make room for him on the bench. Alfie sat behind them with his wife, while Jory's and Gavin's growing families filled the rows ahead of them. And Bronwyn, who'd become mother to a young girl on her marriage the previous year, and now anticipated the birth of her own child.

The Kimbrell section of the church had grown crowded; soon they'd be obliged to purchase another bench.

None of his family's marriages had come about easily. Even that of his sister, whose husband had been remarkably slow to the finish line on account of some trying business with his late wife's family.

Merryn closed his eyes for a moment, thinking of how easily some men made a tangle of their own affairs. He could offer extensive counsel on that particular skill.

His wife's words returned to him. She wanted him to go to London. As her husband.

But he didn't have time to hare off—not with the royal preparations fully underway. His Majesty's visit would either make his reputation or be his undoing, to say nothing of his cousins who had invested so heavily in the effort.

Surely, Gregory Pearce could have no case, no cause to question their marriage. It had been done with a valid license and properly recorded in the parish register.

But Merryn's decision to keep his marriage to himself had been an act of impulse. Or cowardice, if he were honest. He'd had plenty of time to reflect on his stupidity these last years. He'd been young and enamored of his bride. And unwilling, on his return to Newford, to admit that she had left—despite the fact that had been their agreement all along.

But now, just look where his foolishness had got him. Rebecca thought no one in Newford need know the reason for his travels, but he knew better. He was becoming known in London. He'd traveled there twice in the last months in pursuit of funds for his royal project. He could hardly present himself as a married man there and not expect news of it to reach Newford.

He cringed to think of his investors.

He'd allowed everyone to believe the fiction that he was unmarried. He'd even danced with some of their daughters and sisters, for heaven's sake. To reveal his five-year marriage *now* certainly wouldn't project the steady, respectable temperament his investors expected.

Yes, he certainly took the prize for complicating matters. The sooner he could ease his wife's concerns and send her on her way, the better—for both of them.

James shifted on the bench next to him. "Gavin seems to be settling into his role of step-papa," he said with a nod for their cousin.

As if in answer to this observation, a loud giggle came from the other side of Gavin's bench. It was followed by the appearance of little Marianne's tousled curls over Gavin's shoulder and his gentle shushing.

"Though I think he's learning infants have their own notions of proper behavior," James added.

"A ready-made family is no small undertaking," Merryn said.

"Per'aps not," James agreed, "but you know Gavin thrives on a challenge."

Merryn couldn't disagree with James's assessment. "What of you?" he asked. "D'you not have a desire to seek a bride and set up your own nursery?"

"No more than you, I suppose."

Merryn swallowed uneasily. He thought that might have been an end to their conversation until James nodded toward Rebecca's bench. "Although… our newest visitor seems interested in pursuing your acquaintance."

Merryn made a non-committal noise in his throat.

"Per'aps you should invite her to walk with you after the service," James went on.

The vicar rapped twice on the pulpit to signal

the start of his sermon. "Per'aps," Merryn said as quiet fell over the church.

REBECCA BARELY HEARD the vicar's sermon, so anxious was she to continue her discussion with Merryn. The sooner they addressed her cousin's suspicions, the sooner she could return to Paris.

So, when they were outside once more, her hand resting on Merryn's sleeve as he led them back to the Feather, it was a surprise to hear him say, "I cannot go to London."

Her hand tightened on his arm, and she forced it to relax. "Why ever not?"

"I've the royal preparations to oversee," he said. "His Majesty's visit cannot be delayed to accommodate my personal affairs."

Rebecca's eyes widened. "His Majesty? The King comes here… to Newford?" She looked about her, and the pieces fell into place—the extensive construction, the scaffolding, the urgency she'd sensed in everyone's manner. The theater company from London! It all made sense now. "That's what your improvement project is about, isn't it? You're preparing for a royal visit."

"Aye," Merryn said. "We had word just last month that Newford has been added to the King's schedule. We had hopes... Work began last year on the harbor and the roads, but with the news, we could finally begin the pavilion and renovations to the squire's Abbey. 'Tis all for the royal progress." He paused, then added more quietly. "The success or failure of't will determine not only my own reputation, but that of everyone who has invested in these preparations."

Rebecca's breath caught. Even in France they had followed the King's quarrel with his wife—his attempts to be rid of her, and the nation's loud resistance to it. That the coronation was to go on at all seemed something of a triumph. Now talk had turned to the royal progress that must follow, and each town in the King's path strained to make itself worthy of the honor. Newford, it seemed, was no exception.

But, as the scale of her husband's project became clear, the importance of heading off her cousin's accusations only sharpened, for Gregory's claims could only upset Merryn's careful plans.

"I'm afraid that, whether you like it or not, our situation now requires your attention as well."

He lowered his voice as a pair of ladies strolled past. "Your cousin doesn't have any grounds to question our marriage," he repeated.

"Mr. Cross feels there are a number of points in his favor, not the least of which is the fact we live separately—on separate continents, no less."

Merryn lifted an ironic brow.

Warmth climbed her neck, and she hurried to forestall his argument. "I accept the responsibility for that, but what's done is done. I merely point out Mr. Cross's concerns."

"Many couples live separately. It doesn't make them any less married."

Rebecca drew a steadying breath before raising her next point. "And do many couples put themselves out as eligible parties?" At Merryn's frown of confusion, she took her hand from his arm to withdraw her worn copy of *The Newford Inventory* from her reticule. She thrust it at him with perhaps a bit more force than she'd intended.

He took it, and his confusion swiftly cleared. At least he didn't mean to deny it.

"*This*," she said with some heat, "could cast doubt on the validity of our marriage. It could provide Gregory with the grounds he needs to contest it."

Merryn sighed and slowed his steps. After several paces, he said with what seemed like sincerity, "My apologies, Rebecca, truly. I didn't think anything of adding my name to it at the time. 'Twas merely a favor to my cousin Alfie, who'd developed an affection for Miss Darling—the lady who published the Inventory. She needed it to win a competition, but I never thought it would…" His voice trailed off.

"So… you're not…?" How did a lady ask her husband if he sought a bigamous marriage?

"No!" he said, and her relief at his vehemence was stronger than it ought to have been. It was certainly no concern of hers how he chose to conduct himself. Or at least, it wouldn't have been, were it not for Gregory's suspicions.

"We've made a proper muddle of this marriage business, haven't we?" he said.

"Yes," she said. "But I am not the one who forgot to tell people I was married."

He stiffened. Then he sighed once more. "I've not strayed from my vows, Rebecca, if that is your concern."

She blinked. He'd been faithful to their marriage? That had not been part of their terms. She had no intentions of aligning herself with another man, but she'd thought—had rather assumed—he would have taken comfort with another. Discreetly, of course.

His admission, though he couldn't know it, sent a curious warmth spiraling through her.

"But none of this changes anything with Pearce," he said. "Whatever I have or have not told my family is rather beside the point. Our marriage was very properly done, and the parish register will prove it.

I'll write to your cousin's solicitor, and we'll have this sorted soon enough."

Rebecca wasn't sure it could be as simple as he seemed to think. There was a lot of money at stake — not only the balance of her trust, which she'd grown through her own investments, but the thousand pounds she'd paid to Merryn out of it. She wouldn't put it past her cousin to make all the noise he could until he was either satisfied or thoroughly routed.

"Are you willing to risk your project on it?" she whispered.

His frown was immediate. Years before, she'd thought him handsome. Now, she realized with a start, her husband's countenance was... *compelling*.

"If Gregory is successful," she pressed, "you'll lose your thousand pounds."

"I'm not concerned with the thousand pounds," he said. "Though I wouldn't like to see it go, the loss won't break me, if't comes to it."

A thousand pounds was no small amount. Clearly, he'd done well for himself. There was far more than that at risk, though. She should tell him, but she didn't think he would like to know one of the investors in his royal project was his own wife.

She said only, "Well the loss of *my* funds will not be so easily dismissed." He acknowledged that with a short nod, and she pressed her final point. "And that's all to say nothing of the scandal my cousin's questions will create unless we disprove his suspicions from the outset. Whether he's successful in contesting our marriage or not, there will be gossip which neither of us can like. Our marriage cannot remain a secret for long, even in Newford."

And that, it seemed, had his attention. He pulled at his bottom lip until, with a shake of his head, he said quietly, "His Majesty's route is fixed. The preparations must be complete before he arrives. There can be no delays."

Rebecca nodded slowly. "And when is he expected?"

"At month's end. How long before your cousin reaches England?"

"Mr. Cross estimates six weeks, depending on the winds and how quickly my cousin is able to conclude his affairs."

Merryn's expression turned more serious. "The timing is not ideal," he said, "but I will come to you in London once His Majesty has gone."

"But that will only allow us two weeks to... to..."

"To perfect our performance as a loving married couple?"

"A marriage need not be *loving* to be valid," she reminded him.

"Just so."

She frowned. Two weeks to learn how to behave as a true husband and wife—and to convince anyone who might doubt their union that it was genuine. How could they possibly make it appear so?

Rebecca considered her husband. She could not alter the King's schedule, but if Merryn thought she would await him in London, he was mistaken.

She nodded, her decision made. "I have never been to Cornwall," she said, "and I find Newford charming. I shall wait for you here, then we may travel to London together."

His eyes narrowed, and she could see him calculating the implications—not only the risk to his secret, but perhaps the wisdom of her suggestion.

It *was* a good plan.

By remaining in Newford, they would have more time to reacquaint themselves, to learn the small details of one another that would make their performance more convincing, if not precisely *loving*. If they were to persuade her cousin, they must know each other far better than they currently did.

CHAPTER 8

MERRYN KNEW HE must return to London with Rebecca, if only to set his wife's mind at ease. It was his duty as her husband. But her words spun in his mind as they neared the inn. He did not doubt the legality of their marriage, but she was right about the gossip, and the scandal that would follow if her cousin made a fuss. There was every chance his secret marriage would soon be a secret no more.

He ought to tell his family before they heard it from another quarter. There was his sister to consider and his cousins. His mother! She was away visiting her eldest sister in Helston, which was a mercy. But how did one confess five years of deception to a parent?

The situation was not helped by his wife's insistence on remaining in Cornwall—though he'd been mildly surprised she didn't demand they announce their union to all of Newford right then. In his experience, Rebecca preferred things to be done on terms of her own choosing. It was a trait he couldn't fault as it was one he shared. But as he'd grown older, as he'd navigated the demands of his business and his duties as son and brother, he'd learned when to give and when to take. When to temper his demands.

Perhaps Rebecca had learned some things of her own, though the notion that he did not know his wife very well sat uncomfortably on his thoughts.

But with the King's visit drawing ever closer, the timing of her arrival could not be worse. He felt the weight of it all as he delivered his wife to the Feather, but the secret of his marriage wasn't the only thing causing his uneasiness.

When he'd said a thousand pounds wouldn't break him, his wife's eyes had slid away from his. What had caused her discomfort, he couldn't be certain, but he'd never known Rebecca to shy away from talk of financial matters, no matter how much society frowned on ladies discussing money.

Once he left Rebecca and her companion at the Feather, a suspicion began to form. He needed to speak to James. Most of his relations would gather at their grandfather's home for Sunday luncheon.

He collected his horse and made the short ride to the cliffs above Newford. Oak Hill was a rambling manor in the Tudor style with the odd Jacobean chimney to interrupt its lines. It sat at the end of an oak-lined drive with the sea at its back.

His grandfather had acquired the property a generation ago, when high taxes made the free trade a profitable course for enterprising Cornishmen. Alan Kimbrell had been very enterprising in his day, though Merryn doubted his grandfather had smuggled more than an extra sweet from his own kitchen in recent years.

It had been some time since Merryn had last attended a Sunday luncheon, and his builder's eye took in the state of things as he rode up the drive. The slate roof, though well maintained, was beginning to sag a bit. He'd send Dickey and some of his men later to inspect the beams.

He dismounted in the manor's forecourt and gave the reins over to a groom. His grandfather's butler met him at the door.

"Sir," Parsons said. "This is an unexpected pleasure."

"You're looking fit, Parsons."

"Thank you, sir. Your grandfather and the others will be pleased to see you."

"They're on the lawn?"

"Aye," the butler replied as he held out his hand for Merryn's gloves.

Merryn's steps were loud as he strode through the spacious entry and down a large oak-timbered hall. He went through the doors at the end to emerge onto the manor's terrace where the sounds of children's lawn games filled the air. Tables and blankets were arranged to take advantage of the sea view, and servants bustled to and from the kitchen with laden trays.

"Merryn!" Bronwyn came at him to clasp his arm with both hands. His sister was a barnacle, but he'd long been accustomed to her enthusiastic handling of his person. He accepted her embrace and offered a smile in return.

His grandfather's approach was more sedate, though his surprised expression matched Bronwyn's. "'Tis a pleasure to make your acquaintance, lad," the elder Kimbrell said with a wink as he leaned on his cane.

A servant offered a tray with cups of cider, wine and lemonade. Merryn took wine as his grandfather added, "Jests aside, 'tis been nearly a year since you've graced one of my picnics."

"It cannot have been that long," Merryn protested with a laugh.

"Aye, 'twas last summer, after Captain Marsh arrived in Newford with young Emilia."

Merryn's jaw shifted as he considered the past months. Unofficial word of the royal visit had reached their shores long before His Majesty's office confirmed the fact, and Merryn had been busy with the preparations ever since. But had it truly been so long since he'd come to Oak Hill?

"I do apologize," he told his grandfather. "I didn't realize so much time has passed."

"Bah. You've a thriving enterprise to manage, and now this business with the King's arrival. 'Tis understandable, but you'll never find a wife buried in your work like that."

It was only a second before the full weight of Merryn's guilt settled in his stomach.

Oh, to be young again but with the wisdom of age, Merryn might have made better choices in his life. He might not have kept his marriage a secret for all these years, or—he thought wryly—he might not have married in the first place.

Had he not gone to London all those years before, had he not made the acquaintance of William Pearce and his niece, he might now be free to seek a wife in earnest. To have a family of his own and—

"'Tis just what I have been telling him," Bronwyn said to their grandfather. "There are no ladies to be found in his office, to be sure."

Thankfully, someone hailed his sister from across the lawn. She excused herself, and Merryn straightened his sleeve where she'd left wrinkles.

"You know there are no wives to be found in Newford," he told his grandfather. It had long been his standard reply to anyone remarking his marital status. And, in a town with far more males than females, it had worked. For a time.

Jory laid a heavy hand on Merryn's shoulder. "Thanks to Miss Darling's Inventory," he said, "you cannot claim that excuse any longer."

Merryn gave an inward sigh for the blasted Inventory.

James and Alfie joined them in time to hear Jory's comment. "Aye," Alfie added unhelpfully. "And 'twould seem you've already made the acquaintance of our newest visitor. We all saw you walking with Miss Pearce after the vicar's sermon. I believe you've upset the betting."

Merryn rubbed his chin. "The betting?"

"Gavin and Cadan have laid odds on the next Kimbrell to fall, but I don't think you were ever much considered."

"They needn't worry about me marrying."

"Not even a fetching sort like Miss Pearce? She's rather well-traveled, by Bronwyn's report. Per'aps you might consider—"

"No," Merryn said more sharply than he' intended.

Alfie tipped his head with a grin. "Thank you."

"For what?"

"For that confirmation," Alfie replied. "I wagered you'd be the *last* to fall, and your tone suggests I've chosen wisely."

With that, Alfie left them, looking quite pleased with himself.

To Merryn's relief, the conversation soon turned elsewhere. As he waited to catch a quiet moment with James, he watched his cousins enjoying luncheon with their new brides while he'd left Rebecca to take her meal at the Feather. She was his wife; she ought to have been beside him.

He should confess—admit the marriage and accept his relations' surprise or censure. And endure their pity when Rebecca returned to Paris.

No. Now was not the time. His focus must remain on the royal preparations. Only once the King's visit was past could he decide what to say, and when.

Thoughts of the royal project—and of his anonymous investor—pulled him back to his purpose. With a heavy inhale, he drew James aside.

"You said our anonymous investor used an intermediary," he said without preamble.

James didn't hesitate but adjusted quickly to the new topic. "Aye. He won't reveal his client, though. 'Twould be unethical."

Merryn shook his head. "I know. But who was the intermediary?"

"A Mr. Francis Jones. He's a solicitor out of Lincoln's Inn."

"With which firm?" Merryn pressed. James, to

his credit, didn't blink at the urgency of Merryn's tone.

"Cross and Jones."

"Cross and Jones," Merryn repeated. "Nathaniel Cross is the principal?"

"I believe so. You're acquainted with him?"

Acquainted with him? Merryn had been sending letters through the man for the past five years.

Devil it. His anonymous investor was *his wife*.

CHAPTER 9

Merryn marshaled his expression for the duration of his grandfather's picnic. He laughed when he was expected to and entertained his family's questions about the progress of the royal preparations. But when the sun began to sink and his cousins to gather their families, he was the first to retrieve his gloves from Parsons.

His ride down the hill to Newford was made in considerably more haste than his journey up it had been. He left his horse with a groom at the inn's stables and made quick strides through the Feather's entry. With an effort, he forced his expression to relax lest he startle Wynne's serving girl with his frown.

His success at this must have been marginal, though, as Peggy took a hasty step back at the sight of him.

"Sir?"

"Your guest," he said. "Miss Pearce—is she about?"

Peggy's face cleared. "Oh, aye. Miss Pearce be one of the comeliest ladies us 'ave ever served at the Feather. And proper kind, too. She give us a coin jus' fer givin' 'er fork an extra polish."

Merryn prompted her with an impatient lift of his brows.

Peggy swallowed. "Aye, then. Her'll be in the private parlor with her companion."

Merryn nodded and turned in that direction. Then he stopped and, withdrawing a coin, extended it to Peggy. "For your discretion." It wouldn't do for all of Newford to know he'd stormed into the Feather asking after Miss Pearce.

"'Course, sir," Peggy said with a broad smile and an impertinent wink as she pocketed the copper piece.

The door to the parlor was closed, and Merryn rapped upon it. His wife bade him to enter, and her eyes widened at the sight of him. She recovered quickly from her surprise and gave the corner of her mouth a delicate tap with her napkin.

"Merryn."

Miss Denning, astute female that she was, jumped up from her place at the table. "I've just recalled something I left in my room," she murmured.

Merryn nodded as she passed him and pressed the door closed behind her.

"You've frightened my companion off, and now her dinner will grow cold."

"I suspect Miss Denning left out of an abundance of good sense rather than fright. She's always had more of that commodity than either you or I could claim." Indeed, it had been Miss Denning who'd initially opposed the notion of them marrying. Would that he had heeded her concerns.

He removed his hat and hung it on a hook near the door. His wife sat straight in her chair, hands folded one over the other. She was the very picture of poised elegance, though the occasional tap of her forefinger against her hand belied her uncertainty.

"What have I done to put such a frown upon your countenance?" she said as she reached for her wine.

"You are my anonymous investor," he said. He tried to keep the accusatory tone from his voice, but it was there nonetheless.

"Ah," she replied, lowering her glass and setting it carefully on the table.

He was pleased and a little surprised that she didn't deny it or pretend confusion. "Why the secrecy?" he asked.

"Will you sit?"

"I prefer to stand."

"Yes, well, my neck grows stiff from looking up at you."

A growl rose in his throat before he checked it. His demeanor was generally a steady one, but a mere glance from his wife turned him into an impolite, mannerless boor.

Before their marriage, they'd enjoyed one another's company. They'd engaged in flirtation and courteous discourse. He never would have *growled*. But that was before he allowed his hopes to get away from him. He had only himself to blame.

He forced himself to calm and pulled a chair from the table. Sitting across from her, he steepled his hands on his lap.

"Thank you," she said with a regal nod.

"Now, why did you keep your investment in my project a secret?" he repeated.

"Would you have accepted it, had you known the source?"

"No," he said without hesitation.

She responded with a wry look.

"You ought not to have done it," he said.

"Because I am a female?"

"I would be happy to have a lady investor," he replied, "but you are not a lady. You are my *wife*." The slight narrowing of her eyes suggested he may have misspoken.

"And you, husband, are quite rigid in your thinking."

He ignored the accusation. There was probably some truth to her statement, but he'd examine it later. For now, he asked the question that was at the front of his mind. It was what had sent him down from Oak Hill in such haste. "But why would you have invested at all—anonymous or otherwise? We've long since settled our arrangement. You owe me nothing more."

She eyed him across the table as if she weighed her words carefully. Finally, she said, "I expect your improvements will yield a respectable return."

He blinked. The answer was very like her, practical and unclouded with sentiment, but he was nearly certain that was not what she had meant to say. He found himself searching her expression for something more, though what exactly, he didn't know.

"A respectable return," he repeated slowly.

"Yes. I maintain investments for other women—maids and governesses, mostly. Your improvements to the harbor and the roads—they're sound investments." She studied her hands in her lap before bringing her gaze back to him. "I have not forgotten your plans for Newford."

Merryn recalled all too well the occasion when he'd confided those plans. It had been their wedding night. He and Rebecca had retired to separate rooms, both honoring the terms of their arrangement, but neither had found sleep. He'd gone to her uncle's library for something to read, only to find his new wife already there in a demure dressing gown, her copper-threaded hair unbound and falling over her shoulders as she stared into the hearth.

"You're unable to sleep as well," he said quietly.

She turned from the fire to look at him, her hands wrapped around a cup that no longer steamed. "Are you having second thoughts?" she asked in a soft voice.

"No. Are you?"

She shook her head then added with an unexpected vulnerability, "Though I confess, being married feels different from what I expected."

"Our marriage is not the usual sort," he said.

"No."

Her shoulders were slightly rounded, perhaps with weariness or grief for her uncle. The last days had not been easy for her, and now she found herself unexpectedly wed to a man she barely knew.

"I looked in on your uncle," he offered. "He sleeps peacefully."

She nodded. "I cannot think it will be long."

He held out a hand to her, and to his surprise she took it. "Tell me more of him," he said.

He moved them to the settee before the fire, where the quiet wrapped about them. They passed their wedding night trading stories. She spoke of her uncle—of his generosity in taking her in and the lessons she'd learned under his roof. He told her of his own family back in Cornwall.

Gradually, the conversation widened to their hopes and plans for the future. She meant to join her aunt in France now that travel there was possible again. He confessed his uncertainties for his late father's building firm, and his hopes for Newford—that its harbor might be strengthened, its streets improved, and its people given steady work that relied not on the whims of weather or fish.

By the time dawn began to break over London, she'd laid her head on his shoulder. And when the light began to come round the curtains, he shifted. For a moment, her eyes fluttered closed and her lips parted in expectation… until she pulled back from him, murmuring something about the lateness of the hour.

"Or the earliness," she laughed.

He'd married her with a thought to persuade her to return with him to Cornwall. But he'd heard the certainty in her voice that night—her course was set, and to ask her to abandon it would be unconscionable. That they'd always meant to part ways hadn't made a difference to his heart, which had foolishly begun to hope for more.

By the morning, her uncle had passed, and in a few short days, Rebecca was gone.

Nothing about her manner now suggested she thought of that night as often as he did. She said only, "I fear my cousin threatens *both* of our investments."

Merryn shifted. His wife's words, for all their gentleness, struck him. In learning of her investment in his project, he'd thought only of what it meant for *him*. Indeed, since Rebecca had come to Newford, he'd given little thought to what she might lose in all of this.

He still did not think her cousin had solid ground from which to contest their marriage, but he'd learned something of his wife through five years of letters. She *thrived* on her independence. If she thought she might soon lose it, she must be terrified. He sobered to think what an unfeeling man he'd become.

He leaned forward until he could catch her gaze with his. "Your cousin won't prevail," he promised.

Her surprise at this earnest declaration was unflattering, to say the least. But it was soon gone, replaced with a smile that caused warmth to pool in his stomach. "Thank you."

"Now," he said briskly as he stood, "d'you have everything you need at the Feather? Is there anything I can do for you and Miss Denning? D'you need more servants?" Guilt pinched at him anew for keeping his wife at the inn, but he'd do whatever he could to ensure her comfort.

"We've found our rooms at the inn pleasing, and your cousin's hospitality is exceptional," she said, though there was a bit of hesitation in her tone.

"But?"

"But there is one thing. I wonder if I might impose upon you for an escort."

"Of course," he said. "To where am I escorting you?"

"To see your project."

Merryn stilled. He'd thought she might desire an escort to the post office or to see the pretty cliffs at Copper Cove, perhaps. A construction project was no place for a lady. And such an outing was no quick errand. It would require them to spend hours in one another's company—

"I am an investor, after all," she reminded him. "Moreover, I've taken an interest in the rebuilding works in Paris—the bridges and arcades, the restoration projects. One learns a great deal by observing such endeavors. It is not as if I lack knowledge of these things."

He cleared his expression. She had the right of it. Though he couldn't like it, she *was* an investor—one of his project's largest.

He took his hat down from its hook, resigned.

"Tomorrow, then," he said. "We will begin at sunrise."

If she was surprised by such an early hour, she didn't allow it to show.

———

AS HER HUSBAND left the Feather's parlor, Rebecca overheard him tell the serving girl, "When Miss Denning returns, please send in a fresh plate. Her beef has grown cold."

"Aye, sir."

It was a simple kindness, but his manner regarding her investment in his project... that was something altogether different.

She'd expected his irritation. His anger, even. Her father would have ranted unceasingly had her mother ever had the audacity—or the means—to do such a thing. And then he would have locked his wife in her room and barred all visitors for a fortnight so he might gain control of his household once more.

Rebecca knew such despotism was not the norm, but neither was it illegal for a husband to treat his wife in such a barbaric fashion. So yes, she'd expected Merryn's anger.

You are not a lady. You are my wife.

His words reminded her that as his wife, the law afforded her fewer liberties in such matters. And yet, for all his initial sharpness, he'd asked her *why*, as if he wanted to understand her motivation. She had not anticipated that, nor had she expected his biting manner to yield so easily.

Sarah returned and, after peeking round the door, she entered.

"All is well?" she asked as Peggy set a fresh plate before her.

"All is well," Rebecca said, though her tone still held a hint of her confusion. "He knows about my investment in his project."

"Ah. That explains the expression on his face then. Was he very angry?"

"Terribly. But… he's to accompany us to view the progress tomorrow."

Sarah folded her hands to signal a lecture was coming. "You know that I did not approve of you marrying solely for your inheritance," she said in her best governess voice, "but I cannot fault your choice in husband."

"He has held to his end of things."

"He has more than held to it. You kept a rather large secret from him—a secret which has a direct bearing on his business interests. I do not have much experience with husbands, but I cannot think that is something one would take lightly. But in the matter of… what?… ten minutes, yours has overcome his anger and agreed to drive us about."

Rebecca shifted a little at her companion's speech. "When you phrase it thusly…"

"When I phrase it thusly, it's clear for any but the most doltish to see your husband has an affection for you."

"Doltish? Do you mean to say I'm slow-witted?" Rebecca asked in surprise. One could always trust a former governess to be painfully direct.

"Your mind has always been sharp as a pin, but your heart… Well, the heart and mind are two different creatures. But you deliberately ignore my observation: I say your husband holds a fondness for you."

Her words recalled the memory of Rebecca's wedding night. Though their marriage was not a conventional one, she and her husband had confided much to one another that night. Perhaps more than even true husbands and wives might have done. But it was always understood that they would part ways—he with his thousand pounds to build his father's firm and she to her aunt in France.

Perhaps it was that knowledge that had emboldened her to share so much. But when he'd looked as if he meant to kiss her, when she'd leaned toward him in anticipation, she'd come perilously close to abandoning her plans for independence.

That night had nearly changed the course of her existence, for her imagination had conjured a life where she remained in England. Where she set aside her plans for joining her aunt in France and became a wife in truth to Merryn Kimbrell. She feared he needed only to ask, and she would have done it.

The notion had put her heart in a panicked flutter, and she brought their wedding night to a hasty close. Her uncle passed that morning, and amidst her grief and the funeral preparations, she'd asked Mr. Cross the Elder to purchase her passage to France. There was no gilding it: she'd fled.

But even now, years later, the memory of that night and what might have been still sent her heart racing. Sarah believed her husband held a fondness for her. Merryn *had* been fond of her once, but she doubted very much that his feelings were the same now.

"Your dinner grows cold again."

CHAPTER 10

MIST STILL CLUNG to the valley when Merryn arrived at the Feather's stable yard the next morning. He'd chosen his timing deliberately—early enough to draw as little notice as possible, late enough that propriety wouldn't be breached. He hoped his wife wasn't one of those ladies who preferred to sleep until the afternoon, as he'd put aside a dozen tasks for this outing.

A few hours, he told himself. A few hours and then he could return to the things that needed his attention. He would show Rebecca the new pavilion above the harbor and then they'd ride out to the squire's estate. Trevelyan Abbey would host the King for a royal ball and supper, and Merryn's men had worked from sunrise to sunset for four weeks to restyle the man's ballroom.

Mr. Malvern, the Feather's ostler, had two horses saddled and waiting: a steady mare for Miss Pearce and another placid mount for her companion. In a nearby stall, Wynne's boy Leo laid fresh hay.

"Fine mornin' for riding." Malvern's tone held more curiosity than the simple observation merited.

"Aye." Merryn checked the mare's girth, finding it properly secured.

"The ladies be ready and waitin'," Malvern added before spitting into the dust at his feet.

Merryn paused in his task. "Are they indeed?"

Leo's green eyes appeared over the side of the stall. "Oi," he added. "Mrs. Teague says as 'ow the pretty one be breakin' her fast afore the sun was even up."

Malvern chuckled. "Eager to see the sights o' Newford, is she?"

Merryn made a noncommittal sound and strode across the stable yard. The entire town would know by noon that he'd arranged horses for the pretty Miss Pearce. By evening, they'd have constructed a dozen explanations for it, each more elaborate than the last.

He drew open the inn door to find Wynne at her desk and Rebecca coming down the stairs in a blue habit. He was no expert in fashion, but even he could attribute the garment's simple elegance to its Continental origins. She'd fastened a rakish riding hat at an angle that suggested confidence rather than coquetry. The effect was much the same, for it sent his stomach toward his toes.

"Mr. Kimbrell." She descended the last step and came toward him. "You're prompt."

"You're ready." His tone held more disbelief than he intended.

She pulled on kid gloves, smoothing the leather over each finger. "I know you begin your days early, and I did not wish to keep you waiting."

She looked up. He must have worn an expression of surprise, for she stopped fussing with her gloves and her brows came together. Leaning toward him, she whispered, "I did read your letters, you know."

"I thought you found them sparse and business-like," he returned.

The corner of her lip twitched. "And they were. But it does not require a tremendous leap of reason when you close each missive with, 'Dawn arrives soon, and I must go.'"

The back of his neck prickled with heat. Each missive? Surely, she exaggerated. He liked to think he could be more personable than that. The urge to challenge her recollection was strong, but, conscious of Wynne nearby, straining to catch what she could, he merely pressed his lips and nodded.

Her companion joined them at the bottom of the steps, looking less enthused for the early hour than his wife. He stepped to one side and motioned for them to precede him, ignoring Wynne's amused glance as they passed.

At the stables, Merryn moved to assist his wife, a courtesy that brought him close enough to catch the faint but familiar scent of her lavender. She may have dressed herself in elegant French clothes these last years, but she still wore the same scent. Bracing himself against the knowledge, he put his hands to her waist and lifted her into the saddle.

Rebecca settled the skirts of her habit and took up the reins, appearing wholly unaffected by their nearness. "The mare seems steady."

"She is." He stepped back, relieved for the distance, and swung onto his own mount. "We'll take the harbor road first."

They rode three abreast through the stable yard gate, but once they turned onto the high street, the way narrowed with carts and pedestrians. Rebecca's companion fell back, allowing them space that felt both proper and precarious.

His wife still had a fine seat. During their acquaintance in London, they'd ridden twice in the park—occasions when he'd felt his provincial manners keenly.

She'd been polished even then, but now, after five years abroad, she possessed a Continental refinement that made their previous disparity seem modest in comparison.

"It was kind of you to arrange for the horses," she offered. "Sarah and I thank you."

"'Twas merely an expedience." Yes, he was quite charming.

She remained unaffected by his terseness, though, looking about at the bustle around them. Two men went by with surveying equipment. They nodded at Merryn, their gazes taking in his companion with undisguised curiosity.

"Newford is rather more modern than I expected," Rebecca observed.

He looked at his wife sideways. "Did you think to find us herding sheep along the high street?" He glanced about, for while there would not be any sheep bleating down the high street until market day, there was always the chance Mrs. Chenoweth's cow had slipped the gate again.

"I meant no offense, only that for a village this size, there is quite a lot of activity. Is all of it on account of the royal visit?"

Merryn relaxed his hands on the reins and forced an even tone to his reply. *She is an investor. This is a business outing.* He need only get through the next few hours, and then he could return her to the Feather.

"The royal visit has brought opportunity," he said. "Every capable man in three parishes has found work these last months."

"And it's your doing?"

He shook his head, unable to claim an honor that belonged to the collective effort. "Our mayor, the investors, the workers—'tis a shared endeavor."

"But your hopes for Newford are *your* vision. The royal visit has only made them possible."

Before he could make his reply, Mrs. Tretheway and Mrs. Pentreath emerged from the chandler's shop. The matrons stopped abruptly at the sight of Merryn riding alongside Newford's elegantly dressed visitor, and Mrs. Tretheway's eyes sharpened with interest.

"Mr. Kimbrell," she said, forcing them to slow.

"Good morning, ma'am. Mrs. Pentreath." He touched his hat but didn't stop. Rebecca inclined her head politely to the ladies, though without his introduction, she could offer nothing more.

The women's whispers as they passed were not as soft as they might have thought them. Or perhaps they were as loud as they were meant to be, for he caught phrases like "French airs" and "another one seeking a husband."

Wincing, he glanced to the side to see Rebecca's cheeks had colored on hearing herself so discussed, though the corner of her mouth tilted up.

"Your sister warned me about your matrons," she said once they were out of the ladies' hearing. "I believe she called them formidable."

"Bronwyn was in a generous mood then, for I've heard her use much stronger language."

Rebecca's smile widened. "I think I could like your sister very much."

Merryn wasn't certain if that was a comfort or a concern. Perhaps a little of both.

They went past the snug harbor, up and around to a broad, grass-topped cliff. Below, two-masted luggers dotted the water as crews hauled in nets already heavy with the morning's catch.

"Does their gossip trouble you?" Merryn asked.

She made a little shrug. "I've grown accustomed to being talked about. Paris salons may be modern, but they are just as fond of gossip as any London drawing room. An Englishwoman living abroad will always draw interest." She adjusted her grip on the reins. "You did not make introductions."

He drew a breath. "The ladies would not be satisfied with only introductions. They would have required explanations."

Rebecca brought her horse closer to his. "You do realize the impossibility of keeping our arrangement a secret, do you not? Sooner or later, it will come out, and the longer we delay, the worse it will be."

"I am aware." The words came out more clipped than he intended.

She frowned. "If I may ask, why have you—"

Before she could ask why he'd been such an idiot to keep his marriage a secret, he nodded at the rise ahead. "The pavilion is there." The words were unnecessary, though, as the columned structure was clearly visible against a blue sky, nestled in a tangle of timber scaffolding.

All around, the masons' hammers rang against stone, and saws bit through timber. The sights and sounds eased the tightness that had been building in Merryn's chest since his arrival that morning at the Feather. He dismounted and summoned one of the workers.

"See to the horses, Tom."

"Aye, sir." Tom hurried over, his expression curious. It was not unusual for Merryn to arrive at the pavilion with an investor in tow, but the appearance of two gently-bred females amidst the building debris was clearly beyond the man's experience.

Merryn braced himself as he helped Rebecca from her horse. She rested her hands on his shoulders, and for a moment he held her close enough to feel the warmth of her form.

When she looked up, the feather of her hat brushed his chin. He stepped back.

"Thank you," she said in an even voice, giving no indication his hands had felt any different from those of a groom.

Adjusting his cuffs, Merryn led them toward the

pavilion. "Mind your step," he warned. "The way's uneven."

As the ladies picked carefully through the dust and stone and wood littering the ground, he began the speech he'd delivered countless times before.

"The pavilion will serve as the primary reception point when His Majesty arrives. Mayor Moon will present his address, and His Majesty will have a proper view of the sea to his left, and of Newford and the valley on the other side."

Rebecca paused to look out at the sea below. "Is Newford's harbor deep enough for the royal vessel? Sarah and I were obliged to ferry ashore when we arrived."

The question surprised him with its practicality. He shook his head. "His Majesty's yacht will anchor some yards offshore. After the naval escort fires its cannon salute, the royal party will be rowed ashore by barge and driven here. 'Tis but a short ride. The harbor is too small—and too aromatic—for ceremony."

They'd reached the steps of the pavilion and she looked to him. "May I?"

"'Tis sound enough," he said with a nod. As she stepped inside, he wondered what she would make of the structure. It was sure to be plainer than what she expected—not nearly so grand as what might have been done in London or Paris.

She turned a full circle, taking in the view from all sides before directing her gaze to the dome overhead. It was simply done, but pleasing in his estimation—sky-blue with a gilded sunburst at the center. He'd fought a lengthy battle with the squire over the simple treatment and come out the victor. Now, though, he wondered if there shouldn't be more embellishment.

"It is perfection," Rebecca said, and his breath came easier.

"'Tis not too plain?" He immediately regretted the uncertainty. It wasn't his nature to question his work. He made decisions deliberately and stood by them. It was a strategy that served him well—the singular exception being his marriage five years before, and only see where that had got him.

"It is tasteful," she said, studying the sweep of painted blue sky, "and taste seldom offends. One feels the air of Cornwall above, not the ceiling, and the classical lines of the columns lend the space a rare elegance."

He gave a short laugh. "Elegance—'twas precisely the vision I could not convey to the squire. He wished to engage painters from Truro to apply a vast mural or some such to the dome."

"A mural?"

He rubbed the back of his neck. "Aye. His Majesty as Neptune coming out of the waves, being offered the treasures of Cornwall by a parade of sparsely-clad sea-nymphs—that sort of mural."

Rebecca turned wide eyes on him. "Good heavens."

"Just so. We've already plans to gild the top of the dome, and the marble columns are the best to be found. 'Twill be a fitting place to receive a monarch, but Carew believes the King would be honored by such a resplendent scene."

She considered this. "His Majesty has never been accused of moderation."

"'Tis true. But if our King finds this pavilion too modest, at least he cannot find it absurd."

"And that," she said, her tone amused, "is perhaps a greater triumph than you allow."

The corner of his mouth lifted, and she returned his smile. The hammering around them had slowed, and he was conscious of the eyes of his men on them. He raised a brow at a joiner who'd ceased planing a balustrade, and the man jumped to resume his task.

Rebecca directed more questions at him, each more thoughtful than the last. She might not know the intricacies of construction, but she possessed an intelligence that cut straight to the heart of a matter, and she surprised him with a keen interest in joinery and footings.

He found himself warming to the topic despite his earlier reservations about the outing. His words came faster, and he gripped his hands behind his back to keep from sketching shapes in the air as he spoke.

"Of course," she mused as she studied the line of the roof, "the structure must be sound as well as handsome. Pleasing to the eye while practical enough to shelter the royal party from any weather."

"Precisely. See here—" He gestured to where the roof met the dome. "The pitch allows water to run off quickly if a squall comes up, and the orientation shields the royal dais from the winds."

She stepped closer to follow the line he indicated. "You've been deliberate in the placement."

"Aye, though Carew spent a week or more lamenting the angle of the morning light on the balcony."

"Your squire has very decided opinions."

Merryn released a breath. "He's no shortage of them, to be sure."

"And yet you managed to persuade him from his mural."

He lifted a shoulder. He'd worked with enough men like the squire to accept their stout convictions as an inevitable part of the job, and they weren't always wrong. Merryn liked to think he was shrewd enough to recognize a sound idea even when it wasn't his own.

But the squire's mural would have taken weeks to complete, and it would have appeared vulgar in the execution. He'd long wished for Newford's prosperity, but not at the expense of appearing ridiculous.

Rebecca moved a gloved hand along one of the completed columns. "You have achieved a rare thing—a structure both handsome and restrained. Surely, the squire must be pleased with the end result."

"'Pleased' might be overstating the matter. Carew would have the high street paved in gold leaf if't could be done."

Rebecca laughed. "To please the King?"

"To please himself, I think—but if His Majesty should happen to notice, so much the better."

"He has hopes, then, for a commendation from the throne. Let us trust that taste may yet prove as persuasive as ambition, for you have done good work here."

Never had an investor's approval caused his neck to heat, but that was precisely the effect of his wife's simple words. He tightened his hands behind his back and cleared his throat. "We ought to continue on. Trevelyan Abbey is a half-hour's ride."

CHAPTER 11

THE ROAD TO the Abbey took them out of Newford and into the surrounding countryside. It wound upward through farmland and patches of wood, offering glimpses of the sea between the hills. Rebecca maintained a steady but pleasant conversation, asking him questions about the passing flora and sharing stories from her time abroad.

Merryn found himself responding with more ease than he'd managed all morning. He was beginning to think the outing might not be the ordeal he'd anticipated when she turned to him to ask, "How does your mother fare? You've said nothing of her."

The horse sidled beneath him. The reminder that he must still devise some sort of explanation for his marriage for the woman who'd borne him caused the tightness in his shoulders to return.

He adjusted his grip on the reins. "She is presently away to Helston."

Rebecca's expression shifted at his tone. "Forgive me," she said. "I should not have presumed to inquire."

"No, 'tis only—" He caught himself. "She's well. My aunt's health has been troubling her, and my mother has gone to help."

"Ah, yes. I recall she has a sister there."

His brow lowered in surprise. "My letters again?"

They'd been a torture to write, but he'd maintained his duty, sending her funds each quarter and inquiring after her welfare. And all the while wishing to know if she had any regrets or if she was happy in her carefully constructed independence.

"I read them when I'm feeling homesick for England."

Her admission struck him unexpectedly. He'd imagined her filing them away with her other correspondence, never to be seen again. Certainly, he'd never imagined her reading them again.

"I might have made more of an effort to be amusing, had I known."

She tilted her head at him. "Would you have? Perhaps you would have told me more stories like the one about your squire's son and the plaster."

Merryn chuckled. He'd shared the tale with her during their wedding night conversation. His firm had just completed improvements to the squire's dining room. The next morning, the man's youngest son, having emptied his father's brandy after a sideways encounter with a lass, was found asleep against the wall, hair firmly fixed in the newly-dried plaster.

It had required two men and a razor to free him, and the lad had taken to wearing his hat at all hours.

"Per'aps," he agreed.

She smiled as Trevelyan Abbey came into view. The medieval manor dominated the hillside with thick grey walls and mullioned windows, behind which burned the extravagance of daytime candles. The squire's carriageway swept in a broad arc before the entrance, where topiary yews stood sentinel on either side.

"Trevelyan Abbey," Merryn said unnecessarily.

A footman took their horses at the end of the drive, and Carew himself met them in the entry. His cravat, which was usually rather limp, had benefited today from a liberal application of starch. The points were sharp and crisp beneath his jowls.

"Kimbrell!" His eyes took in the cut of Rebecca's habit and the tilt of her hat. She must have passed his judgment, for he nodded. "This must be the honored guest of whom you spoke."

"Squire Carew, may I present Miss Pearce," Merryn said, "lately of Paris."

"Paris! How delightful. You must tell me how our preparations compare to French standards. Naturally, Trevelyan Abbey spares no expense for His Majesty."

Rebecca gave Carew one of her engaging smiles. "I'm certain His Majesty will be gratified by your hospitality."

"Indeed, indeed. Come, you must see the improvements. The ballroom chandeliers alone have cost—well, suffice to say, it was a considerable sum. The finest workmanship this side of the Channel."

Carew led them through the house, pontificating on every improvement he'd commissioned over the years—and there had been many. Merryn said little but watched as Rebecca navigated the squire's bluster. She made appropriate sounds of admiration, asked questions that flattered the man's knowledge, and managed to redirect his more tedious monologues without causing offense. Merryn did not doubt she would have persuaded Carew from his mural notion far more readily than he had.

Carew showed her his dining room first, where the King and his entourage would be treated to a Cornish supper fit for royalty. To hear the talk in Newford, the squire's cook had already sent away to London for pineapples and hothouse grapes, which to Merryn's thinking, seemed counter to the notion of a Cornish supper.

"Had Kimbrell in to do the room some years

ago," Carew said. "He did a proper job of it too, though there were some problems with the plaster — had to redo it, you know."

As the squire bent to wipe a smudge from the polished mahogany table, Rebecca caught Merryn's eye, her lips pressed against a laugh. He was hard put to hold his own mirth.

"I think you were wise to engage Mr. Kimbrell," Rebecca offered, "for he strikes me as a man who doesn't settle for anything less than perfection. Not everyone has your discernment in choosing their associates."

"What's that? Discernment? Quite right."

They moved on to the squire's ballroom, which was still in the throes of renovation. Much of the floor, a new parquet in a herringbone pattern, lay beneath canvas while the painters finished their gilt work on the ceiling. The squire's expensive new chandeliers hung from chains, and their crystal prisms caught the light from the tall windows. In the musicians' gallery above, workmen were installing the final balustrades.

Rebecca gathered the skirts of her habit in one hand and accepted Merryn's assistance over a pile of timber.

When she stood safely clear of the debris, her hand remained on his arm. The weight of it was light and warm through his sleeve as Carew pointed out where the King's dais would occupy the front of the room.

"Now, the gardens," Carew announced, leading them through French doors that opened onto a broad terrace. "I've had a hedge maze installed with a temple at the center—classical design, very fashionable, though the expense was not inconsiderable. His Majesty will be most impressed."

The maze stretched before them, its yew hedges neatly trimmed, and the white stone columns of the squire's temple rose from the center.

"And here," Carew gestured to a raised platform at the edge of the terrace, "is the royal box, where His Majesty will have a fine view of the gardens and the fireworks display. The temple provides an excellent focal point, you see."

"Fireworks!" Rebecca said. "You have thought of everything, sir."

The squire preened at this while Rebecca made appropriate noises over the King's box. It had been constructed with carved railings and a canopy overhead.

Cushioned benches offered seating, and Merryn could not fault the view, for the structure did indeed command both the temple and the valley beyond—precisely as it had *before* Carew insisted the whole thing be dismantled and rebuilt an inch and a quarter to the left.

"It is remarkable," Rebecca said, stepping into the box to better see the gardens.

As Merryn followed her, voices drifted up from the maze. Gardeners, by the sound of their hedge clippers. The squire frowned in their direction then left them to stride quickly down the path.

Rebecca turned. "Is that the Feather?" she asked, motioning to where the inn's roof could just be seen through the trees. Merryn started to answer but was interrupted by the squire's bellow.

"No, no, you fool! Not that hedge—the other one! Can you not tell the difference?" His voice carried up to them as clearly as if he stood beside them on the terrace.

"Mind the corners—His Majesty will notice if they're uneven!"

Rebecca's eyes widened slightly. Merryn leaned closer to her and whispered, "Though 'twas not intended to, the squire's temple acts much as a stage—sound carries dreadfully from the stone."

Carew gave another sharp command, and Rebecca pressed a hand to her mouth, clearly fighting amusement at the squire's unwitting performance.

"Dreadfully indeed," she murmured.

Carew emerged from the maze moments later, looking well satisfied with his corrections. "Well then! Shall we return to the house?"

To Merryn's relief, Rebecca declined the squire's offer of refreshment, citing no wish to keep him from his important duties. After collecting their horses, they turned back to Newford.

The return journey passed more quickly than the outward ride, and Merryn was surprised to find their conversation came even easier. They compared French and English architectural preferences and debated the merits of various types of stone. Somewhere along the way, they ended up discussing Cornish sweets versus French pastries.

"I cannot credit you prefer a French puff to a proper saffron bun," Merryn said.

His wife's eyes gleamed with amusement. "I can and I do. Though I will admit your cousin Wynne's raspberry tarts are superior to anything in Paris."

"A concession at last."

Her pert, "Do not grow accustomed to it," drew a smile from him.

Their wry teasing was the sort Merryn might have shared with one of his cousins, were he inclined to notice his cousin's light hand on the reins or how the afternoon light caught the copper threads in his hair.

"Speaking of your cousin's tarts," she said, "I have brought you one from the Feather's kitchen." She produced a small linen-wrapped parcel and offered it to him.

Merryn stared at it, caught by the unexpected gesture.

"You needn't look suspicious," she said, her tone light. "It's only a tart. I understand you've a fondness for them, and I thought you might enjoy it after your supper this evening."

He took the parcel, his gloved hands brushing hers. "Thank you."

The words felt inadequate, but her wide smile suggested they sufficed. He tucked the linen carefully into his coat.

As they descended the final hill into Newford, Rebecca cleared her throat delicately. "Sarah and I thank you for a pleasant morning. I fear we've taken up quite a bit of your time."

They were nearing the bottom of the lane where it joined the bustling high street. In moments, they'd reach the Feather where Merryn could deposit his wife, his duty discharged. Soon he could go about his day and the tasks he'd left undone. He ought to be relieved. Instead, he was reluctant to see an end to their outing.

"There's another project," he heard himself say. "If you'd care to see it."

Rebecca turned, her gaze unreadable beneath the small veil of her riding hat. "Oh?"

"The bridge works, per'aps a quarter hour's ride north. The men will set the final stones today."

He paused, feeling foolish. There was nothing particularly engaging about the bridge to Truro. It certainly wasn't designed to impress like the pavilion, nor could it claim the opulence of the squire's Abbey renovations. It was unlikely the King would even notice the work as the royal carriage passed over it, but unlike the pavilion and the Abbey's ballroom, the bridge was *needed*.

Just like the new pump he'd installed last month near the village green and the drainage works below the high street. Improvements that might not stir admiration but were vital to the people of Newford.

The royal project had made them all possible with funds and workers they wouldn't have had otherwise. Merryn had been careful with his spending, stretching every farthing to cover what was needed alongside what would impress a king for a day.

"The bridge—'tis nothing so grand as the pavilion," he warned, "but the old timber crossing has been unsafe for years, more so when the river floods in winter. It delays the mail, and the fishermen's catch spoils before it can reach the market—"

"I should like to see it."

His wife's simple statement shouldn't have made his pulse quicken, but it did. Or perhaps it was the smile that accompanied it.

There were a dozen tasks awaiting his attention, and spending more time with Rebecca would only add tinder to the gossip that was certainly beginning to burn. But her questions and their teasing talk of saffron buns and raspberry tarts had put him in mind of the time he'd spent in London. Of their rides in the park and outings to Hatchards and Gunter's before they'd made their marriage bargain. Of that night in her uncle's library before she'd gone.

Each hour in her company had left him eager for the next, and the next after that.

For better or worse, he nodded and turned them north.

CHAPTER 12

MERRYN KEPT THEM at an easy pace as the horses wound through sheep-dotted farmland. Presently, the road descended toward the stream that marked the parish boundary. Rebecca rode tirelessly beside him while, away from Newford's crowded streets and watching eyes, Sarah gave up any pretense of chaperonage to trail a fair distance behind.

Adjusting the reins in his hands, Merryn explained, "The bridge serves the Truro road. The crossing has stood for some forty years, but the timber supports rot more each winter."

"And the King's visit has made its replacement possible?"

"Not only possible, but necessary. His Majesty's royal coach will travel this road when he leaves Newford."

"And after? You believe the bridge will turn a profit?"

He turned to look at her. He'd allowed himself to forget for a moment that she was an investor. That her interest in his bridge was a financial one.

"You shall have your dividends."

"Do not turn stiff," she said. "I've a dozen ladies who've entrusted me with their funds."

"Aye," he said on a breath. "The tolls will turn a profit. A sound bridge shortens the journey by nearly an hour. Merchants will pay for that."

"When I directed Mr. Cross to send on my investment, he warned me that such improvements seldom enrich anyone."

"Then he has never seen Cornish mud after a storm. Every man spared a broken wheel will happily give up a farthing for't."

She smiled, which caused his frown to grow.

"Why d'you smile?"

"Because your practical heart warms my own."

Her words surprised an answering laugh from him. "You thought me otherwise?"

"Well," she said, a hint of teasing in her tone, "some might argue that building a bridge to improve the common good—at considerable risk to your own capital—is less practical than it is idealistic."

"Nonsense. 'Tis a prudent investment. The tolls will yield returns."

"Of course they will. But that's not why you're building your bridge, is it?"

He shifted in the saddle. "I fail to see the distinction."

"The distinction," she said, "is that a truly practical man would invest in ventures with better margins and less risk. You've chosen this because it helps people. That's idealism."

"A man should be able to earn honestly by improving what others rely upon. I take no shame in that."

"Nor should you."

Her tone suggested she believed him incapable of choosing sense over sentiment, which rankled. He turned the conversation back on her. "And what of you? D'you not have a bit of the idealist in you?"

"Me? I am the most practical female you will chance to meet."

"Maintaining investments for governesses and maids—you could put your efforts anywhere. Instead, you've chosen to help women who've little means and less standing." He paused. "That seems rather idealistic for one who denies it."

"It is nothing of the sort," she countered. "Small investors can achieve far better returns through collective management than they ever could individually. There's nothing idealistic about sound financial strategy."

"Per'aps. But you could apply that same strategy to wealthier ladies and profit far more from't."

"Profit isn't everything."

"Which is precisely my point."

She pressed her lips together, though whether in irritation or suppressed amusement, he couldn't tell. "I believe you are being deliberately obstinate," she said.

"I am being *practical*," he replied, and the absurdity of their debate struck him. He found himself smiling as he added, "D'you see? There's not a trace of sentiment between us."

"None at all," she agreed, though her eyes held a spark of laughter. "We are both exceedingly sensible people making exceedingly sensible choices."

"Then we shall be partners in practicality."

"Partners," she said, and he couldn't tell if she meant the word as agreement or was merely testing it.

They rode in silence for a few minutes, passing hedgerows thick with wild roses and fields of grazing sheep. A lark sang somewhere overhead, its song lifting on the warm summer air.

The bridge came into view as they crested a hill. The old timber crossing stood to one side with its weathered planks and listing posts. Beside it, a new stone structure rose from the banks of a wide stream. Scaffolding surrounded the crown where a three-foot keystone with its carved royal cipher would complete the arch.

Merryn counted nearly a dozen men on the banks. Several prepared the ropes and pulleys that would hoist the stone into place, then there were men from the surrounding farms who'd ridden over to witness the event. And his cousins: James, Jory, and Gavin.

He cursed his stupidity. He should have known they would come to see the bridge completed. They had argued its necessity for as long as Merryn had. He might have been able to avoid the matrons' curiosity, but his cousins would not be put off so easily.

"Your family?" Rebecca asked, following his gaze.

"Aye," he said. "They are investors as well." As the horse shifted beneath him, Merryn considered briefly whether a retreat was possible. It was not. The workers had already spotted them, and James lifted a hand in greeting.

"Then I shall have the pleasure of meeting them," Rebecca said simply.

With a sigh for the inevitability of it, Merryn descended toward the bridge. A boy hurried forward to take their horses, and his cousins approached, their interested and none-too-subtle gazes taking in Rebecca and her companion.

"Gentlemen," Merryn said. "Allow me to present Miss Pearce and her companion, Miss Denning. They are lately from Paris."

The words lodged in his throat as he introduced his wife by her former name to his family. Each word of the lie felt heavier than the last. How much longer could he keep the truth from them? More to the point, why had he ever been so foolish to hold his silence to begin with? Pride—it was a cursed thing.

His throat had gone dry, and he cleared it before continuing. "Miss Pearce is one of our project's investors."

James's brow lifted toward his hairline, and Gavin's expression shifted from curiosity to keen interest, his constable's instincts stirring. Jory looked between Merryn and Rebecca with clear speculation.

James was the first to recover. "An investor—from Paris?"

Rebecca inclined her head. "Your cousin has been kind enough to show me how my investment has been employed. It is pleasing to see such clear results."

"A lady investor," Gavin mused with a tone of faint bewilderment.

Rebecca's chin lifted. "My uncle was a banker. He taught me that one might have opinions about how their money is used or sit idle while others manage one's fortune." She paused, meeting Gavin's gaze directly. "I find the former more engaging, and a comfort to my peace of mind."

Merryn's cousins exchanged glances, clearly trying to reconcile the elegantly clad woman before them with their understanding of the world.

"Besides," Rebecca continued, "investments such as this—practical improvements that serve communities—these have value beyond mere profit. A sound bridge protects lives, enables commerce, connects families. My uncle believed one's wealth could benefit more than one's own purse."

"He sounds like a wise man," James finally said.

"He was." A shadow crossed her features, quickly mastered. She took a step toward the bridge, studying the arch's curve. "Local stone was used?"

Jory stepped forward. "Aye. 'Tis from the Carnmenellis quarries," he offered. "Same granite used for the harbor improvements in Falmouth."

"And the engineering—you've employed a single span design."

His cousins' surprise appeared in more arched brows, and Merryn hid his smile as he answered. "Aye. 'Tis stronger than multiple arches for such a width, and less likely to catch debris during the winter floods."

There was movement at the bridge as several men hoisted the keystone from its sled, the ropes straining under its weight. There were a few shouts and shifting feet as the block swayed before the men steadied it.

Rebecca studied the wooden scaffolding surrounding the arch's crown and the system of ropes and pulleys attached to a heavy timber frame. "How will they maneuver it into place?" she asked. "The weight must be considerable."

"Nearly three thousand pounds," Merryn confirmed. "The men will use a timber frame with a block and tackle—you can see the arrangement there."

He gestured to where thick ropes ran through iron pulleys mounted on a sturdy oak beam. "They'll lift the keystone with the pulleys, swing it into position over the crown, then lower it into place. The benchmarks cut into the stonework on either side of the arch will guide the placement to within a quarter inch."

Lifting the hem of her habit, Rebecca moved closer to the place he indicated while the workers continued their preparations.

As soon as she was out of hearing, James caught Merryn's eye. "An investor—she is the source of your anonymous amount?"

Jory and Gavin drew closer, and Merryn's jaw tightened. "Aye."

Gavin's eyes narrowed. "How does a lady in France come to invest in Cornish improvements?"

"Her solicitor is out of London."

"Her solicitor," James repeated with a hint of

suspicion in his tone. "'Twouldn't be Nathaniel Cross, would it? Of Cross and Jones?"

Merryn gave a tight nod and waited while his cousin worked through the implications. It didn't take him long.

"You asked me about Cross and Jones at Oak Hill. You must have suspected even then... Just *how*, precisely, are you acquainted with Miss Pearce?"

Before Merryn could fashion a proper response to such a sensible question, warning shouts rose from the men at the bridge.

CHAPTER 13

Rebecca's habit was caught on a coil of rope. She bent to free the cloth when the first Cornish shout went up.

"*Warya!*" The language was foreign to her, but the warning tone was clear enough. She looked up to see the keystone swaying where it hung from its large pulley.

Everything happened quickly after that. One of the ropes holding the stone slipped, and the massive block swung wide, striking one of the support timbers with a force that shook the entire scaffold. Wood cracked and splintered.

There were more shouts in Cornish and then "Stand clear!" as the timber broke free and tumbled toward her.

She gave a final, desperate yank at her skirt. The cloth yielded with a fantastic tear, but her escape came too late. The falling timber filled her vision. Something struck her from behind just as pain exploded across her temple.

The world tilted, sky and earth trading places. Strong hands caught her before she hit the ground, and she found herself held against a solid form that smelled of leather and soap.

She lay motionless, disoriented.

"Rebecca."

Merryn's voice was close and urgent. She tried to bring his face into focus, but the edges of her vision had gone soft. Something warm trickled down her temple. She lifted a hand to it, and her glove came away red.

"Well," she heard herself say, though her voice sounded distant to her own ears. "This is rather dramatic."

She attempted a smile—surely things weren't as dire as Merryn's expression suggested—but the movement sent fresh pain lancing through her skull. Slowly, she became aware of the sound of raised voices and boots thudding across planks. She caught fragments of Cornish mixed with English, all of it far more urgent than her little tumble required.

"Rebecca!" Sarah's voice came from a distance.

Rebecca tried to rise, but Merryn commanded her to, "Lie still." She complied. It seemed too much of an effort to do otherwise. He shifted, drawing something from his coat. A moment later, a square of soft linen pressed against her temple.

She replaced his hand with her own, their fingers tangling briefly until he conceded the handkerchief to her. Already, it was damp with her blood.

She moved to rise again, but Merryn held her firmly. She blinked at the fierceness of his frown and tried for a bit of levity. "Is your concern for my bruised head or has your bridge been damaged?"

A muscle moved in his jaw. He was not in the mood for jests then.

"That rope should not have failed," he said roughly. There was a new tension in his arms.

"Surely, these things happen."

"I should have checked it. I should have—" He broke off, but his arms tightened around her.

"I am perfectly all right," she said. "In fact, I think I can stand…" She wasn't entirely certain that was true. The world had taken on an odd, distant quality, and forming coherent thoughts required an unusual degree of concentration.

"Rebecca, please. Just… be still."

The raw note in his voice stopped her more effectively than his command, and she subsided against his chest. Through the soft haze of pain, she was aware of his heartbeat, quick and hard beneath her cheek. Of all the improper things to notice at such a moment, but there it was—her husband's pulse racing.

THE BLOOD WOULD not stop. When Rebecca's hand loosened on the handkerchief, Merryn replaced it with his own and gently pressed the wound. She was conscious and speaking—even attempting humor—but there was a pinched look about her eyes.

"Here is Miss Denning," he said when her companion reached them, though he made no move to give his wife over to the woman's care.

"Rebecca, my dear girl," Miss Denning knelt beside them. "I turned away for only a moment, and then I find you lying on the ground, bleeding."

Rebecca's eyes fluttered closed. "It is only a scratch," she assured her.

"Gavin has gone for Rowe," James said. The news ought to have been a relief, but it would take half an hour or more for the surgeon to reach them.

"How bad is't?" Jory whispered.

Merryn didn't answer immediately but studied Rebecca's pale face. Her lashes lay thick against her cheek. The timber had struck her with some force, and the cut at her temple continued to bleed beneath his handkerchief.

Why hadn't he checked the blasted ropes? If only he'd—

He stopped, for nothing would be gained by worrying over what was done. His thoughts would be better put to addressing his wife's comfort. He drew a breath and composed himself—there was no purpose to alarming Rebecca or her companion with his concern.

"'Tis only a scratch," he replied, echoing Rebecca's own words. She must still have been conscious, for the corner of her mouth lifted.

Miss Denning looked up from where she crouched at her employer's side. "We must return to the inn. She needs proper tending."

Rebecca stirred and opened her eyes again. "Yes," she agreed. "That sounds just the thing. I should like a proper lie-down."

She would hear no more arguments. When she moved to rise, Merryn assisted her to her feet, his own breath catching with the effort. He held one arm firmly around her waist when she swayed. Her hand found his, gripping it with more force than she likely intended. He shifted closer and let her lean against him.

"D'you think you can suffer the journey back to Newford?" James asked, his eyes moving between them both. "The surgeon can meet us at the Feather."

"I believe so," Rebecca replied.

"Wait," Merryn said, though he didn't know why. Returning Rebecca to the Feather was a logical course. It would take less time than waiting for Gavin to fetch the surgeon to them. They would meet Rowe, and he could tend her there.

But the notion of his wife recovering in a public house felt... wrong. Though Wynne kept a clean and warm establishment, Rebecca could not be as comfortable there as in a proper home.

He shook his head. "Not the Feather."

The words came out rough, and he cleared his throat. His cousins turned to look at him. Merryn, in turn, looked at Rebecca. Her brown eyes met his, wide and uncertain.

"But—" Jory began.

"Miss Pearce will recover at my home."

His words fell into a sudden quiet, like stones dropped in a dry well. Even the workers at the bridge had slowed their tasks to listen.

"Merryn..." Gavin's tone held warning, question, and concern in equal measure. "Did the beam strike your head as well?"

"'Twould be unseemly," Jory added. "Your mother is away—"

Merryn shook his head, halting his cousin's words. Regardless of the years and distance between them, Rebecca was his wife, and she'd been hurt at his bridge because he'd brought her here.

She should not be made to recover at a public inn. Not when it was his pride, his cowardice, his stubborn silence that had brought them to this point of secrecy.

He covered her hand with his. "She'll recover at my home," he repeated. "Miss Pearce is my wife."

His cousins stood frozen, mouths open in identical expressions of disbelief that would have been amusing were the situation anything else. Miss Denning's eyes were wide, and even the workers were caught in the moment with their hammers and chisels half-raised.

Rebecca had gone very still at his side. She'd abandoned all attempts at humor, and he wished he could read her thoughts. This was why she'd come to Newford, after all—to claim her husband and settle her cousin's suspicions. But her face was pale, her thoughts as hidden from him as they'd ever been.

There was no mistaking the matter, though. Once her cousin's threat was resolved, she would board a ship back to France. And he would remain in Newford, exactly as he'd been five years before—wed but alone. Only now, everyone would know it.

CHAPTER 14

LATE AFTERNOON LIGHT fell in amber ribbons across an unfamiliar ceiling. Rebecca studied the plaster roses that formed a delicate pattern around the edges, trying to place where she was. There was a soft heather scent coming from the bed linens—she was not at the Feather then, for Mrs. Teague used rosewater.

Her head ached with a dull persistence that made thinking difficult. She turned then winced as the motion sent a sharper pain through her temple.

Beside the bed, Sarah dozed in a chair, a book open on her lap and a candle guttering on the table. Rebecca's riding habit hung on a hook by the door, the hem trailing the floor from a spectacular tear.

It came back to her in a rush. Merryn's bridge, the swaying keystone and falling timber. Her husband's arms around her, his heartbeat quick beneath her cheek.

And then his unexpected declaration and the ride to his home.

His home.

There'd been a pair of wide-eyed maids and a housekeeper at the door. Mrs. Tilbury, he'd called her. The older woman had been understandably shocked when Merryn directed her to ready a room for his wife.

This, then, must be a guest chamber. It was nicely appointed but impersonal—solid furniture, quality curtains in a pale green that matched the bed linens. A landscape painting hung on the opposite wall next to a washstand and mirror.

Everything was tidy and clean, but it lacked the refinement of her aunt's apartments in Paris, or even her uncle's home in London. There were no gilt cherubs or marble mantelpiece, no ormolu or Aubusson.

Sarah stirred. "You're awake," she said. Setting aside her forgotten book, she began fussing about with the bed pillows.

"The housekeeper has sent up water," she continued, "but I'll ring for tea. I doubt they can round up chocolate, though I will ask."

"I'm fine," Rebecca said. "Truly."

"You were struck rather forcefully by a falling timber, my dear. You are decidedly not fine."

Rebecca lifted a hand to the plaster at her hairline and touched it gingerly. The surgeon had wrapped it in clean linen, secured beneath her hair. "The surgeon was here," she said as the memory of an older gentleman returned to her. "I believe he said I shall make a full recovery."

"He also said you require rest and quiet." Sarah poured a glass of water from the pitcher on the bedside table. "Here, take small sips."

"You have always said I have a thick skull," Rebecca said. The cool water began to clear some of the fog from her thoughts.

Sarah drew herself up. "I have said no such thing." Then, frowning, she added truthfully, "At least, not since you were a girl."

Rebecca returned the empty glass to her. "My husband's secret is out, it would seem." The plaster at her temple pulled when she frowned, so she forced her expression to clear.

"And none too soon, I say. What's the world come to when a man and wife keep their union a secret?" Sarah mused. Then, huffing a soft laugh, she added, "I thought his cousins might turn themselves inside out in their bewilderment, but they rallied soon enough. When it was clear Mr. Kimbrell meant to bring you here, they jumped to secure a cart."

Rebecca remained silent as the import of her husband's actions settled on her thoughts. His secret was out, and she was uncertain what she ought to feel.

"Shall I see if I can arrange for a light repast? Some broth, perhaps? You've had nothing to eat since dawn."

The thought of food caused Rebecca's stomach to turn, but she nodded. Sarah moved toward the door then paused. "Rest, my dear, then eat. I shall arrange for our things to be brought from the inn."

The door closed with a soft click and Rebecca was alone. The house around her was quiet but not silent. She could hear footsteps somewhere below, the distant clatter of what might be pots in a kitchen, a door closing.

Her head ached, but beneath that, was an awareness that she was in Merryn's home. The place where he'd grown from a boy to a man. Where he laughed and ate and slept. The notion of her gruff husband sleeping with his face relaxed was an intriguing thought. She wondered if he snored. The thought caused a smile, which in turn caused her temple to throb.

She threw off the bedclothes, only to find she was clad in nothing but her chemise. She shivered despite the warm summer air and studied the room again, searching for some hint of her husband in this space. There was nothing to suggest this room was anything more than a stopping place for visitors.

Even the books on the bedside table were the sort one provided for guests—a book of sermons, a guide to Cornish landmarks, a bit of poetry.

The irony wasn't lost on her. She was Merryn's wife in name, but she was a guest in his home. Their arrangement had ensured that, hadn't it?

She'd taken her inheritance and left, as they'd agreed. Made her life in Paris, as planned.

For five years, it had worked. She had her independence, and he had the sum she'd promised him—one thousand pounds of her inheritance. Enough to fund his construction ventures. There was never supposed to be anything more to it.

And yet, he'd caught her when she fell and refused to let her convalesce at the inn.

My wife, he'd said, and there had been something fierce in his voice. Something that went beyond duty or propriety or the terms of their arrangement.

Male voices rose from somewhere below, too muffled for her to make out words but clear enough to recognize Merryn's deep timbre among them. His cousins, perhaps? They would have questions. Five years of a secret marriage surely demanded an explanation.

Putting her feet gingerly onto the floor, she gripped the bed post. When the dizziness subsided, she rose, head throbbing, and moved toward the door. She leaned close to listen through the wood, but she couldn't make out their words. How would Merryn explain?

Yes, we married in London.

Five years ago, yes.

No, I never thought to mention it.

A laugh escaped her, though there was little humor in it. The movement caused her head to pound anew, and she pressed a hand to her temple before moving back toward the bed.

There was a light knock, and the door opened again. It wasn't Sarah but a woman in her middle years wearing a housekeeper's neat grey dress and white cap. Mrs. Tilbury.

She entered bearing a tray. "Begging your pardon, ma'am," the woman said, bobbing a curtsy. "Your companion requested a repast. I've come with bread and butter and some broth, if you care for't." Steam curled from a bowl on the tray, and the warm fragrance of freshly baked bread reached Rebecca. Despite her earlier nausea, her stomach rumbled.

"Thank you, Mrs. Tilbury," she said with a nod.

The housekeeper crossed to the small table beside the hearth and set down her tray. As she began arranging dishes, her gaze darted to Rebecca, then away and back again, as though she couldn't quite comprehend this new turn in her employer's circumstance.

"I imagine it must be something of a shock," Rebecca said gently.

The woman completed her task and straightened. Hands folded before her apron, she said, "Be there anything else you require, ma'am?"

"I am quite comfortable, thank you."

Mrs. Tilbury's mouth was a flat line in an otherwise unremarkable face. She bent her knee in a shallow curtsy but didn't move to go.

Rebecca waited.

"If I may say so, ma'am," the woman began, "'tis… well, 'tis a surprise, is all. Mr. Kimbrell never said… That is, we had no idea he'd married."

Rebecca couldn't blame the woman for her confusion, but neither could she explain her husband's actions, for she didn't understand them herself. Still, there was her cousin Gregory to convince, and it wouldn't do for those closest to Merryn to show surprise on the matter of their marriage. Even the servants—*especially* the servants—must believe it was properly done.

"I assure you, our marriage was quite properly made in London five years ago. As to the privacy surrounding it—" She paused, choosing her words carefully. "Mr. Kimbrell believed discretion was the best course at the time. I trust that satisfies your curiosity on the matter."

"Of course," Mrs. Tilbury replied, though her

tone suggested she had her own thoughts about such irregular doings. She nodded again and withdrew.

Rebecca knew she ought to feel relief that Merryn's secret was out. Perhaps now they could get on with the business of preparing for her cousin's return. Instead, she felt... uncertain.

The housekeeper's skepticism was only the start. How many more would look at them with the same doubt?

She couldn't deny a flicker of irritation for her husband. If he'd simply told his family about their marriage from the start, none of this awkwardness would exist.

And yet, she hated the thought of what he now faced for his silence—the questions, the astonishment, the whispers sure to follow. He was downstairs now, addressing the first of what were sure to be many such interrogations.

Whatever the terms of their marriage had been, he now bore the weight of its revelation alone, and that knowledge unsettled her more than the pain in her head.

CHAPTER 15

MERRYN STOOD OUTSIDE the parlor and scrubbed a hand over his jaw. His cousins waited on the other side of the door, and it was foolish to think the conversation could be avoided. He set his mouth and went in.

The sun was lower in the sky, and the room was cool. The grate had been swept, the fire laid for the evening but as yet unlit. On the mantel, the clock announced the hour.

Jory and Gavin rose. James stood before the window, arms crossed and the late afternoon light casting his features in unreadable shadow.

"How does she fare?" Jory asked after a small beat.

"Rowe is satisfied," Merryn said. His voice was even, though he couldn't credit how he managed it. "He advises quiet and rest."

"And you?" Gavin said. "You took the force of the beam before it struck Miss Pearce. I daresay she has you to thank for her life."

Merryn rolled his shoulder and hid a wince for the pain in his ribs. He would have a spectacular bruise come the morrow, but he would survive. He told them as much.

No one sat until Merryn, with a motion of one hand, bade them to do so. He remained standing by the hearth, his back to the cold grate and the clock ticking at his shoulder.

It was Jory who broke the stillness with a throat clearing. "I was not... rather—"

Gavin interrupted. "We were unaware you had made a marriage, cousin."

Merryn clasped his hands behind his back and studied the pattern in the rug. His mother had acquired it some twenty years before, and it was beginning to show wear. His mother—she would have to be informed, of course. Now that his secret was out, he'd not have her hearing of his marriage from one of the matrons.

He answered Gavin with a nod. "'Twas done in London, five years agone."

No one spoke as they took this in. He could imagine their thoughts turning as they recalled the last five years, searching for any hint that their eldest cousin had carried such a secret.

"'Twas the summer you sought funds for your father's firm," James said slowly.

"Aye. I was a guest of William Pearce, of Pearce and Hanford. Miss Pearce—Rebecca—was his niece and ward."

James nodded as if this were a sufficient explanation. Merryn knew he could not be so fortunate. Outside, a bird called to its mate. Inside, Jory looked once toward the sideboard where the brandy decanter sat, and Merryn thought they could all use a bit of fortification. He crossed the room and poured, then distributed the glasses round.

Gavin studied the swirling amber liquid as Jory emptied his in one swallow. "We would have stood by you, had we known," he said. "At the least, we could have given your wife a proper welcome."

Merryn drew a slow breath and released it. "There was little time. The arrangement was quickly done."

Gavin set his untouched brandy aside. "An arrangement."

"I remember there was something..." Jory spoke slowly until his recollection firmed. "Your host—he took ill while you were there."

Merryn nodded. "Pearce suffered an apoplexy on my last visit. 'Twas why I remained longer than I planned. I couldn't leave—" Merryn cleared his throat before continuing. "It didn't seem right to leave his household with such uncertainty. There were creditors to manage, accounts to settle... At any rate, Pearce's situation was grave, and he desired to see his ward settled. His son and heir, Mr. Gregory Pearce, has been away to the West Indies these last years, but even had he been in England, I do not think Pearce would have liked to see his niece's welfare given over to him. Marriage was the only recourse."

"He did not trust his own son?" Gavin said with a frown.

Merryn shook his head. "The two were estranged. I gather they did not agree on most matters, but especially those regarding money and how it ought to be spent. 'Tis why the younger Pearce left in the first place."

"And Miss Pearce?" Gavin asked. "What were her thoughts during all of this?"

"Miss Pearce was very fond of her uncle and dismayed by his condition. She had no wish to marry, but her inheritance would otherwise fall to her cousin's trusteeship. She desired her independence," Merryn said. "We found our interests aligned. She required a husband to claim her portion, and I required funds to grow my father's firm. I agreed to her terms." Then, seeing his words had little effect on their frowns, he added, "The discretion was mine entirely. She bears no blame for't."

Gavin's jaw worked. "As… practical… as this arrangement sounds, it doesn't answer for why you couldn't speak of't. We're blood, and if that is not enough for confidences, we thought ourselves friends."

"You are," Merryn said through the tightness in his throat. He looked between them, these men who'd come up with him, who'd stood by him when he'd been a lad of seventeen with the unexpected charge of his mother and his sister and his father's firm. Gathering his thoughts, he tried his best to explain.

"When Miss Pearce repaired to France—as we'd agreed—it seemed the easiest course was to simply go on as I had done. What purpose would explanations have served? But you have cause to be vexed, and for that, I beg your forgiveness."

A long moment passed before Jory said, "Of course, you have it." Merryn held his breath another moment until Gavin inclined his head in agreement.

"Why has she come now?" Gavin asked. "Does she mean to remain in Newford?"

Merryn shook his head and explained her cousin's impending return to England. "I imagine Rebecca will return to France when all is settled."

His cousins' matching frowns at this statement did little to ease the tightness that had settled in his chest. He resisted the urge to ease it with his fist.

"Irregular," Gavin murmured, and Merryn could

not disagree. But it was the bargain he'd made, and he was nothing if not a man of his word.

James, who'd been quiet for some time, said, "Devil it, Merryn. What were you thinking?"

Merryn blinked as his cousin began pacing.

James turned sharply at the end of the rug. "You've lived separately for five years, with her in France and you—good God." He wheeled around. "Eliza's Inventory. You've put yourself out as a bachelor. Her cousin will argue you never intended a true marriage. That 'twas contracted solely to secure her inheritance."

"There is no law that requires a man and his wife to share the same household for the marriage to stand. If there were, then half of England would be bastards."

"Aye," Gavin said, stepping boldly into the debate. "Many couples live separately."

"For a season or two, per'aps," James conceded. "But not for five years, with no acknowledgement of the union."

"Her uncle approved," Merryn said.

He didn't tell them he'd already sought William Pearce's permission to court his niece properly—mere hours before the man's apoplexy struck and necessity replaced courtship. Rebecca thought she'd persuaded Merryn to the match. In truth, he'd already set his course in that direction. But it was better his cousins think she'd left behind a marriage of convenience than know he'd harbored hopes of a more tender nature.

James pressed on. "I assume the marriage has been consummated? There's no chance of annulment?"

Heat climbed the back of Merryn's neck. Jory found fascination in a loose thread on the rug, while Gavin shifted on the settee.

"I don't see how—" Merryn began.

James slashed an impatient hand through the air. "I don't want to know. But if it wasn't, then her cousin would be within his rights to petition for an annulment." He resumed his pacing. "The banns weren't even called."

"There was no time. Her uncle—"

"Was gravely ill—aye."

Merryn straightened to his full height, which was an inch or two above that of his cousins. "We obtained a license," he said. "'Twas all properly done."

James released a breath. "Good, good. But if her cousin is successful in dissolving it?" he pressed, his voice quieter now. "What then? You could be liable for your bride's inheritance—and any income earned on it." He paused. "Can you even imagine what that sum might be after five years?"

"Aye," Merryn replied on a sigh. He could imagine it, and the sum was considerable. He knew, because Rebecca had invested much of it in his royal project. If Pearce prevailed, the project could fail. And if the project failed, his cousins would lose their own stakes.

But it was more than that. It wasn't just Rebecca's funds at risk, or his cousins', but every man who'd invested time and money in the project—all of it could crumble because he'd been too proud to speak the truth five years ago.

He squeezed his temples with one hand as his cousins sorted the implications for themselves. James swore again, creatively, while Gavin and Jory sat silent, brows furrowed.

Finally, Jory cleared his throat. "What is your plan?" he asked.

Merryn's jaw shifted. His plan?

His silence had got him into this noose to begin with, and now, his impulsive declaration at the bridge had only tightened the rope. He feared making another misstep, but Jory was right. He needed a plan if he and Rebecca were to convince her cousin of their marriage.

His wife had been right all along. They must present themselves as a married couple.

"Miss Pearce and I must give every appearance of a proper marriage," he said. "I must become a husband."

"'Tis not such a chore," Gavin offered by way of consolation.

"Aye, but you and Mari hold a genuine affection for one another," Jory reminded him.

Merryn closed his eyes. He was no stranger to affection when it came to Rebecca, but now he must perform what he'd spent five years concealing. The prospect sat ill with him.

"What can we do to help?" Jory asked.

"I suppose you'll be needing husband lessons," Gavin said with a sigh.

Merryn's eyes flew open. Gavin's mouth was tilted in a smile, and Merryn realized his cousin was having him on. "I think I can manage it," he said dryly, "but thank you all the same."

Gavin ignored him. "To begin, you cannot continue to call her Miss Pearce."

Jory nodded. "'Tis true. D'you know her given name?"

"Rebecca," Merryn answered with a frown.

"And you should know how she takes her tea—"

"She dislikes tea."

Jory pulled his head back at this. "Dislikes tea? Then what does she drink?"

"She favors chocolate, preferably from France."

"That could be a problem."

"When you offer your arm," Gavin added, "it should appear natural, not awkward."

"I do not appear awkward," Merryn protested. "I have walked with a lady before."

"Ah, but a wife is not just any lady. She is another creature altogether."

Merryn looked to James for help and received none. His cousin had resumed his place by the window, arms crossed. He wore an expression of reluctant amusement as their cousins continued their "lessons," despite Merryn's assurances that such tutoring was unnecessary.

"Refer to common memories," Jory continued, "even if you must invent them."

"Learn to finish her sentences," Gavin said. "Married folks—"

"—do it without thinking," Jory finished. He and Gavin were a wellspring of marital advice that had just been tapped.

"Defend her in conversation—even when she's wrong," Gavin said.

"Especially when she's wrong," Jory added.

"Inquire after her plans for the day."

"Exchange the occasional smile with your bride. 'Twill look as if you've secrets between you."

James straightened. "And for heaven's sake," he interjected. "Do not look as if you've swallowed a dodgy pilchard whenever someone mentions your bride."

"I do not—" Merryn began but stopped when

Gavin and Jory shook their heads.

James went to retrieve his hat from the stand. Brow pitched low, he added, "We are blood, Merryn, 'tis true—but more importantly, we *are* friends. We will stand with you."

"Aye," Jory added. "This cousin's accusations have no grounds. Everyone knows you to be a man of honor. If anyone should question the circumstances of your marriage, we will put their concerns to rest."

Merryn nodded as gratitude pricked at him, unexpected and inconvenient. He cleared his throat. "Thank you."

Gavin leaned forward. "What d'you know of this Gregory Pearce?"

"Little enough. He's been abroad these several years."

"Then we should remedy that," Jory said. "Grandfather's connections might know of him—particularly if he's engaged in trade. And James has associates in Plymouth and London who could make inquiries."

"Discreetly," Gavin added. "We'll learn what we can of his circumstances and his character. If he's foolish enough to challenge your marriage, there may be debts or other pressures driving him."

Merryn's shoulders eased slightly. They were right. And to have allies in this—it was more than he'd hoped for when he entered the room. "I would be grateful."

James nodded and took his leave of them. He'd not been gone more than a moment when the familiar, quick tread of slippered feet came from the hall outside the parlor. There was the murmur of a feminine voice, and before Merryn could fully prepare himself, Bronwyn came through.

The afternoon's warmth had put color in her cheeks. Her bonnet hung by its strings from one hand and her gloves were crushed in the other. She stopped just inside the threshold.

"'Tis true?" she said, not sparing a look for their cousins. "You're married?"

"Aye."

Jory and Gavin collected their hats at once, all lessons in marital accord forgotten.

"Craven milksops," Merryn muttered as they left him to face his sister.

CHAPTER 16

TRUE TO SARAH'S word, she arranged for their things to be brought from the Feather. Rebecca stood at the window of her guest chamber in a simple afternoon dress of pale blue muslin, watching the shadows lengthen across the garden below. The plaster at her temple pulled when she turned her head, a persistent reminder of the day's events.

Below, the front door opened, and Bronwyn emerged. Rebecca watched as her sister-in-law descended the front steps. Bronwyn paused to adjust her bonnet ribbons before striding toward the stables and a waiting pony cart.

Rebecca's chest tightened with an uncomfortable sensation. Merryn's sister had been kind to a stranger—she'd invited Rebecca to tea, had included her in conversation about Newford's theatrical productions and the Feather's raspberry tarts. Rebecca had begun to like her.

Now, Bronwyn knew she'd been deceived, and not only by her brother.

Bronwyn accepted the reins from a groom, and without another glance for the house, the cart rolled forward. Long after it disappeared down the lane, Rebecca remained at the window questioning her life's decisions.

A knock came at the door.

Straightening, she smoothed skirts that required no smoothing. "Come in."

The door opened, and after a moment's hesitation, Merryn crossed the threshold. With his coat removed, his linen shirt stretched across his shoulders beneath a simple grey waistcoat. He appeared worn but composed, and his expression lightened when he perceived her at the window. Whether it was relief at finding her awake or finding her dressed, she couldn't say.

His gaze went to the bandage at her hairline. "How d'you fare?" he asked.

Rebecca shrugged. "Well enough." She gestured toward the settee before the hearth. "Would you care to sit?"

He crossed to the hearth but remained standing, hands clasped behind his back in a stance she now recognized as uniquely his.

Rebecca stepped away from the window. "Your sister has been here."

Something flickered across Merryn's features before he mastered it. "Aye. Understandably, she has questions."

Rebecca held a surprised laugh. Her husband had a talent for understatement. She moved to the settee and took a seat for herself, folding her hands in her lap.

"Understandably," she repeated as she arranged her gown. "What answers did you give?"

He released a short breath. "The truth, or something of it." She lifted an encouraging brow, and he added, "That our marriage was a matter of convenience, and when you left for France—per our agreement—it seemed the easier course to simply go on as I had done. Nothing was truly changed. What purpose would explanations have served?"

It sounded reasonable when he put it in such terms. Nevertheless, a flash of irritation warmed Rebecca's throat. "But you must have expected our marriage would come out eventually."

"I expected we would go on with our arrangement," Merryn said with some asperity. He bent to light the fire that had been laid. "I didn't anticipate your return or your cousin's challenge."

Her irritation faded as quickly as it had come, and Rebecca sighed. "No. I don't suppose either of us did."

Not for the first time, she cursed the terms of her

father's trust, which would have required months of petitions to the Court of Chancery to alter. Marriage had been the only way to secure her inheritance.

The clock on the mantel ticked steadily, marking the awkward beats between them.

Rebecca moved them to safer ground. "Sarah arranged for our things to be brought from the inn. I hope it wasn't too presumptuous, but it seemed necessary. If we're to convince anyone, that is."

Merryn glanced over his shoulder at her trunk against the wall. "'Twas the practical course." The fire caught. Rising, he cleared his throat and looked about. "This room… 'tis adequate?"

"It is quite comfortable," she assured him.

A heavy silence followed. A log shifted, and sparks showered the hearth before winking out. Her husband turned back to face her. When he spoke, his voice was even.

"For the sake of appearances, I can have your things moved closer to…" He stopped and cleared his throat. "That is, there's a room that adjoins my own."

Heat warmed Rebecca's cheeks until she thought they must be as red as the settee's cushions. But his suggestion made sense. She nodded, licking her lips and cursing the nervous flutter in her stomach. "That would be prudent." Practical. Prudent. She was beginning to sound like her husband.

Merryn nodded, hands returning to their position behind his back. "I'll see to it tomorrow then."

She observed her husband standing before the fire. There was an endearing stiffness to his posture, but there was honor in it as well. She was flooded with a sudden, unexpected affection, and the knowledge that whatever may come, she could not regret her marriage.

Of all the gentlemen she might have chosen, she was glad she had chosen *him*. Five years before, she'd sensed that she could trust him, and he'd proved her right, never asking for more of her or her funds than they'd agreed upon.

Once they were wed, he could have insisted she remain in England, that they live as man and wife. He could have spent the entirety of her inheritance on horses and wine. Or on his building firm, for that matter. He could have cost her the very independence she'd sought. Instead, he'd let her go.

He may have complicated matters with his silence, but the marriage had been her idea to begin with. Now, they must find their way through it together.

"Thank you," she said softly.

His brows lifted in surprise. "For what, precisely? The beam that landed on your head or the scandal broth I've created?"

She huffed a laugh. "For marrying me. For keeping to our arrangement when I went to France. And for acknowledging me as your wife now."

Merryn gave a short nod, rubbing the back of his neck. Silence settled between them again, but it felt less awkward now.

"Your sister," Rebecca said after a moment. "She'll manage?"

"Aye. She's a force. She's already addressed Mrs. Tilbury and the maids, ensuring the household understands the situation. She'll speak to Wynne and Morwenna on the morrow."

"And what of your cousins from the bridge?" she asked. "Are they as accepting as Bronwyn?"

With a tight nod, he replied, "They will stand by us." He hesitated for a beat before adding, "They have offered husband lessons, if you can believe it."

She laughed. "Lessons? Dare I ask what their tutelage entails?" She adjusted her place on the settee, making room for him. To her surprise, he sat.

"They've an endless supply of advice," he said. "To begin, I ought to become a mind reader, so that I might finish—"

"—my sentences?" she teased.

He gave her a repressive frown. "Just so."

"Being a husband does not seem so very difficult then. What other advice do they offer?"

"We're to exchange looks and secret smiles and such, and I must alter my demeanor. Apparently, I look like I've swallowed a fish that's gone off whenever my bride is mentioned."

She couldn't help a surprised laugh.

"'Tis a habit I will strive to improve," he assured her.

"Do I elicit such an unpleasant reaction then?"

"Never," he said. "Surprise, per'aps, or alarm at having swallowed the thing whole, but never unpleasantness."

Pushing aside the unexpected warmth his words brought, she steered them toward practicalities. "I imagine Newford will be abuzz with gossip by morning."

"Aye."

"It is not only your family and servants we must convince," she said quietly. "Everyone must believe in our marriage. If even the slightest hint of irregularity were to reach my cousin…" She stopped, unable to complete the thought.

Merryn stood and began to pace, three steps to the window, three steps back. Rebecca had seen him do this years before when they'd negotiated the terms of their arrangement. It was how he sorted problems. She waited.

"We cannot allow speculation to run unchecked," he said. "We must meet it directly."

He was right. The way gossip traveled here couldn't be that different from London or Paris, and the sooner they corrected any misassumptions, the better. She recalled Bronwyn's warning about Newford's matrons and the women she and Merryn had encountered—heaven's, had it been only that morning? So much had occurred in the intervening hours that it seemed as if days had passed.

"Your matrons," she said. "Mrs. Pentreath and Mrs. Tretheway, is it?"

He nodded warily. "Aye, and Mrs. Clifton."

"They are dreadful gossips, are they not?"

"They make it their business to spread about everyone else's."

"Then we ought to ensure they have the correct version of events."

Merryn considered this, his expression thoughtful before a smile touched the corner of his mouth—the first she'd seen since before the bridge. "The post."

She lifted a brow in question.

"The ladies frequent the post office," he said. "I daresay they watch to see what letters come through and for whom. 'Twould be an easy enough thing to encounter them there."

"Then we must go."

He shook his head. "*I* will go. Your injury—"

"Is naught but a scratch. Truly." Merryn's jaw tightened in that stubborn way she was beginning to recognize. He didn't like it, but she pressed on. "We must be seen together, and when we encounter one of your matrons, we give them a tale to put about."

He released a breath. His gaze met hers and held, and something shifted in the air between them.

"We must ensure we've a credible explanation for everything."

Merryn nodded and resumed his position by the hearth. "The reason for our marriage is simple enough. Your uncle was ill and wished to see you settled."

"And the last five years?"

"The truth. You desired to visit your mother's family in France. With the war's end, you finally had the opportunity to do so." He considered. "I don't suppose your aunt has been ailing…? We could put it about that you were tending to her."

Rebecca shook her head. "My aunt is remarkably hale. But among London and Parisian society, it is not uncommon for couples to live apart."

"For a time, aye."

She swallowed. "Five years is longer than usual."

He nodded, frowning. "But if you and I appear… pleased… with our reunion…"

His words hung unfinished between them. Five years *was* a long time. But if she and Merryn appeared accepting of it, if they were amicable in one another's company as if their reunion had been anticipated all along, then who could gainsay them? It would require a performance. Wifely glances and secret smiles, much as Merryn's cousins had advised with their husband lessons.

She watched her husband stab the fire with the poker. His movements were efficient and capable, and as she recalled the accord they'd found with one another in London, she didn't think the performance would be a taxing one. She would have no trouble affecting enjoyment in his company.

But when he turned, it was clear his thoughts did not travel a similar path, for there was frustration evident in the tight line of his jaw. "People will ask, rightfully, why I never spoke of't. 'Tis not the usual way for a man to neglect to mention his marriage. Certainly, 'tis not the manner of a man who expects to reunite with his wife after her visit abroad."

"No," she said. "It is not. What will you say?"

He rubbed the back of his neck, and her breath was tight in her chest as she waited to hear his reasoning. Despite what he'd told his sister, she sensed there was more to his silence than simply taking the easier course.

With a slow exhale, he said, "Newford is not London or Paris. Arrangements of convenience may be understood there, but here, 'tis difficult to explain that you've married a lady who departed so soon for the Continent. And by design, no less. They'd have thought me a fool for entering such an arrangement."

He shifted to face her more fully, his jaw firm above his neckcloth.

"I admit, I didn't think it through properly when we made our bargain. It seemed straightforward enough, but I'd not accounted for what it would mean to bring that arrangement home to Newford. I'd not accounted for my pride—I thought it a sturdier thing than it turned out to be."

The corner of his mouth lifted in an ironic smile that made her heart flutter even as an uncomfortable warmth climbed her throat—not quite guilt but something close to it. She'd been so set on securing her future that she'd given little thought to what he would face when she left.

Their arrangement had been practical, fashioned for their mutual benefit. She'd have her freedom; he'd have his funds. She'd assumed his life would go on unchanged, but his words revealed complications she'd not considered, though she should have.

He could have called her back. Their bargain aside, he would have been within his rights to insist on her return. Instead, he'd protected her independence at the expense of his own comfort.

"I—I don't suppose I thought it through properly either. I proceeded with my plans without thinking of the explanations I'd left you to make."

"You were grieving your uncle's loss."

She shook her head, but before she could protest further, he turned away, his gaze going to the darkened window. "But none of this addresses your original question, does it? I still don't have an answer for them—not one that will satisfy."

"We needn't have all the answers tonight," she said carefully. "We shall manage it together."

Something that might have been surprise crossed Merryn's features, and she felt it too. That word—*together*—settled between them differently than it might have days before.

His expression softened a fraction. "Tomorrow then. Only a short outing, and if your head pains you overmuch—"

"Then I shall say so."

Merryn gave her a brief, reluctant nod before moving toward the door. He paused with his hand on the latch, and when he spoke, his voice was quieter than before. "I regret the necessity of this. You came seeking help, and I've made everything more complicated with my silence."

She said quietly, "You could have made everything simpler for yourself by holding your silence at the bridge, but you did not. I could have convalesced just as easily at the inn, but you brought me to your home."

"You are my wife," Merryn said. "Where else would you go?"

Rebecca had no response to such a simple question. She said only, "Sleep well."

"*Nos da*," he answered in Cornish.

The door closed softly behind him, and Rebecca was alone once more. But when her thoughts turned to wondering what might have been different had she remained in England, she didn't immediately shove them away. Instead, she let the question linger, as dangerous and persistent as the ache in her temple.

CHAPTER 17

MERRYN ADJUSTED HIS stride to match Rebecca's as they descended the lane toward the high street. The elms overhead waved and rustled in the breeze to send dancing, dappled light onto the hard-packed lane. He'd walked this route his entire life, but never with his wife beside him.

Through the trees to one side lay the valley, endless and rolling and speckled with sheep. To the other side, Newford's chimneys and the sea. He wondered what Rebecca made of it, though he didn't have to wonder long, for they soon rounded the bend that afforded the very best views.

"Oh," she breathed. "It's a very pretty prospect."

"I imagine in your travels, you must have seen many as pretty or prettier."

"Yes, but none that seemed quite so… fresh, I suppose. There's something about the air here—"

"The scent of fish, per'aps?"

She laughed. "No—well, yes. Near the harbor, of course, there's that. But away from the fish, it all smells… clean. There's the salt from the sea, and the pine and gorse, but there is something else I cannot put my finger on."

He nodded, for he knew precisely what she meant. Those who'd never left Newford couldn't understand, but he'd been to London a few times, and to Bath. And each time he returned to Cornwall, he smelled what she described.

Home, he wanted to say. It was the scent of home, but he held his silence, for they'd reached the lane above Newford.

"You're certain we'll encounter your matrons at the post office?" Rebecca asked, returning them to their mission.

"Aye." He glanced at her. "Are you ready?"

She tilted her head at him, and the movement showed the plaster at her temple beneath her bonnet. He hid a grimace—for her injury and for the necessity of their outing. He'd offered again to postpone it, but she'd refused of course. Stubborn, vexing woman.

"I've navigated the salons of Paris for five years," she replied. "Surely, I can manage a few busy matrons."

"You've not met our Mrs. Pentreath."

"Then it is time I did."

They passed the bakery where Mr. Clifton swept his front step, and the chandler's, where the doors and window trims were getting fresh paint. Tom Hatch paused in his task and touched his cap in greeting. His gaze lingered on Rebecca before flicking to Merryn with poorly concealed curiosity. By noon, all of Newford would know Merryn Kimbrell had walked to the post office with his wife.

Which was rather the point, he reminded himself.

Rebecca's hand rested lightly on his arm, and he was conscious of the weight of it. Light enough to seem natural, firm enough to suggest familiarity. He wondered if he would ever become accustomed to it.

They'd discussed their strategy again over eggs and ale. Or tea, rather, for Rebecca—he'd have to see about acquiring chocolate for his wife. But for all their discussion, he still had no answers for why he'd held his silence for five years. At least, no answers that would satisfy anyone of sense.

The explanation he'd given Rebecca the previous evening—that his pride had got the better of him—was not meant for public circulation. Even so, it was only a half-truth.

The whole truth was rather more than that, for though his pride had been bruised, it was his heart that had truly ached when he returned to Newford alone. He'd wanted nothing more than to nurse it in solitude, but there had been bills to pay. His mother and sister to see to. And so he'd thrown himself into his work and put his marriage from his thoughts.

A heavy cart rumbled past, drawing Merryn from his thoughts. He guided Rebecca closer to the shop fronts to avoid the splash of mud that rose from the cobbles. Her shoulder brushed his arm. When she didn't immediately step away, he reminded himself this was a performance. Much like the theatrical Newford would soon host for His Majesty, he and Rebecca trod a stage of sorts.

They soon reached the post office near the end of the high street. Through the bow window, he spied his cousin Cadan behind the counter. There was no sign of the matrons yet, though a pair of young ladies shopped the dry-good shelves.

Merryn reached for the door but paused when Rebecca squeezed his arm.

"All will be well," she whispered, and something in her steady gaze loosened the knot in his chest.

"Aye."

The bell above the door chimed as they entered. Cadan looked up from his work, and his brows lifted a fraction. His gaze went from Merryn to Rebecca then back again before he gave them a short nod. He'd heard then.

"Cousin," Merryn said, conscious of the ladies browsing the tea tins.

"Merryn." Cadan didn't wait for Merryn to make

the introductions but offered Rebecca a smile as if her five-year marriage to his cousin were not a surprise to them all. "And Mrs. Kimbrell. 'Tis a pleasure, ma'am."

Rebecca inclined her head. "The pleasure is mine, sir. It is nice to finally meet my husband's relations, though we do wish circumstances had allowed for it sooner."

The way she said "we" was ingenious, as if she and Merryn had planned all along for things to come about as they had. In the shop's corner, the ladies bent their heads close.

Cadan set down the letters he'd been sorting. "Circumstances often have a habit of ignoring our will, do they not?" His reply was loud enough for the ladies to hear, and Merryn knew a sudden rush of affection for his cousins. They didn't know all the whys and wherefores of his marriage, but still they stood with him.

"They do," Rebecca agreed.

"I trust Verity is well?" Merryn asked.

Cadan's expression brightened at the mention of his wife. "Aye. The early weeks were difficult, but she's much improved now."

"I am pleased to hear it." To Rebecca, Merryn added, "My cousin is newly wed. Cadan and his wife Verity anticipate the arrival of their first child in the spring."

"What happy news," she said. "Please convey my felicitations to your wife."

Cadan agreed to do so then cleared his throat. "I'll just look to see if you've any letters."

As he turned to check his bins, the bell above the door chimed again. Mrs. Pentreath entered, followed closely by Mrs. Tretheway. Merryn knew a mixture of satisfaction for having predicted the matrons' arrival and wariness for the encounter to come.

Both women stopped short at the sight of him and Rebecca.

"Good morning, ladies," Merryn said, inclining his head.

"Mr. Kimbrell," Mrs. Pentreath replied before turning an expectant gaze on Rebecca, whose hand remained on his sleeve.

Merryn stepped forward and performed the introductions. He remembered to smile at his wife, though he feared he looked like a bedlamite rather than a besotted bridegroom.

"Ladies." Rebecca greeted them with a generous tip of her head. "It is a pleasure to make your acquaintance."

Mrs. Tretheway murmured a courtesy while Edith Pentreath pressed her lips. "You must pardon my confusion," she said, "but we have heard the most extraordinary thing. Is it true, Mr. Kimbrell, that you have been married these last five years?"

Mrs. Tretheway pressed forward, her brow furrowed with curiosity. Merryn kept his gaze from straying to the dark hair curling from a mole on her chin.

"'Tis true," he confirmed, and Mrs. Pentreath sucked in a breath.

Before she could form another question, he added, "My wife has been away visiting her family abroad. We thought it best to delay the announcement of our nuptials until her return."

"But… five years!" Mrs. Pentreath said.

Mrs. Tretheway mirrored her colleague's frown. "'Twas an exceptionally long visit."

"And there were no banns."

"We were married in London," Merryn explained, "by license."

Mrs. Pentreath tucked her chin. "A license! How… irregular, to say nothing of the expense!"

Merryn looked to Rebecca, who offered him a gentle, wifely smile. "It was our misfortune that we had no other recourse," he said. "My wife's uncle was unwell and wished to see his ward properly settled."

Mrs. Pentreath merely hummed at this, for who could argue against such sentiment? She rallied, though, tapping her cane once against the oak floor. "But that does not answer for why you could not announce it. It was poorly done, sir."

Merryn checked his irritation, for he could hardly fault the ladies for his own foolishness. But the best way to endure a cold bath was to simply plunge in, so he nodded. "You are correct, ma'am."

But before he could elaborate further on the pride that had held his tongue, Rebecca leaned forward with a rueful smile.

"Please, do not hold my husband's silence against him."

Merryn's brows lifted just as the matrons' did.

"My uncle passed so soon after we were wed," Rebecca continued, "and it would have been improper to celebrate our union when I was obliged to put on my blacks."

Mrs. Pentreath's expression shifted, her suspicion yielding to something more grudging. "You were in mourning?"

Rebecca nodded. "My uncle was very dear to me." She looked at Merryn with a soft expression. "But I'm afraid I have made my husband wait far longer than either of us intended."

Mrs. Tretheway nodded, the curls beneath her cap bobbing. "How dreadful for you, ma'am. To lose your uncle so soon after your marriage. And your parents...?"

Rebecca inclined her head. "Gone since I was a girl."

Mrs. Tretheway clicked her tongue. "You poor dear."

Mrs. Pentreath was not so easily persuaded. "But five years... that is quite the trial for a young husband." Her eyes narrowed on Rebecca. "Where have you resided all this time?"

Rebecca met her gaze steadily. "I was obliged to join my aunt in Paris. She has no other family, you see, and I could not leave her alone."

"Your aunt," Mrs. Tretheway said, her expression softening. "That was very kind of you."

The ladies wore matching frowns until, with another tap of her cane against the planks, Mrs. Pentreath harrumphed. "I still say it is an irregular business"—she paused to direct her frown at Merryn specifically—"but no one can fault a lady's tender feelings for her elders."

"My wife's affection has been well worth every day of waiting," Merryn assured them. Rebecca's eyes widened the merest bit at this statement, but her surprise quickly fell into a pleased smile that caused his chest to tighten.

Before Mrs. Pentreath could pursue the topic further, Rebecca spoke. "Ladies, I wonder if I might beg your advice. I am in need of buttons, but I do not know where such things are best acquired in Newford. Will I be obliged to order them from Truro?"

Her words had the desired effect. Mrs. Pentreath gasped while Mrs. Tretheway pressed one hand to her ample bosom. "Truro? Heavens, no! Why, Mr. Cadan Kimbrell stocks an acceptable assortment right here."

"Excellent," Rebecca replied. "Will you show me?"

Her hand slipped from Merryn's arm. As the matrons led her toward the button bins, Cadan came to stand beside Merryn.

"Your wife," he said with a nod for the ladies. "She is rather... persuasive."

Merryn couldn't help his smile. "She is."

Cadan extended a stack of letters and Merryn took them, though his attention remained on his wife. Mrs. Pentreath's lips actually curved upward in what he thought was meant to be a smile. Rebecca was really very good at this sort of thing.

"Chocolate," he said suddenly to Cadan. "D'you have any?"

Cadan tugged his ear. "I've two bricks of't."

"The quality is good?"

Cadan gave him a look for the unnecessary question. "I don't make a habit of stocking items of poor quality."

Merryn nearly smiled at his cousin's affront. "But are they comparable to what one might find in France?"

Cadan's frown eased, and he gave a nod of understanding. "They come from Fry's in Bristol, so aye. They'll do."

Satisfied, Merryn directed his cousin to add a brick of chocolate to his weekly order.

Finally, the matrons left, and Merryn and Rebecca took their leave of Cadan. Outside, Rebecca leaned toward him. "That went rather well, don't you think?"

Merryn smiled at the faint flush of victory that colored his wife's cheeks. Were she boastful, he would not have liked it, but he could never fault confidence when it was fairly placed. It was precisely this capability, this quiet certainty in her own abilities, that had drawn him to her from the start.

"Thank you," he said, "for standing in my defense. You made it seem as if my silence was your idea, when we both know it was not."

She gave him a sideways glance. "Appealing to the ladies' sense of propriety seemed the most practical course," she replied. "And we are partners in practicality, are we not?"

"Nevertheless, you could have left me to flounder. 'Twas a kindness that you did not."

She turned her gaze more fully on him, one brow lifted slightly. "A kindness—much like purchasing chocolate?"

"You heard?" The notion that she'd been aware

of him even as she spoke with the matrons sent warmth twisting through him.

"I did, and I thank you for it."

She smiled, and his breath caught until the plaster at her temple took his notice again. "Your head—does it pain you?"

"Only a little."

"We should have waited. I'll summon Rowe—"

Predictably, she assured him she had no need of the surgeon, but she didn't protest when he slowed their pace.

CHAPTER 18

By the time they returned to Merryn's home, Rebecca's things had been moved into the room adjoining her husband's. She stood on the threshold looking in. The space was larger than her guest chamber and done in shades of cream and blue. Light spilled through a pair of tall windows to stripe the rug. To one side of the dressing table stood a door, which she assumed led to Merryn's chamber.

"'Tis acceptable?" he said from behind her. "We can change the color if you prefer another."

"It's lovely," she said before taking a tentative step into the room.

"My mother had it done a couple of years ago," he said ruefully. "Wishful thinking, I suppose. I could have told her there was no need, but…"

She nodded before he could finish. "Well, there is a need for it now," she said. "Your mother has excellent taste."

He reached for the doorknob. "Rest," he ordered.

Rebecca was only too happy to comply, and she felt much refreshed by the afternoon. She left her room to find paper and ink so she might write to her aunt in France. Her husband must have some.

As she neared Merryn's library, though, she heard the low murmur of voices inside. She hesitated at the door, not wishing to intrude if her husband entertained his business associates. But then she recognized one of the voices as that of Dr. Rowe, the surgeon. Merryn had summoned him, although she'd assured him there was no need.

"And how does Mrs. Kimbrell fare?" Rowe said on the other side of the door.

From farther away came Merryn's response. "She claims she is much improved, but I think her head must pain her still, hard though 'tis."

Rowe chuckled, and Rebecca frowned. She entered without knocking, a sharp rebuke on her tongue, but stopped at the scene that greeted her.

Rowe stood over his black surgeon's bag while her husband reached for his shirt hanging over a chair. He was bare above his trousers, and the shoulder which faced her was smooth and carved. She was intrigued to see he was, in fact, formed much like her aunt's alabaster statues—the most notable difference being the supple way his skin slid over bone and sinew when he moved.

It seemed an impossibly long moment before she recalled herself. When she did, it was only because he turned, revealing a darkening bruise on his left side, and she gasped.

The surgeon looked up and inclined his head. "Mrs. Kimbrell. I hope you'll forgive the intrusion, but I've come to see how you both fare after yesterday's misadventure. I must say, Kimbrell here is a fortunate man."

Rebecca remembered to close her mouth. Licking lips that had gone dry, she replied, "How do you mean?"

"I daresay if that timber had struck him more squarely, it would have done far more damage than a few cracked ribs." Rowe snapped his bag shut and nodded at a small jar on the edge of the desk. "I've brought a liniment for the swelling. If he heeds my instruction, he will make a full recovery."

Merryn drew his shirt over his head, and she didn't miss his slight wince at the motion. She'd caught a similar expression on him as they'd walked to the post office, but she assumed his discomfort was for the task ahead. All the while, the foolish man had been nursing cracked ribs. And to hear the surgeon's report, his injury could have been far graver.

She frowned, trying to recall the events at the bridge. Everything had happened so quickly. She'd hardly had time to make sense of it all. One moment, she'd been tugging at her skirt and the next had her looking up into her husband's worried gaze. He must have moved quickly to put himself between her and the falling timber, and he'd taken the brunt of it for his effort. The notion caused an uneasy quiver in her belly.

"I—I shall ensure that he does. Heed your instruction, that is." Where had her wits gone?

Rowe inquired after her head, and she assured him she was indeed feeling much improved. He inspected the plaster at her temple and, satisfied, took his leave of them.

Turning, she gave her husband a look. "You are injured. Why did you not say anything?"

His head was down as he worked the buttons of his waistcoat. She tapped her foot, waiting, until he dropped the button with a sigh. "Would you believe 'tis naught but a scratch?"

She ceased her foot-tapping. "I would not. I saw the bruising on your skin. 'Tis far more than a scratch," she said, mimicking him.

"'Twill heal. Any man who's not suffered a cracked rib or two is no proper Cornishman."

"Well, that is about the most absurd thing I have ever heard."

He gave her a tilted smile that sent her stomach into a graceless dive. "Is that wifely concern I hear?"

"It is wifely irritation." Lifting her chin a notch, she added, "If you cannot tell the difference, then I fear your cousins' lessons have failed you."

He began retying his neckcloth, and she found it hard to look away. Though she'd been a married lady for five years, she'd never had occasion to witness the masculine ritual of cravat-tying, and she was fascinated by how deftly he twisted and flicked the ends until they lay tucked once more beneath his vest.

"Per'aps I ought to keep notes then. When my wife's eyes are particularly bright and her color high, 'tis a sign I have thoroughly vexed her."

Rebecca feared his words had sent her color even higher. She cleared her throat. "You are being deliberately provoking," she said, "but I will not be turned from the topic. You are injured, and the surgeon has left you with a remedy. Do you intend to heed his instruction?"

He looked as if he might make light of her question, but then he stopped and came closer. He took her hand. His fingers were warm and rough against her own, which curled of their own accord into his palm.

"You *are* concerned," he said softly. "There's no need for't, truly. I've suffered far more than this little bump, but if 'twill ease your thoughts, then I will heed Rowe's instruction."

Rebecca released a breath. Of course she was concerned—any woman of sense would have been, given the mottled hue of the bruise on his ribs.

But she was not only a woman of sense. She was Merryn's *wife*, and despite the sensible nature of their arrangement, she cared about him. Far more than she would have thought possible five years before.

Frowning, she studied him. He was close enough that she could smell his shaving soap. It was clean and faintly herbal—the same soap he'd favored five years before. She'd smelled it that night in her uncle's library as they'd sat hip to hip on the settee. Her heart thumped heavily at the memory.

Marriage to Merryn had made her independence possible. But now, standing close enough to feel the warmth of him, she wondered if he was content with their bargain.

"Do you ever regret our arrangement?" she whispered.

His eyes tightened at the corners, but he didn't look away. She expected a denial, so she was surprised when he said only, "Do you?"

"No." She swallowed. "I am glad it was you."

He took a step back and rubbed a hand over his mouth. "D'you ever wish for… more?"

She began to shake her head, to assure him she was content in her life. But then she stopped, for it would be a lie to tell him she'd never desired a family. A husband in the true sense. She enjoyed her independence, but sometimes she wondered what it would be like to have another to share her joys and burdens with.

"It is the natural order of things," she said carefully, "to marry and make a family."

"That does not answer the question."

She inhaled a long breath. "It doesn't," she agreed. "But yes, I have sometimes wondered if what I have will be enough."

He fixed his gaze on her face. So intent was his expression that she thought he might kiss her. The idea of it swooped and twirled in her belly, until he turned away. He held a hand to the back of his neck and stood motionless for a long moment.

When he turned back to her, his expression was dark and unreadable. "I mean to honor our arrangement," he said. "I will not ask for more than we agreed to, but neither will I refuse should you ever desire a true marriage."

Rebecca's heart nearly stopped, she was certain of it. She took a step back from him. Part of her told her to run, to flee back up the stairs. She could not return to France if she were wedded—*truly* wedded—to Merryn Kimbrell. She knew without asking that he would not let her go if their marriage was real.

She ought to refuse what he suggested before it had a chance to take root. The sensible answer—the answer she would have given him five years before—was a firm no. She'd worked too hard to create a life of her own to cast it aside so carelessly.

But the refusal would not come. Somehow, with his letters and his honorable nature, his wit and intelligence and love for his family, this man had found a corner of her heart. She clasped her hands together, as much to avoid reaching for him as to steady herself.

"I... I shall think on it."

I shall think on it? The words were as much a surprise to her as they must have been to him, but her husband had that effect on her wits.

Before she could utter anything else, she turned and fled, forgetting until much later that she'd gone down for paper and ink.

CHAPTER 19

That night, Merryn lay in his bed, conscious of Rebecca on the other side of the wall. How he was supposed to find sleep was beyond him, but somehow he did. His first thought on waking the next morning was the same as his last thought the night before.

I shall think on it.

His wife's words were not an acceptance, but neither were they an outright refusal. She was not entirely averse to the notion of making a real marriage between them.

There was the sound of birdsong outside his windows and the particular quality of light that suggested a fine morning lay ahead. He rose and washed. As he shaved, a Cornish tune came to him, something light and quick, and he hummed a few bars before catching himself. He sang hymns in church but never did he *hum*.

Light showed beneath his wife's door. Rebecca was awake as well, preparing for her day. Through the wall came the sound of water pouring into a basin. Soft footsteps crossed the floor, then a drawer opened and closed with a click. Five years they'd been married, yet these small rituals of her morning remained unknown to him.

He reached for his shirt, wincing at the pain in his ribs. The bruise was a rather spectacular shade of violet today, and every breath was a reminder of the events at the bridge.

His foreman informed him the damage to the structure had been far less than the damage to his person, much less his peace of mind. If the falling timber had struck Rebecca fully... He wouldn't contemplate it. Cracked ribs were a small price to pay for her safety, and if they earned him his wife's concern as well, he would count them well paid.

The jar of Rowe's liniment sat on his dressing table, largely ignored since he'd placed it there the day before. But he'd promised Rebecca. Setting aside his shirt, he opened the jar, relieved when the substance inside smelled faintly of pine rather than pig fat. As he applied the liniment, a notion began to take shape.

I shall think on it. What if his wife could be persuaded? He'd seen her concern for him the day before. She was not unmoved.

Five years before, she'd been set on her course. Her mother's unhappiness in her own marriage had cemented Rebecca's determination to avoid the same fate. No matter how strong the urge to follow her to France had been, he'd known to do so would be to lose her altogether.

Added to that, she'd been worried for her future and grieving her uncle. There'd likely been no room in her thoughts for anything else. Certainly, not a marriage she neither wanted nor expected.

Merryn had been a solution to a problem, though she'd never made him feel less for it, nor had she ever been untruthful in her dealings with him.

But now… what if she was no longer opposed to a true marriage? He pondered the thought as he drew on his shirt.

She'd agreed to think on it. Would he not be the worst sort of fool if he didn't make some effort to secure her affections? She might still return to France after this matter with her cousin was settled, but at least he could have no regrets. He began humming again. He would court his wife.

He finished dressing and descended to the breakfast room. Rebecca was already seated by the window where the early morning light caught the copper threads in her hair. She held a steaming cup in one hand, and even from the doorway he could smell the rich, slightly bitter scent of chocolate.

She looked up when he entered and smiled.

"Good morning." She lifted the cup slightly. "Your cook sent this in. It's delightful—thank you again."

"I'm pleased it suits."

He took the chair across from her, cleared his throat to speak, then stopped when Mrs. Tilbury bustled in to set a plate of steaming eggs before him. Only after the housekeeper had gone again did he say, "I trust you slept well. How d'you find your new room?"

"It is very comfortable, thank you." She took a small bite of toast then pressed the serviette to her mouth. "What plans have you made for the day?"

The question was the sort one spouse might ask another, according to his cousins' lessons. But Mrs. Tilbury had already gone. There was no audience to witness their performance. It was, in fact, the perfect opportunity to invite her to walk with him, but his tongue felt thick in his mouth.

"I've a meeting with the plasterers at the Abbey," he said instead. "And you—how will you spend your day? You should make yourself free with my library. Bronwyn has probably left some novels there." He nearly winced at his words—his wife would not be content to while away her day with novels. How *did* his cousins go about this wooing business, he wondered.

She sipped her chocolate. "I've put off my correspondence for too long. I mean to write to my aunt and the ladies of my investment circle."

Investments. Much safer ground, and something he could speak to. She'd mentioned the group before—he'd even quizzed her for her idealism—but he knew little of the particulars.

"How many ladies are there?"

She lowered her cup with a smile. "Twelve, although I suspect Sarah will leave me soon for a cottage near her sister. She's nearly achieved her goal, for she has been investing much longer than the other ladies."

He lifted his brows. "Miss Denning means to leave your employ?"

Her smile grew. "She will have her independence soon," she said. "Or three thousand pounds, to be precise."

He stared. Three thousand pounds—a small fortune. That Rebecca had helped her companion achieve it through prudent management of her funds spoke to a talent he'd clearly underestimated.

"It was never Sarah's intention to become a governess," she continued, "much less a companion to me. But her brother was incautious with her family's fortune. When the funds were gone, so too were Sarah's marriage prospects. Twenty years ago, she had few choices left to her."

"But now, thanks to your investments, she has choices again."

"It owes as much to Sarah's diligence. She could have taken her funds long before now and spent them, but she has trusted that the end result will be worth the wait."

"I think she has trusted *you*," he said.

His mother and sister were both very capable women, but aside from managing the household accounts, they refrained from any more rigorous discussion of money. And properly so, for ladies did not concern themselves with such matters. His wife's open flaunting of the rule caused him equal measures admiration and consternation.

She'd nearly finished her breakfast. She would take her leave of him soon. If he meant to speak, he must do so now.

"I've some time before I must leave for the Abbey," he began.

She set down her cup, tilting her head at him.

"I wondered if you might like to take a walk. The morning promises to be a fine one. If your head does not trouble you, that is."

The clock ticked in the silence, and doubt crept in. He'd spoken too soon. He ought to have waited, perhaps—

"I should like that," she said with a smile. "If your ribs do not trouble you."

Relief loosened the knot in his chest. When she rose to fetch her shawl and bonnet, he stood as well.

"Shall we meet in the parlor at half past the hour?" she said.

"Half past," he agreed.

MERRYN LED THEM along the lane that rose beyond the house. Fog still hung in the low places like cotton wadding, and the morning smelled of gorse. The yellow blooms were heavy on the bushes, their faint scent mixing with salt from the sea, and wildflowers dotted the hedgerows.

"Cornwall is very pretty," Rebecca said. "The wildflowers grow so freely here—they are not ordered about as they are in Paris or London."

"'Tis certainly wilder," Merryn agreed. "Though I'd wager you'll find more than one gentleman who prefers his gardens disciplined. Carew has been at war with his hedgerows for months."

"The poor man. I imagine the hedgerows must be winning?"

A laugh escaped him. "Every day."

They walked in silence for a time. The lane narrowed as it climbed, drawing them closer together. Her shoulder occasionally brushed his arm, and each time the contact sent awareness through him.

The lane curved right, but on their left, a footpath led to a hedged pasture. Beyond it, the land rose toward the clifftops.

"The prospect is better from the high ground," he said with a nod toward the path. "It requires crossing the field, though. Your gown—"

"Will surely survive an encounter with the grass," Rebecca said with a smile. "I should like to see this prospect."

He led her to a narrow stile in the stone hedge. "Careful. The stones can be slippery," he said, offering his hand.

She placed her fingers in his, and he steadied her with his other hand at her waist. For a moment they were close enough that he could see hints of amber in her brown eyes. He followed her over the stile and they continued up a gentle rise, the grass springy beneath their feet. Sheep watched them with mild interest before returning to their grazing.

They crested the hill, and the view opened. Rolling green fields fell away to dramatic cliffs above a pretty cove. Here, the morning's fog was gone, and the sea stretched endless and brilliant blue beneath a cloudless sky.

Rebecca stopped. "Oh," she breathed. "It's magnificent. Even better than the view above Newford."

She moved forward, drawn by the view, and he followed. When the wind threatened his hat, he removed it, grateful that the exaggerated curls men wore in London had never taken hold in Cornwall, else he'd have quite the tangle fluttering about his head.

"I think I see France," she said, laughing.

Her words erased all thoughts of his hair. In the first months after their marriage, he'd often looked out over the sea as they were doing now and imagined he, too, could see all the way to France. Was his wife wishing herself across the water?

"'Tis a fine, clear morning," he managed. "Per'aps you can."

"Oh, do not think me so simple as that," she said with mock severity.

Her tone drew a smile from him. "Simple is the last adjective I would choose for you."

She considered him. "What is the first?"

"Determined," he answered without thinking, then cursed his tongue. Although the word fit her perfectly, he didn't think that was what a lady wished to hear. A string of more complimentary words came to him then: beautiful, compassionate, charming, intelligent, elegant. Any would have been better than *determined*. Perhaps he should not have been so quick to dismiss his cousins' lessons.

Her eyes narrowed as she pondered his reply. Finally, she brightened. "Thank you," she said. "Although I think 'determined' is just another way of calling me strong-headed, it is possibly the most honest thing I've heard in some time. Any other gentleman would have played to my vanity instead."

He wondered if she had gentlemen paying her court in France. He thought she must—the society there was far more sophisticated than in the English countryside.

"They would not be wrong to call you charming or clever or beautiful," he said. "You are all of those things, but 'tis your determination which defines you. You do nothing by half measures."

"I think that you and I are more alike than we are different," Rebecca mused, "both of us determined in our own way. It is one of the reasons I suggested our arrangement in the first place."

"One of the reasons?"

Her expression turned teasing. "Do you wish me to play to *your* vanity now?"

"I would not be averse to a bit of flattery."

"It is not flattery to point out your kind nature or your honor. That is to say nothing of your shrewdness! You used the King's visit to bring a much-needed bridge to your neighbors."

Merryn held his gaze on the sea, turning his hat behind him as heat crept up the back of his neck.

"You understand what it is to strive for something just beyond your reach," she went on. "I—I think often of that night in my uncle's library."

He cut his eyes to her. "You do?" Her admission caused his heart to beat more rapidly. It was one thing to know she'd kept his letters, quite another to learn the same night lingered in her thoughts.

A curl slipped loose from her pins to flutter about her cheek. She brushed it aside with an impatient finger. "Do you not? Sometimes in Paris, when my aunt's salon grows too loud or too…" She stopped and made a vague flutter with her hand.

Curiosity burned through him. What had she begun to say? That she'd been lonely for England? That she'd thought of home? Of him? He waited but then she shifted and gave him a too-bright look. She would say no more on it.

They stood for a time, watching the sea and looking out toward France. Her skirts fluttered in the breeze. Gulls wheeled overhead, their cries carried away by the wind. The fishermen were out, and their distant boats were tiny shapes on the water down below.

After several moments Rebecca turned to him again. Her cheeks were flushed. "Your walk was an excellent suggestion. Thank you," she said with a smile.

Whether she wished herself in France or not, her smile was worth it. It was the sort he felt clear to his center. "The pleasure was mine." He hesitated before adding, "We could walk here again, if you would like to."

"I would like it very much."

Some of the tension left his shoulders. Perhaps wooing was not so difficult as his cousins made it seem. Perhaps they'd been going about it all wrong.

His wife looped her hand through his arm, though there was no one about to see them. "I do not wish to keep you from your work," she said as they began moving back toward the lane. "How do things progress at the Abbey?"

They spoke of his royal project as they walked, and of her investment ladies. When she inquired after his cousins, many of whom she'd met but whose place in Newford and the Kimbrell family tree escaped her, he obliged her with an accounting.

"James, Jory and Gavin you met at the bridge. James owns the bank," he explained, "as did his father before him. He's as yet unmarried. Gavin, the constable, is wed to Mari. They've the care of Mari's young niece. Jory tunes church bells—I'm given to understand there's a fair bit of mathematics to the art. He is married to Anna, and they've a young daughter, Tamsyn."

He continued ticking cousins off his fingers. "Gryffyn is my uncle Thomas's son—one of five. He's recently wed to the mayor's daughter."

"He's the sculptor?"

"Aye, his latest work decorates the High Cross in Truro. And then there's Alfie—"

She smiled. "I gather from the frequency of his smiles that he is the least serious of your cousins."

Merryn couldn't help his own smile. "Aye. That is a generous way of putting it. Alfie's manner is untroubled, to say the least. Irreverent, the matrons might say, though he is steadfast when it matters. He operates a cidery on the other side of the cove and is married to Eliza."

Rebecca's brows drew together. "Eliza Darling, of *The Newford Inventory*?"

He rubbed the back of his neck. "Aye. 'Twas on account of Alfie's courtship of Miss Darling that I— we all, rather—lent our assistance to her inventory. 'Tis true that no good deed goes unpunished. Ladies and their mothers have been coming to Newford ever since to have a look at the bachelors."

"How unfortunate for all of you."

Merryn twisted his mouth ruefully. "It seemed harmless enough at the time, though I see now how such actions could be mistaken... 'Twas carelessly done. For that, you've my apology."

She waved a hand, dismissing his words. "Did it work at least? Did Miss Darling's publication win her competition?"

He nodded. "She won, and now she manages her newspaper in Newford."

"She operates a newspaper? Here?" She looked about them as if she expected to find the sheep manning the press.

"We do read," he said, which earned him a chiding look for his sarcasm.

It struck him then how alike his wife and Eliza were, both of them possessing ambitions beyond what society expected of gently-bred ladies. The obvious difference between them was that, despite Eliza's independent ways, she'd found contentment in her marriage to his cousin. Whether Rebecca might see possibilities in that, or dismiss it as irrelevant to their circumstances, he couldn't say.

Keeping his tone even, he suggested, "You might enjoy making Eliza's acquaintance."

Rebecca tilted her head at him. "I think I would."

The rest of their walk passed quickly, and they soon reached the drive again. Merryn knew he ought to leave directly for the Abbey—the plasterers would be there soon, and he had no wish for them to begin without the proper instruction.

Rebecca looked toward the house, likely thinking of the letters she meant to write, but neither of them moved.

"Until later, then," she said finally.

He cleared his throat. "Until later."

She dropped her hand from his sleeve. As she reached the door, she looked back at him, her lips curving in a small smile. When he turned for the stables, his step felt lighter than it had in some time. Years, perhaps.

REBECCA WALKED WITH him again the next morning, and the morning after that. Each day, he left her at the stables and went about his tasks while she tended her correspondence or joined his sister for tea at the Feather. On the third day, he entered the stables with a lightness he was unaccustomed to feeling.

"Morning, sir." Jem looked up from one of the stalls, pitchfork in hand. "Yer mare's ready when you are. Saddled as you requested, and the shoe's been reset proper-like."

Merryn checked the horse anyway, as was his habit, running a hand down the foreleg and examining the shoe. The mare nuzzled his shoulder, seeking treats, and he obliged her with an apple from the basket by the door.

He should have been considering the work that awaited him at the Abbey, but his mind was already turning to another walk with Rebecca on the morrow. Was it too presumptuous of him to expect it? Too eager?

He nearly laughed aloud—they'd been married five years with not a kiss between them. Whatever accusations might be leveled at him, undue haste could hardly be among them.

"Your uncle was here," Jem said conversationally. "Delivered your mother from Helston not twenty minutes past. Pity you missed him—said he meant to make the tollgate before dark."

Jem's words took a moment to penetrate Merryn's thoughts. When they did, the pleasant warmth of the morning evaporated like fog before a wind.

"My mother?"

"Aye, sir. Mrs. Kimbrell—the *other* Mrs. Kimbrell, I s'pose—is returned from her sister's."

His mother. Here.

His letter must have reached Helston quickly. He'd hoped for a few more days, but he should have known better. Of course his mother, on learning of his marriage, would have flown back to Newford as soon as she was able. The sinking sensation in his stomach made him feel like he'd been caught filching Cook's biscuits—except he was a man nearing thirty, and the biscuit in question was his wife.

"Unsaddle the mare," he said, surprised that his voice remained even while his heart hammered his sore ribs.

"Sir?"

Merryn didn't respond but turned toward the house, his stride quickening with each step.

CHAPTER 20

Rebecca entered the house, the ribbons of her bonnet dangling loose about her throat. She paused to draw them free then worked the buttons of her gloves.

Her morning walks with Merryn had become a welcome routine over the past days, though each one left her thoughts more disordered than the last. It wasn't only the ease of their conversation as they looked out over the sea but the ease of their silences as well.

The thought of returning to France felt less certain now, complicated in a way it had not been before. When Merryn had suggested a real marriage between them, the prospect hadn't alarmed her as it ought to have done. But she couldn't forget her aunt, her investment ladies, her independence—all awaited her return once matters with her cousin were settled.

Her thoughts, which were usually well ordered, were proving disobedient. They scattered like a flock of startled birds every time she tried to arrange them properly.

She must keep her attention on her aim—her cousin's threat could not be forgotten—but neither could she ignore the feelings her husband stirred. They bore no resemblance to the orderly satisfaction she felt for a successful investment—that solid, measurable pleasure when careful study yielded profitable returns. These new feelings were... precarious. Soaring and light, like standing on a clifftop with the wind at her back.

She looked forward to the distraction of her ledgers and correspondence. The morning room had a pretty desk that served nicely for the task. She moved toward the stairs, tugging the tips of her gloves as she went. She slowed her steps, though, when she heard voices coming from the parlor.

"...a most unusual circumstance, to be sure..."

Mrs. Tilbury. Rebecca recognized the housekeeper's low tone.

"I should like to understand it for myself," said a second, unfamiliar female. The accent was educated but softened with the cadence particular to Cornwall.

"And arriving with only a companion and maid to accompany her, no family to speak of—"

"No more talk, Mrs. Tilbury, if you please." The stranger's voice turned firm. "I should like to form my own opinion of this woman."

Rebecca's fingers stilled on her glove. *This woman*. Was there any mistaking their subject?

She pulled the glove free and set the pair on the hall table. Was this another of Merryn's cousins come to assess his secret wife? Or perhaps another of Newford's matrons?

Irritation increased her pulse, but she forced her breathing to calm. Merryn may have chosen to keep his marriage to himself, but she had chosen to go to France and remain there. She could hardly expect to avoid scrutiny. Indeed, there would likely be much more of it when her cousin reached England.

She smoothed her walking dress and straightened her spine. Putting a welcoming smile upon her countenance, she drew open the parlor doors.

Mrs. Tilbury stood near the tea service, hands worrying her apron. In the best chair sat a woman in her early fifties with a teacup halfway to her mouth. She was handsome rather than beautiful, dressed in well-made but unadorned traveling clothes. She looked up at Rebecca's entrance with intelligent eyes.

Intelligent eyes in a familiar shade of blue. That was Rebecca's first indication. Then she noted the tilt of the woman's mouth, the angle of her nose, the dark hair with a slight curl at the temples. Though it was threaded through with silver, the similarity could not be mistaken.

This, then, was Merryn's mother.

Rebecca's mouth dried as her mother-in-law replaced her cup in its saucer. The older woman rose and studied Rebecca the way one might examine a horse before purchase. Her scrutiny was not unkind, but it was thorough.

Mrs. Tilbury looked from one to the other, eyes wide, apron twisting in her fingers.

"Mrs. Tilbury," Merryn's mother said without taking her eyes from Rebecca. "Cake, if you please."

Mrs. Tilbury's eyes widened further still. She had clearly hoped to remain and hear what would be said, but her employer's tone left no room for argument.

"Of course, ma'am." The housekeeper cast one last glance at Rebecca before complying. Her expression bore the faintest hint of satisfaction about the mouth, as though all her suspicions about secret wives had not been misplaced.

The silence stretched until the door clicked shut behind Mrs. Tilbury. Rebecca resisted the urge to glance toward the window. Merryn would be halfway to the Abbey by now. There was no aid coming from that quarter.

Not that she required any. She had entertained

countless dignitaries in her aunt's salon, and worldly businessmen in her uncle's home before that. She could certainly manage one mother-in-law.

She made a respectful curtsy. "Mrs. Kimbrell. I am pleased to make your acquaintance."

"Mrs. Kimbrell," the older woman greeted her with a wry tone. Her expression revealed nothing of her thoughts. "I confess you have me at a disadvantage," she continued, "for I was unaware we shared the name."

The words were direct but not hostile. The elder Mrs. Kimbrell did not hesitate to say precisely what she meant. Given the situation, Rebecca could not fault her manner.

"I regret the circumstances of our introduction," she said. "They are irregular, to say the least."

"Irregular. 'Tis one word for it." Then, to Rebecca's surprise, Mrs. Kimbrell's tone softened a fraction. "But I suppose that cannot be remedied now. Please, won't you sit?"

Rebecca didn't mistake the woman's words for an invitation. They were a direct order. She sat, taking the place her mother-in-law indicated and folding her hands upon her lap.

Merryn's mother returned to her chair and reached for the teapot. Her hand hesitated a moment before she pulled it back. She looked at Rebecca, and something shifted in her expression.

"I would offer you tea, but I suppose 'tis your place to do that now."

The words hung between them. Rebecca swallowed. How would it feel, she wondered, to find you'd been replaced without ceremony in your own home? And by a stranger, no less.

She met the other woman's gaze. "I should be honored to learn your preferences, ma'am. I am yet a stranger in this house."

Her mother-in-law studied her a moment longer, then nodded. "Prettily said. Milk, if you please, no sugar."

Rebecca moved to the tea service. Her hands remained steady as she poured, though she had no notion how she accomplished it. She added milk, no sugar, and carried the cup to Mrs. Kimbrell.

"Thank you." Mrs. Kimbrell sipped, eyeing Rebecca over the rim. "My son wrote to me of your marriage. I confess his letter has raised more questions than it answered."

Of course it had. A flutter of irritation competed with reluctant amusement. Irritation, for Merryn had written to his mother, but he hadn't thought to warn Rebecca of the fact.

And amusement at the thought of her stoic husband attempting to explain five years of silence—in a letter! *Mother, I've been married these last five years and neglected to mention it. Please do not be alarmed.*

It was almost enough to make her smile, despite the gravity of the situation.

"I imagine it must have been something of a shock," Rebecca said gently.

"You have been in France, I understand."

Rebecca nodded. "Yes, ma'am. In Paris."

"And what has brought you back to England after all this time?"

Rebecca chose her words with care. "An inheritance matter requiring my attention."

Mrs. Kimbrell sipped her tea, her gaze never leaving Rebecca's face. "Do you intend to stay?"

Rebecca released a startled breath. Her mother-in-law did not mince words. Rebecca could appreciate the other woman's forthright nature, even as she resisted the urge to shift in her chair. "I am undecided," she admitted.

"At least you are honest," Mrs. Kimbrell said with an approving dip of her head. "My son did not mention that you are also comely."

Rebecca blinked. Whatever she had expected, it was not that.

"I do not believe my appearance weighed in his considerations."

"No." Mrs. Kimbrell set her cup in its saucer. "Merryn has never been easily swayed by a pretty head. He has always been too fixed on his business interests."

"I think he has been fixed just the right amount," Rebecca ventured.

Mrs. Kimbrell stilled before adding, "I should be curious what considerations *did* persuade him to such an unusual step."

One thousand pounds, Rebecca thought, though she didn't say it aloud. If Merryn's mother thought him too fixed on his business interests, what would she say to his reasons for marrying? She could not think how to answer—in truth, it was not for her to do so—but to her relief, the doors opened, sparing her the necessity.

Merryn came in, his hair slightly disordered as if he'd run a hasty hand through it. He swept the room, taking in his mother in her chair and Rebecca on the settee. His jaw tightened.

"Mother, you're returned. I did not expect you so soon." He crossed to her and pressed a kiss to her cheek.

"That much is clear, else you might have better prepared your wife for our first meeting." Mrs. Kimbrell's tone was wry as she glanced pointedly between her son and Rebecca.

A flush climbed Merryn's neck—discomfort or guilt, perhaps. An awareness, at least, that he'd failed to mention he'd written to his mother.

Mrs. Kimbrell looked at Rebecca. "If you will excuse us, I should like a word with my son."

It was not a request but a dismissal. Rebecca stood, smoothing the fall of her dress and offering a smile.

"Of course, ma'am."

She moved toward the door. As she passed Merryn, she allowed herself one brief glance. His eyes met hers, and she thought there might have been an apology in them.

She continued past him into the hall. Only after the parlor door closed behind her did she release the breath she held.

MERRYN FACED HIS mother. She regarded him with the expression she had reserved in his boyhood for moments that required confession. Admittedly, they had not been many, but he knew the look well.

"Sit." She gestured to the chair Rebecca had vacated. When he hesitated, she added, "I'll not be obliged to bend my neck at you."

That Rebecca had spoken similar words to him in the Feather's parlor brought an inappropriate urge to smile. He stiffened his jaw against it and sat.

His mother studied him with equal parts determination and irritation—as if he were an unwelcome knot in her embroidery thread. He crossed his legs then crossed his hands over his midsection.

"I imagine you must have questions," he began.

She didn't let him finish. "I received your letter the same day others from Newford scolded me for keeping secrets."

He winced, but she went on.

"My son—married five years and I had to hear it from Edith Pentreath."

He forced himself to hold her gaze. "Aye."

"Why?"

Straight to the heart of it, as always. He scrubbed a hand over his mouth. The explanations were growing tedious, but of all the people he'd kept his secret from, she deserved one the most. She was his mother.

"'Twas naught but a marriage of convenience," he said.

"No marriage is 'naught but' anything. You spoke vows before God."

He nodded, for he had no other answer to that.

"What I wish to know," she continued, "is... why?"

"Miss Pearce—Rebecca—needed a husband."

Her eyes narrowed, and he hastily assured her, "'Twas not like *that*." He explained the matter of Rebecca's trust and her uncle's illness.

"This is the matter which has brought her back to England?"

He nodded and told her of Gregory Pearce's impending return and his challenge to their marriage.

When he finished, she shook her head. "So Miss Pearce needed a husband. What of you?"

"I needed funds."

"Funds! Whatever for?"

He swallowed. "I wished to grow what Father started."

His mother's mouth thinned. "Your father built a respectable trade. He provided for his family. Was that not enough?"

The question struck harder than any rebuke.

"'Twas enough for him," Merryn said quietly. "But I want it to be more. I want it to endure."

She studied him then, not in anger, but with something like regret. "Ambition is a fine thing, Merryn. But it has a way of persuading a man that what he has is never quite enough. But even so, you could have appealed to your grandfather for funds. There was no need to go to the banks, much less to such lengths as… as marriage to a woman you barely know. There is nothing Alan Kimbrell adores so much as watching his grandchildren succeed—you all are his legacy."

Merryn nodded but remained silent. It was true. He could have gone to Oak Hill with an appeal. His grandfather would have readily given him the funds, but Merryn had wanted to succeed on his own merit.

The London banks, though, were reluctant to lend their funds and their trust to an untested man from Cornwall. He'd gone there again and again, pleading his case. But eventually, the reason for his travels, the explanation he gave his cousins, began to wear thin to his own ears.

In truth, it was the lady at her uncle's table who had captured his interest far more than any banker might have done.

"Regardless of your reasons for marrying," she went on, "there is no explanation for your silence."

He rubbed his jaw. "As I said, our marriage was only a... transaction. Rebecca left for France soon after, as we agreed she would do. There seemed little point in speaking of't."

"A transaction," she repeated, and he couldn't miss the note of disappointment in her tone. "But why you? Why could some other gentleman not have served her purpose?"

"Because she asked me," he said simply.

"And you agreed to such an arrangement straightaway?"

The silence stretched between them.

"No," he said finally, his voice rough. "There was nothing 'straightaway' about it."

His mother waited.

The truth rose up, impossible to push back down. "I had met her many times before, at her uncle's table. She was different from other young ladies—intelligent, forthright. I thought—"

He broke off, the words caught in his chest.

"What?" she whispered. "You thought what?"

He forced the words out. "I thought I could persuade her to remain in England."

"She was determined to go?"

He met her eyes. "She made her intentions clear before we married. She cannot be blamed for keeping to the terms of our agreement."

Her expression softened. She reached across the space between them to press his arm. "Do you feel an affection for her?"

He flinched. But this was his mother, and she had never been one for circling a subject.

"Aye." The word came out rough.

His mother's hand tightened on his sleeve. "Oh, my son."

He straightened, uncomfortable beneath her sympathy. She spoke as if he'd fallen and scraped his knee or broken a favorite toy. "'Tis something of a muddle," he murmured.

She gave him a sad smile. "You have always been one for understating things."

She rose briskly then, smoothing her skirts. He stood with her as she began to tidy the tea things.

"I suppose I ought to tell Mrs. Tilbury not to unpack my trunks," she said.

He stared at her. "Why? D'you return to Helston?"

"No, I shall remove to Oak Hill," she said. "Your grandfather will welcome the company." At his open-mouthed stare, she added, "You, my son, have courting to do, and you will not accomplish it with your mother underfoot."

Heat climbed his neck beneath his cravat. "Mother—"

She gave him a look. "Do not be missish."

"I was not—that is—" He could not find the words.

"Merryn." Her voice gentled. "Whatever her reason for returning, you have another chance to make things right with your wife."

"She has only returned because of her cousin's challenge. I do not think she will stay," he said. It was one thing to allow his own hopes to catch flame, another altogether to raise his mother's expectations.

"You cannot know that. 'Tis not a certainty unless you do not try, and in that case, no woman would stay." She shook her head. "This wife of yours—she is not what I expected."

He could not read her tone. "No?"

"When I read your letter, I imagined someone grasping. A woman who saw your fine prospects and seized her opportunity."

When he shook his head, she held up a finger. "Do not gainsay me."

Of course, his mother would see him as a prize, but Rebecca was not like that. She would much rather make her own way in the world than to rely on a man with prospects. His mother, however, wasn't finished.

"She is guarded and holds fast to what she's won, though I wonder if the victory still suits her. She is not unaffected by you. A mother can tell these things."

Merryn stilled, though his pulse quickened.

She rose up to kiss his cheek. "I think perhaps you chose better than you knew. When I return, I expect you will have got the thing done. Do not let her go this time."

He could not speak past his embarrassment. It was bad enough that his cousins offered their husband lessons unsolicited, but now he had courtship directives from his mother.

She smiled. "Do not look so scandalized, love. Now, I expect I will see the pair of you at church."

Church. Of course, he and Rebecca would be expected to attend on the morrow, and afterward, they would drive to Oak Hill for luncheon. No matter how he might wish to keep his wife to himself, to court her in private with idyllic walks along the cliffs, it couldn't be avoided.

At his silent nod, his mother took herself off to have her things readied for the drive to his grandfather's home. Merryn fell back onto the settee, elbows on his knees and hands in his hair. He sat like that for a long moment, until a noise drew his attention back to the doorway.

Rebecca stood with her hands clasped loosely before her. She entered when he looked up.

"Your mother is kind," she said, "to accept a strange woman into her home."

He rose. "She is," he agreed and instantly regretted it when his wife lifted a wry brow at him. "I did not mean—" He cleared his throat. "You are not strange. Unfamiliar to her, per'aps, but—"

"I took your meaning," she said with a hint of amusement in her dark eyes.

"You are enjoying this," he accused.

"Only a little." The corner of her mouth quirked as she came toward him. "Though you ought to have told me you'd written to her. I could have been better prepared for her arrival."

He rubbed the back of his neck. "I confess, it didn't occur to me to do so."

"I thought perhaps it didn't. But we must appear of one mind. We are married, after all."

He released a short breath. "I shall endeavor to remember it."

CHAPTER 21

THE CARRIAGE ROLLED up a tree-lined drive to Merryn's grandfather's home, and Rebecca's fingers worried the ribbons of her reticule.

"You're uneasy." Merryn's observation carried no judgment, merely fact.

She released the ribbons and stilled her hands. "Is it so obvious?"

He leaned forward, his shoulder blocking the window's light for a moment. "They will welcome you, Rebecca. You needn't worry."

But she did worry. Not about their welcome — the Kimbrells had proven warm enough when she'd been merely Miss Pearce. That they had questions now was only understandable.

No, what troubled her ran deeper. Today she would be introduced as Merryn's wife. She would become a part of his sprawling family, expected to attend future gatherings. To belong.

And belonging meant staying.

That the notion didn't terrify her as it might once have done... well, that alone was rather alarming.

The carriage slowed as they rounded the manor's forecourt. Merryn stepped down first, then turned to offer his hand. His palm was warm through her glove, his grip steady as she descended.

The doors opened and an aging butler appeared at the top of the steps.

"Sir, Mrs. Kimbrell." His greeting acknowledged her new status without ceremony. "The family is gathered on the lawn. Shall I announce you?"

"No need, Parsons," Merryn said. "We'll find our way."

"As you wish," he said, closing the doors behind them. "And sir," he added as Merryn led Rebecca through the spacious entrance hall.

Merryn stopped and turned.

"You've my felicitations on your marriage," Parsons said with a smile tipping the corner of his mouth.

"Thank you, Parsons."

They went through toward the back of the house and soon reached doors opening onto a broad terrace. The sound of children's laughter reached them first, followed by the murmur of adult conversation. A freshly-scythed lawn was set with tables and blankets, and children darted about in some game that involved a great deal of gleeful shrieking. Beyond it all lay the sea, fading into the horizon.

The sound of the children's laughter recalled a spring afternoon when Rebecca had been six or seven. She'd found her mother at the drawing room window, watching the neighbors having a picnic in the square across the street. When Rebecca asked if they might join them, her mother's face shuttered.

The week's accounts made no provision for a picnic, she said. They must wait for her father to approve the expense. But he was out, and by the time he returned that evening, the neighbors had long since packed their hampers.

Her mother drew her close instead and told stories of France, of running wild through the countryside with her sister Eugénie, of summers that had seemed endless before the Terror.

"We were so free then," she whispered.

Not until years later, as Rebecca watched her mother request permission for everything from new shoes for their growing daughter to an extra candle in the winter's darkness, did she understand. Her mother had fled the Revolution for England, only to trade one danger for another sort of prison entirely.

She pushed the memory aside as an elderly gentleman approached them. His eyes—the same deep blue as Merryn's—sparkled with warmth and something that might have been reproach.

"So this is the bride you've kept from us all this time." Alan Kimbrell's voice carried across the terrace. "I begin to see why—you feared one of your cousins might steal her."

Rebecca felt Merryn stiffen beside her, his jaw tightening though his grandfather's eye twinkled. She curtsied. "Mr. Kimbrell. You've a lovely home. How kind you are to welcome me."

"Stuff," he said as he clasped her hand between both of his. "You're a Kimbrell now."

Before Rebecca could form a proper response to this, Merryn's mother appeared. She accepted her son's kiss to her cheek before taking Rebecca's hands in hers with a firm but not uncomfortable pressure.

"Rebecca, dear—you do not mind if I call you Rebecca?" There was a firmness to the question that Rebecca dared not contradict.

"Of course not, ma'am."

"We are pleased you've come. You must persuade my son to join us more often," Mrs. Kimbrell said, her tone lighter though still pointed. "A wife's influence in such matters cannot be overstated."

Rebecca blinked at this greeting, but Merryn's mother's aim was clear. By not hesitating to greet her new daughter-in-law, by acknowledging her as a wife, she made her acceptance of the match clear. Though Rebecca didn't think her actions would fool anyone, she appreciated the gesture nonetheless.

"Merryn," Mrs. Kimbrell continued. "Take your wife about and introduce her properly."

"I was about to do just that, Mother, before you swooped in."

"Don't be pert," she warned him with a tap of his arm that had Rebecca concealing a smile.

She allowed her husband to lead her across the lawn toward several women gathered near one of the tables. They looked up, their conversation pausing at Merryn's approach. Rebecca recognized the dressmaker, Morwenna, and Wynne from the Feather. A pair of aunts, and another woman in a blue day dress with dark, curling hair caught in a simple chignon.

Eliza, Alfie's wife. The newspaper woman. Merryn had pointed her out to Rebecca that morning in church. Her gaze was direct but not unkind, and Rebecca was struck by the pretty, almost-violet hue of her eyes.

Merryn made the introductions, and Rebecca was soon caught up in conversation with the women.

Presently, her husband was drawn away by his cousins, and a commotion with one of the children drew the other ladies' attention. Rebecca found herself alone with Eliza Kimbrell.

"I'm delighted to meet you," Eliza said. "Alfie tells me you've upset the Kimbrell betting book. He has me quite curious about the lady who has captured his cousin."

Rebecca smiled, drawn to Eliza's forthright manner. "And as a newspaper woman, I suspect you must suffer from an excess of curiosity," she said, matching the other woman's directness.

"It is true," Eliza admitted. She motioned to a nearby bench. "Would you care to sit?"

They sat, and the children's laughter carried across the lawn as servants moved between the tables.

"Perhaps I will appease your curiosity sometime," Rebecca said, "but first you must satisfy mine. Will you tell me more about your newspaper? Merryn tells me you acquired it in Truro."

Eliza's expression brightened. "Yes, the *Cornwall Monthly Journal* was my father's. I was fortunate to purchase it from his successor and brought it to Newford when Alfie and I married."

"I imagine it must be quite the undertaking, managing such an enterprise."

She laughed. "To say I 'manage' the paper is generous—some days it feels like I am the one being managed. But I can tell you that no day is ever the same as the one before it," she said. "Some might find that exhausting, but I find it…"

"Invigorating?" Rebecca suggested.

Eliza smiled. "Just so."

Her attention was caught then by her husband, a tall, dark-haired man across the lawn. Alfie Kimbrell laughed with a group that included Merryn and several of their cousins, and when he turned, his gaze found his wife's immediately. His smile widened, and Rebecca watched, amused, as color climbed Eliza's throat.

When she looked back at Rebecca, her expression had softened. "I confess, as much as I love the newspaper, it is not the whole of my life anymore."

The admission surprised Rebecca, and her eyebrows lifted before she could school her features. She cleared her throat. "Have you and Mr. Kimbrell been married for long?" she asked.

"Nearly a year." Eliza's gaze strayed to her husband once more. "Sometimes it seems I've known him all my life, and other times, it's as if we've only just met, and I am discovering him all over again." She brought her attention back to Rebecca and wrinkled her nose. "Heavens, I sound like a goose."

"Not at all."

"But what of you, Mrs. Kimbrell?" Eliza turned the conversation neatly. "What interests do you pursue?"

Rebecca hesitated. She and Eliza were strangers still, yet something in the woman's direct gaze invited confidences. "I have been studying the funds," she said. "I lead a group of ladies in Paris, and we've been rather successful in our efforts thus far."

Eliza's eyebrows rose. "The funds?"

"I have shocked you."

"No," she said slowly. "It's only… That is a rather unusual pursuit for a lady, is it not?"

"No more so, I expect, than publishing a newspaper."

Eliza considered this. "Quite so," she replied with a grin.

Their conversation was interrupted by the arrival of an enormous wolfhound and a black collie. The dogs loped toward them, tongues lolling. On their heels trotted a small brindled terrier, towing one of the lawn blankets behind him. He danced about his larger companions with far more confidence than his size warranted, which only served to tangle the blanket about his stubby legs.

Behind them, Bronwyn followed at a more sedate pace, shaking her head at the little dog's antics.

Eliza laughed. "The large one is Brioc—he belongs to Alfie's grandfather—and his lady is Trout. And that," she said, indicating the little terrier, "is Alfie's dog, Hero. Never was there a more perfect example of optimism. Come, you mangy thing." She collected her husband's dog, untangled him from the blanket, and turned back to Rebecca. "I expect we'll have a chance to speak again soon."

"I hope so."

Rebecca rose to greet her approaching sister-in-law. Bronwyn wore a sunny yellow dress that was at odds with the storm cloud gathered between her brows.

"Mrs. Kimbrell," she said, tapping a stick against her leg.

Rebecca grimaced at Bronwyn's overly formal address. "Please," she said, "you must call me Rebecca if we're to be friends."

Bronwyn crossed her arms, stick dangling from one hand to tease the wolfhound. Brioc dropped to his haunches, panting at her side. Bronwyn ignored him, her slippered foot tapping the ground beneath her skirts.

"Are we?" she said. "To be friends, that is."

Rebecca held her gaze. "I should like it if we were," she said carefully. Honesty compelled her to add, "I cannot say how long I will remain in Cornwall, but I should like us to be friends, for whatever time I am here."

The storm cloud on Bronwyn's brow darkened. She eyed Rebecca for a long moment then turned her gaze across the lawn to where Merryn stood with James. She sighed. "I do not know why you married my brother, or why the pair of you have kept it to yourselves, or why you could not remain here. I do know, however, my brother can be confoundedly silent when he should not be."

"It is true," Rebecca admitted.

"I would not be at all surprised if the secret nature of your marriage was his doing."

Rebecca would not lie to her sister-in-law, but neither did she wish to toss her husband so neatly onto the fire. She said only, "He had his reasons."

"You defend him."

"He is my husband."

Bronwyn considered this before giving a brisk nod. "We cannot prevent them from being idiots, though we may try." She tilted her head then, studying Rebecca with a shrewdness that reminded her of Merryn. "As a married woman myself, I know that simple things have a way of becoming more complicated than they should. Still—five years of separation strikes me as beyond the usual muddle."

Her words surprised a laugh from Rebecca.

Bronwyn's lips curved in a reluctant smile, and she tossed the stick. The dogs bounded after it, kicking up clods of grass and dirt in their haste.

Then, as if she'd just recalled it, Bronwyn said, "The squire's ball—'tis at week's end. Have you got a proper gown?" Before Rebecca could answer, her sister-in-law shook her head. "What am I thinking? You've come from France—of course you have dresses."

CHAPTER 22

Merryn watched his wife toss a stick for the dogs with his sister. The sight should have been absurd — his fashionable Parisian wife entertaining his grandfather's enormous wolfhound — but instead it sent his pulse skipping like a stone over water.

His family, once they had got over their initial shock, was accepting of his marriage and his wife. Rebecca had charmed the matrons at the post office. Was it possible news of his secret marriage was not the disaster he'd feared?

"Merryn," James murmured. "A word?"

The serious expression on his cousin's face, to say nothing of his quiet tone, caught Merryn's attention. He followed James a few paces to the edge of the garden where the warm scent of their grandmother's roses was heavy on the air.

"I've had a letter," James began.

"About Pearce?" Merryn asked.

James shook his head. "My contact in Plymouth has learned nothing thus far. The man is either careful or lucky." He paused. "The letter was from Trewyck."

Merryn's stomach dropped. "What does he say?"

James's jaw was tight. "He means to pull his funds. Says the costs concern him, that per'aps the project's scope exceeds your capacity." He hesitated before adding, "He claims Sir Felix is prepared to step in."

Merryn's hands curled into fists behind his back. Trewyck—the same investor who'd expressed concerns weeks before. Merryn thought he'd eased the man's worries then with his anonymous investment, but clearly he'd been mistaken.

The work was nearing completion. Bills were due. If Trewyck pulled his funds now, they would be hard pressed to finish. "We're nearly at the end," he bit out. "If Trewyck abandons us—"

He stopped when he saw the look on James's face. His cousin appeared deeply uncomfortable.

"He's not the only one," James said miserably.

"Who?"

"Alderton means to join him, as does Killigrew. And Pentreath, it seems has got Enys's ear."

Merryn grimaced. If Pentreath had got Enys's ear, that could only mean his wife had got Pentreath's ear. Merryn and Rebecca had been too hasty to think they'd routed the matrons, for Edith Pentreath loved nothing more than stirring pots in kitchens other than her own. The speed of the lady's letter to his mother was proof enough of that.

But *four* investors.

If they pulled their funds, more would follow. The timing couldn't be worse—His Majesty's royal barge would land in just over a week, and there was still much to complete. Without funds, he couldn't pay his men or purchase the remaining materials. Everything would collapse.

He thought of the bank book in his desk at home. It would solve the problem, if only he could bring himself to use it. No. He shook his head, forcing his breath to steady.

"What did you tell them?"

"That the work proceeds apace. Their concerns are unfounded."

"Aye." The project would finish. Merryn would make certain of that one way or another. There was the house—perhaps James would agree to a mortgage. He swallowed at the thought. His father never would have countenanced such a thing. "What reason do they give?"

James paused, and the muscle in Merryn's jaw jumped. "Say it."

"Trewyck mentioned your personal circumstances specifically..."

"Aye?"

"He expressed concerns about the scent of scandal tainting the project. He specifically questioned the integrity of"—he cleared his throat—"the project's builder."

Merryn swore. He glanced toward Rebecca—she was laughing at something his sister said. His wife. His secret. His potential ruin. If he didn't stop this wave of discontent, he'd be washed overboard.

"Invite them to dine," he said. "The sooner the better."

James didn't look convinced, but he nodded.

As his cousin left him, Merryn stood watching gulls wheel overhead much as his thoughts swooped and turned. He had little more than a week to finish the work. Wavering investors and a wife who might leave again the moment her cousin's threat was resolved. The weight of it all made it difficult to draw a full breath.

There was a tug at the bottom of his trousers. He looked down to find Jory's daughter Tamsyn at his feet. She pulled herself up, using his leg for balance.

Jory followed, beaming at his daughter. "Have you ever seen a cleverer lass?"

"Never," Merryn agreed. He bent and tossed Tamsyn into the air. She giggled, her golden curls catching the light, her cheeks rosy as cherries. Her unbounded glee at being so flung about was infectious. It was hard to be dismal, though Merryn couldn't escape his mood entirely.

Jory moved to stand beside him. "When you have one of these," he said with a nod for his child, "your perspective changes. 'Tis hard to worry over trifling things when you've a child's laughter in your home—though you'll have new worries to keep you awake at night." He glanced at Merryn. "Whatever troubles you now—'twill sort itself."

Jory tickled his daughter's chin, setting off a new peal of giggles. Merryn couldn't help a smile—until he recalled that of all his troubles, this might be the worst. If Rebecca returned to Paris, he would never have a child of his own. And what was it all for—the sleepless nights, the irksome investors—if there was no one to pass his legacy to? Why build something enduring if there was no one to carry it on?

He held Tamsyn against his chest, breathing in the sweet scent of her baby-fine hair. It was late, and he was suddenly tired. The sun would begin its descent soon. He should collect his wife.

Tamsyn squirmed to be let down. He set her at her father's feet, and when he stood again, he found Rebecca watching him. He put on an untroubled smile and crossed the lawn.

REBECCA LISTENED WITH half an ear as Bronwyn chattered about Newford's upcoming theatrical—apparently, there was some confusion with the actors' costumes. Her attention strayed, though, to where her husband stood across the lawn with Jory.

He lifted the man's daughter and tossed her into the air. The child's squeal carried across the distance, and Rebecca's breath stopped. Her ribs felt too tight, as though she'd been running. She'd never seen Merryn like this—tender, with the stern lines of his face softened. He spoke to Jory though his attention remained on the girl, his large finger caught in her tiny fist. A smile crossed his face, unguarded and wistful, before it was gone again.

He wanted this. Children. A family. If she'd remained in England, would they have one of their own by now?

Bronwyn's voice cut through her thoughts. "They always find my brother—children, that is. They're drawn to him like bees to heather." Her gaze drifted to the roundness beneath her skirts. "He'll make an excellent uncle to this little one."

Rebecca only nodded; she couldn't speak through the tightness in her throat.

Bronwyn added more quietly, "And a father to his own."

The words were pointed enough that Rebecca glanced sharply at her sister-in-law.

Bronwyn met her gaze steadily. "I don't pretend to understand the circumstances of your marriage, but I know my brother. I see how he looks at you when you're not watching."

Rebecca swallowed. "I do not think—"

Bronwyn held up a hand. "I do not mean to meddle. Well, per'aps just a bit. I'm saying only that… whatever has kept you apart before, it needn't do so now."

Across the lawn, Merryn set the girl down and looked up. His gaze found hers, and her pulse quickened. Ridiculous, that a mere glance should cause such a reaction, but then he began to cross the lawn toward her, and she thought her heart might stop altogether.

As he neared them, Bronwyn drifted away with timing that was too perfect to be coincidence.

Rebecca's mind churned. She'd told herself she was content with the arrangement they'd made. Content with her independence, with her life in Paris. She persuaded herself that *he* was content. He'd gained what they'd agreed upon, after all.

But the afternoon when he'd suggested a true marriage between them, she had asked him if he regretted their union. It occurred to her now that he'd not given his answer.

REBECCA WATCHED MERRYN'S profile as he looked out of the carriage window. His expression was tight, shoulders rigid. There was a weariness about his eyes. A heaviness that hadn't been there before, though he tried to hide it. There was something more than their marriage pressing on him. Finally, she broke the silence.

"Something troubles you."

He glanced at her then away. "'Tis nothing to worry over."

She should ask him again if he had regrets, but she couldn't do it. Instead, she observed, "I saw you speaking with James. Are there problems with one of the building projects?"

The muscle in his jaw worked. He was quiet for a long moment before saying, "Some of the investors are wavering. They have concerns about the costs and my... personal circumstances."

Rebecca's midsection tightened. Her return had made everything more complicated. "What will you do?"

"Calm their fears. Show them the project is sound, that their concerns are unfounded." He looked at her then, uncertainty shadowing his features. "James is relaying an invitation to dinner."

She understood immediately. This was something she could help him with. She'd managed enough salons for her aunt to know just how to go on.

"How many will attend?"

"Four investors and their wives."

"I shall speak with Mrs. Tilbury directly."

His eyebrows lifted slightly. "Aye?"

"Of course." She kept her voice steady. "I'm not without experience in such matters, you'll recall."

His shoulders lowered a fraction, and some of the tension left his frame. "Thank you."

He was quiet after that, his gaze fixed on the darkening landscape beyond the window. She settled more comfortably against the carriage seat. The silence that followed felt different. Lighter somehow.

But the image of Merryn with his cousin's daughter wouldn't leave her mind. The carriage swayed around a corner, and Rebecca gathered her courage.

"I asked before if you regret our marriage. It has occurred to me that you did not answer."

Merryn's eyes came back to hers. He opened his mouth then closed it again with a frown. Finally, he said, "You needed protection and I had the means to provide it. And I did not walk away empty-handed, either."

"That is not what I asked."

His knuckles went white. "What d'you want me to say?"

"The truth."

There was another long pause, filled only with the sound of the carriage wheels on the lane. When he spoke, his voice was rough. "I do not regret our marriage," he said. "We made an agreement. You were clear about your terms, and I accepted them. If the cost proved higher than either of us anticipated, 'tis no one's fault."

The admission hung in the air between them. Rebecca's chest constricted. He was right—they had both paid a price far dearer than either had anticipated. She had chosen her independence, as they'd agreed, but in so doing, she had denied them both all that a true marriage might have offered.

The carriage slowed—they were nearly home.

Rebecca searched for words and found none that were adequate to the situation.

"I'm sorry," she whispered finally. "When I suggested the arrangement, I never meant to—I didn't realize—"

"I know." His voice was gentler now. "As with any investment, we made the best decision we could with what we knew."

"And now?"

The question hung between them as the carriage rolled to a stop. Merryn helped her down, his hand lingering on hers a moment longer than necessary.

"Now," he whispered, "I suppose we decide how much we're willing to risk on this venture."

His eyes held hers. "You know better than most that the safest investments yield the smallest returns."

She frowned. "They also yield the smallest losses."

"'Tis true," he said. "But I do not think you are a safe investor. Prudent, per'aps. Diligent, certainly. But not safe."

He released her hand and stepped back, leaving Rebecca standing in the dusk, her heart beating too fast, her mind churning.

The safest investments yielded the smallest returns. How many times had she said as much to her ladies? But she'd also taught them to carefully weigh the risk, to understand the stakes.

Five years before, she'd married to protect her inheritance. The choice then had been practical—a business arrangement that had served them both. She'd known precisely what she risked and what she stood to gain.

Now, nothing was straightforward. She had her independence, it was true, but also a husband she'd grown rather fond of. She had her home in Paris, but Cornwall and its bevy of Kimbrells also drew her.

Prudent, he'd said. Diligent. But not safe. He was right. When had she become so timid in her approach?

She'd spent the last years protecting what she

had, never considering what she might be sacrificing in the process. What she was only beginning to understand was that the choice before her now was far more complicated than the one she'd made five years before.

CHAPTER 23

Mrs. Tilbury's voice had all the warmth of a December wind. "You wish to organize a party? For Tuesday?"

Rebecca stood in the doorway to the kitchen, heat from the cooking fire warming her cheeks. The smell of fresh bread hung heavy in the air from loaves cooling on the rack. Mrs. Tilbury sat at the table with the account books spread before her.

"I understand the timing is unfortunate—" Rebecca began soothingly.

Mrs. Tilbury was not one to be soothed. She set down her pen. "Unfortunate? 'Tis impossible. There is silver to polish, linens to press, china to lay out—to say nothing of the menu to plan, and market day already passed. A proper gathering requires a week's planning, at least." She drew herself up, her grey dress as crisp as her tone. "Beggin' your pardon, ma'am, but the first Mrs. Kimbrell would never have suggested anything so ramshackle."

Rebecca kept her voice even. "Not even to help her son?"

Mrs. Tilbury stilled. "'Tis for Mr. Merryn?"

"It is. The guests are his investors for the royal project."

Mrs. Tilbury's shift was immediate. Her expression softened, her posture losing some of its starch. Despite having just assured Rebecca of the task's impossibility, she said, "Well, why didn't you say so? If 'tis for Mr. Merryn's project..." She rose and went toward the pantry. "Cook, we must talk about the menu."

Cook emerged, wiping flour-dusted hands on her apron. She was a round woman with large arms that had clearly turned out a loaf or two.

"Dinner for ten?" she said when Mrs. Tilbury explained their charge. "On Tuesday?"

"Aye. For Mr. Merryn's investors."

Rebecca held an irritated huff, for the housekeeper's tone lost its chill entirely as the pair began conferring in rapid succession, cataloguing what must be done.

"Jane must away at once to Falmouth," Cook declared. She took Mrs. Tilbury's place at the table and began a list. "The fishmonger for turbot, if't can be had. The butcher for capons—two, per'aps three. Vegetables..."

"Perhaps we might begin with a clear soup," Rebecca suggested. "And a savory pie—gentlemen always appreciate something substantial."

Cook's eyes narrowed. "Aye," she said after a moment's consideration. "A clear soup would be servin'. And the pie—a proper game, per'aps."

They refined the courses together: soup, fish, roasted capon, savory pie, herbed vegetables. Then Cook hesitated, her pen hovering above her list. "'Tis the dessert course what troubles me."

"What do you mean?" Rebecca asked.

"A gathering like this requires a trifle or syllabub, but there be no time for fresh strawberries, nor hothouse grapes." She looked toward Mrs. Tilbury with a crease in her brow.

The housekeeper's face fell. "We cannot serve gentleman investors a dinner without a proper dessert."

"I suppose I could make a lemon pudding," Cook mused, though her tone suggested she found the idea wanting. "Or per'aps a flummery…"

The two women swiftly spiraled into worry, listing options and finding each inadequate to the task. A plain pudding would not impress. A cream would be too simple, a jelly beneath the occasion.

"What about chocolate?" Rebecca said.

The women stopped speaking. Mrs. Tilbury looked as though Rebecca suggested serving tea cakes for the main course. "Chocolate? We cannot serve cups of chocolate at dinner."

"Not 'cups' of chocolate." She turned to Cook. "But surely you can make a sauce of it. Or a chocolate blancmange, perhaps?"

Cook's frown deepened. "A chocolate blancmange? I never heard tell of such a thing."

"In France—indeed, in London—such desserts are not so uncommon."

Mrs. Tilbury's chin lifted. "With respect, ma'am, this is not France."

Rebecca kept her gaze from straying toward the ceiling, but only just. "No, this is not France. But Cornwall has always been a place where merchants trade with the world. Surely we can contrive to serve my husband's guests something that reflects both quality and sophistication."

She didn't wait for an argument but turned to Cook. "You've a book of receipts—perhaps one might be amended to include chocolate. If you've a pretty mold to turn it out, we have our dessert."

Cook hesitated. Her hands pleated the edge of her apron, and Rebecca could see pride warring with uncertainty in her expression. She was skilled—that much was clear from the woman's well-ordered kitchen. But venturing into unknown territory… "I'll have a look at my books," she said at last. "Per'aps there's something that'll do."

The rest of the morning became a flurry of activity. The scullery maid was dispatched to Falmouth with Jem and a lengthy order for the market. Mrs. Tilbury organized the household with impressive haste, directing the maids to beat the rugs, to check the candelabra for wax drips, to ensure the table linens had neither spot nor wrinkle.

By midday, the Kimbrells' best silver service had been brought out. Rebecca found Mrs. Tilbury in the pantry, spreading cloths over the worktable and arranging her polishing supplies.

Rebecca had already removed her morning dress's delicate fichu. Now, she took down an apron from the pantry's wall pegs and began tying the strings.

Mrs. Tilbury looked up, startled. "Ma'am?"

"I do not doubt your efficiency, Mrs. Tilbury, and I am grateful for your diligence. But even you cannot polish all of this silver by tomorrow. I shall help."

"But—" The housekeeper's eyes widened, her hands suspended above a serving platter. "'Tis unseemly. You are the mistress."

Rebecca nearly smiled to hear the woman admit it. She said only, "And it is my husband's dinner." Taking up a polishing cloth, she settled onto a stool beside the housekeeper. "I do not mind the work, truly."

The silence lengthened as Mrs. Tilbury studied her. At last, she gave a little, grudging nod. "I suppose you may begin with the spoons."

Rebecca nodded and began to polish. She had done such work before—not often, and certainly not in her aunt's grand household where such tasks fell to the servants. But her uncle's establishment had been more modest, and she had learned that capable hands served a woman well regardless of her station.

Cook passed by the pantry door and stopped short at the sight of them. Her eyebrows climbed toward her cap.

"Do not be gettin' ideas," she warned. "I'll not have you peelin' turnips in my kitchen."

Rebecca couldn't help her smile. "I assure you there is little risk of that."

THE CANDLES HAD all been lit, and they reflected in the dining room's gleaming silver. Merryn stood at the head of the table, hands clasped behind his back, as Rebecca directed his guests to their places.

She wore a gown of deep green silk with her hair arranged in a style that struck him as both fashionable and practical—no elaborate construction of curls, but something that framed her pale face and caught the candlelight. The effect was simple but elegant enough to take his breath whenever he chanced a glance at her.

Which, admittedly, was rather often.

The table's formal arrangement placed them at opposite ends. It was proper, of course. But the distance felt vast, and he longed for the intimacy of the breakfast room, where they'd grown used to taking their meals. It was odd, he thought, that he could grow used to anything in such a short time.

Mrs. Trewyck sat at his right hand. She was a faded sort of woman, pleasant enough but given to nervous smiles and softly murmured agreements. On his left was Mrs. Killigrew, a livelier matron whose numerous rings caught the candlelight with every lift of her wine.

The middle was taken by the Enyses and Aldertons—the latter pair's pinched expressions suggesting chronic cases of dyspepsia.

The first course arrived promptly. To Merryn's surprise, it was delivered by two footmen borrowed from Oak Hill. Of course, his wife had thought of everything.

Conversation, though, moved slowly about the table. Mrs. Trewyck made a shy comment to Merryn about the weather, while at the other end, her husband complimented the soup. Killigrew, seated on Rebecca's other side, remained silent.

It wasn't until Rebecca directed a comment to that fellow about the royal festivities that the conversation picked up. "I understand the ball at Trevelyan Abbey is to crown His Majesty's visit. Have you had occasion to see the squire's new ballroom?"

Before the man could reply, his wife interjected. "Oh, would that we have!" She leaned forward, her enthusiasm overriding decorum as her voice carried down the table. "Margaret Carew has been maddeningly tight-lipped about the whole affair, though we've all hinted we should love a glimpse."

The lady's eyes widened as she seemed to realize her breach. "Oh! Forgive me, I did not mean to speak out of turn."

"Not at all," Rebecca assured her from the other end. "I have grown a bit continental in my manner, for I do enjoy a lively exchange across the table. Pray, think nothing of it."

Mrs. Killigrew glanced uncertainly at the other wives, as if awaiting their judgment. Mrs. Trewyck's nervous smile flickered, and even Mrs. Alderton seemed unsure whether to approve or censure her colleague.

A brief, awkward silence settled.

Then Mrs. Enys cleared her throat. "I hear the squire has installed new cut-crystal chandeliers from London."

Rebecca directed a prompting look at Merryn. "Aye," he confirmed.

"I'm told there will be fireworks at midnight," Mrs. Trewyck offered tentatively.

Rebecca gave them a conspirator's nod, lowering her voice. "I had occasion to see my husband's work at the Abbey. I do not think I give away anything I should not when I tell you the King will have a fine view of the squire's fireworks."

The ladies murmured their anticipation of this, and more than one envious glance was exchanged over his wife's advantage.

The conversation began to flow more easily then, voices crossing the table as the ladies—and even Enys—offered their thoughts on the squire's preparations. Mrs. Trewyck wondered aloud whether the King would tour the Abbey's gardens. Mrs. Killigrew expressed her hope that the weather would hold.

Much of the stiffness that had marked the first courses had all but disappeared.

Merryn watched from the other end of the table, bemused, as Rebecca turned his proper Cornish dining room into something resembling a Parisian salon. He ought to have felt alarm—surely, Newford's matrons would be scandalized—but he knew only the keenest admiration. The tightness in his chest began to ease.

At a pause in the conversation, Rebecca added, "The King's visit shall be a day Newford long remembers. So many have invested their time and funds—indeed, their very reputations—in making it a success. It would be a shame if anything were to undermine such an effort."

Mrs. Killigrew nodded vigorously. "Indeed, Mrs. Kimbrell. We are all doing our part to ensure Newford's honor."

The fish course arrived—turbot in a delicate sauce, as fine as anything his cook had ever produced. The ladies exclaimed over its presentation, and even Mrs. Alderton's dyspeptic expression softened slightly.

Killigrew set down his fork. "Excellent fish, Mrs. Kimbrell. You've a capable household."

Rebecca inclined her head. "It is our admirable Cook who deserves the credit for the fish."

"And Cornwall's bountiful waters, no doubt," Enys added with a chuckle.

Rebecca smiled at the jest, and talk then turned to the harbor improvements Merryn had been overseeing. It was Alderton who inquired about the progress.

"Ahead of schedule," Merryn responded. "His Majesty's barge will find excellent accommodation."

"And the marine pavilion?" Enys inquired.

"Two days shall see it completed. I should be

happy to show you—all of you—the progress before His Majesty arrives."

The men exchanged glances as the roasted capon was brought out. Non-committal, but not hostile.

More courses followed: a savory pie with a rich and flaking crust, vegetables dressed with butter and herbs, and a macaroni Merryn had never before seen at his table. He began to hope. This might actually work, though he'd yet to gauge Trewyck's stance. The man had said little enough throughout the evening.

At the other end of the table, Killigrew, emboldened by good wine and excellent food, was holding forth to Enys about his latest investment forays.

"The key to sound investing is diligence and concentration," he declared, gesturing with his wine glass. "I have told my son-in-law repeatedly—spreading one's capital across multiple ventures means profiting from none."

Merryn had shared enough conversation with his wife to know she grasped these matters as well as—or better than—any man at his table. The diversification of funds was a principle she employed to protect her ladies' modest savings, spreading their funds across multiple ventures so no single failure could ruin them.

She'd stilled at Killigrew's words, her fork held over her plate. Merryn held his breath, waiting for her to correct the man. In Paris, he suspected she could have turned his comments into a lively discussion, much as she had the squire's ballroom. Cornwall, however, was not Paris.

But the moment passed, and she remained silent. Lifting her wine glass, she took a small sip, finding his gaze along the table with a knowing smile. *This*, he thought. *This* was the secretive look his cousins were going on about. He returned her smile with one of his own.

Rebecca addressed a comment from Enys, and Merryn tucked into his pie, nearly overwhelmed with gratitude for his wife's talents.

She could have asserted her expertise. She could have proven her worth to these men who would never expect a woman to understand such matters. Instead, she had chosen discretion. Though he knew it was silly to think it, he couldn't help feeling she had chosen *him*.

The dessert course arrived to murmurs of wonder and appreciation: a blancmange, though the color was darker than any Merryn had ever seen. Chocolate, he realized, turned out onto crystal serving dishes.

"How elegant," Mrs. Trewyck breathed.

"I have never seen the like," Mrs. Killigrew added.

"It is a French preparation," Rebecca explained,

"though made with the finest English chocolate from Bristol."

The ladies tasted it, and expressions of delight went round the table until Trewyck set down his glass with emphasis.

The sound cut through the pleasant chatter, and everyone fell silent.

Trewyck looked at Merryn. His face reddened. "Kimbrell, I think I have been patient long enough. What have you been playing at, keeping your marriage a secret all this time?"

The words landed like stones in still water. The confrontation Merryn had hoped to avoid was happening anyway, here, in front of everyone.

Trewyck didn't wait for a reply, but continued, his voice rising. "The good ladies of Cornwall ought to know whether a man is eligible or not!"

His wife murmured, "Trewyck, perhaps this is not—"

He ignored her. "Good heavens, man! You danced with my brother's girl in Truro!"

The room fell silent.

The wives looked uncertain, their gazes darting between their husbands and the rigid set of Merryn's shoulders. Enys studied his dessert with an intensity even chocolate couldn't command. Alderton and Killigrew exchanged glances—Merryn was certain they had been warming to him over the course of the evening, but this... this was the scandal at the root of their doubts.

He opened his mouth to say something—to explain, to apologize—but what could he possibly say that would not make things worse?

Before he could speak, Rebecca's clear voice cut through the tension. "Ah, Miss Trewyck! My husband wrote to me of what a delightful young lady she is. He found her conversation most engaging."

Every head swiveled toward Rebecca.

Merryn stared at her. He had written no such thing, and they both knew it.

But some of the wind left Trewyck's sails at her words. His face remained red, but confusion competed with anger now.

"Miss Trewyck..." Enys mused. "She married last spring, did she not?"

Mrs. Killigrew nodded quickly. "Yes, to Sir John Eddy from Penzance. He does quite well for himself, I hear."

"Nearly three thousand a year," Mrs. Enys added.

Trewyck slumped in his chair, though his eyes remained narrow. "Still. Five years—"

"Is an unusual arrangement, certainly." Rebecca's voice remained steady. "But surely we have all known marriages that began a trifle... unconventionally. The important thing is that my husband

and I find ourselves quite ordinary now."

She looked at Merryn as she spoke. Her expression remained composed, but there was a softness in her eyes that he almost believed was real.

He found his voice. "Indeed. I apologize for any confusion. 'Twas never my intention to mislead anyone."

Trewyck harrumphed, but his bluster had subsided.

"I suppose no lasting harm was done," Enys murmured.

The wives began speaking to fill the silence, and Mrs. Killigrew complimented the blancmange again. Mrs. Alderton wondered aloud if her own cook might attempt such a dish. Even Trewyck's high color began to ebb.

Dessert was cleared, and Killigrew, to his wife's frowning displeasure, turned them back to business. "This anonymous investment of yours, Kimbrell—I confess myself curious how you came by such funding. I'm sure we would all feel more secure in our own investments if we knew the source."

There was no mistaking the question in his tone, but Merryn was feeling optimistic. The food had been excellent. The investors seemed open, if not entirely mollified. And his charming wife had handled Trewyck's displeasure so capably.

"It came from someone who knows investments well," he said. "My wife." The words left him before he could consider them.

Faces around the table shifted—confusion, surprise, something approaching disbelief. Finally, Killigrew's furrowed brow smoothed.

"Ah, the mysterious investor was you all along!" he said. "Clever strategy, Kimbrell, using your own funds to make it seem like fresh capital."

Merryn opened his mouth—to correct the man? To agree? He was not sure.

"John," Mrs. Killigrew murmured. "Perhaps such matters might wait until the ladies have withdrawn."

Rebecca rose. "You are quite right, Mrs. Killigrew. I believe it is time to leave the gentlemen to their port."

She led the women from the table, and Merryn watched her go—this wife of his, who would rather be privy to their conversation. Who would rather participate in the discussion as an investor in her own right. In a Paris salon, perhaps she might be able to. But here, she would always be relegated to the drawing room with the other wives.

It was how things were done. The smile she gave him as she closed the door made his heart ache with pride and regret, sadness and hope. His chest hurt in a way his bruised ribs could not account for.

CHAPTER 24

AT LAST, THE final carriage faded into the darkness beyond the window, leaving only the sound of summer crickets in its wake. Rebecca watched as Merryn closed the front door and turned the latch.

The candles in the hall sconces had burned low, their flames guttering in melted wax. Shadows fell across his shoulders. She could not see his face, but there was tension in every line of him.

The long evening had worn them both thin.

She returned to the parlor, where a lamp still burned on the side table. Mrs. Tilbury could put the room to rights on the morrow, but for now, it was blessedly still.

Merryn's footsteps followed her and a moment later, he appeared in the doorway. He tugged at his cravat, loosening it as he strode to the hearth.

He took up the poker, and Rebecca lowered herself onto the settee. She was tired to her bones. She felt keenly the last day of preparation, to say nothing of the last hours' performance. But she would not sleep until she knew what the investors had decided.

The embers stirred at Merryn's prodding, sending up a shower of sparks that briefly illuminated his features before settling into a steadier glow. He added a log from the basket beside the hearth, positioning it carefully. Testing its placement. Adjusting it until it sat just so.

Rebecca's fingers drummed a quiet rhythm against the cushion. She had been patient through the meal's endless courses. She had been patient while Merryn navigated the investors' doubts and Trewyck's outburst. She had been patient when the gentlemen discussed their business over port while she poured tea for their wives.

But patience had its limits.

"Well?" she said.

Merryn straightened from the fire and turned to face her. He rubbed the back of his neck, and the gesture sent a spiral of anxiety through her. Had the gentlemen not been persuaded after all?

Her stomach twisted to think of all that Merryn had worked for, possibly lost for the capricious whims of a few men. She was calculating how quickly she might convert some of her French investments to sterling, composing a letter of instruction to Mr. Cross and wondering if she might use more of her own funds to step into the breach, when he spoke.

"I apologize," he said, "that you could not remain while we discussed business matters."

She nearly laughed. Of all the things she expected him to say, an apology for the natural order of dinner parties was not among them.

"I am not so lost to propriety that I expected to take port with the gentlemen," she said. "But never mind that. What have they decided?"

He was quiet for a moment, his blue eyes catching the firelight. The new log had begun to burn in earnest now, casting warmth across the room and painting everything in shades of amber and gold. She watched his face, trying to read his answer before he spoke.

The corner of his mouth lifted, raising her spirits with it.

"They have agreed not to withdraw their funds," he said.

The triumphant noise that escaped her was unladylike, to say the least. It surprised her as much as it did her husband, but Rebecca could not bring herself to care. She jumped up from the settee and crossed to his side.

"I knew they would," she said. "How could they not? Tell me everything."

He did, recounting the conversation that had followed the ladies' departure. Rebecca listened to the smooth timbre of her husband's voice, her earlier exhaustion falling away.

Killigrew, he said, was happy to follow where the others went.

Enys complimented the quality of both the meal and the company.

"Alderton blustered about the cost, of course."

And Trewyck had made one final complaint about his niece before subsiding into grudging acceptance. Merryn's mouth quirked as he said this, his eyes finding hers with something that might have been appreciation or amusement for the letter he'd never written.

He turned to pace before the fire, his long legs quickly eating up the distance. "But I suspect 'twas his wife's pointed glances throughout dinner which moderated his objections. In the end, he agreed the project appears sound and he sees no reason to withdraw his support."

Rebecca smiled. She had observed the softly-spoken Mrs. Trewyck's pointed glances herself. The woman was not as meek as she appeared.

As the fire cracked and the candles burned down, as the clock on the mantel chimed, Rebecca became aware of the lateness of the hour. The house around them was silent. She and Merryn were alone, much as they'd been that night in her uncle's library. The thought sent a curious ripple along her spine, though she could not have said whether it was anticipation or alarm. Perhaps both.

They had been alone before, of course. They had shared a breakfast table, a carriage, their walks to the cliff. But this felt different. The hour was late, the fire was low, and the requirements of the evening had fallen away. There was an unusual charge to the air.

Merryn stopped his pacing to stand before her. "You were splendid," he said into the silence. "The party you organized—on a day's notice, no less. How you managed the conversation, the way you handled Trewyck... you made everything seem effortless."

She laughed. "It was not effortless, I assure you, though I'm pleased the effect was convincing. But you're mistaken—it was *you* who were splendid. They cannot argue with such an orderly accounting of the project."

He shook his head. "I have hosted dinners with these gentlemen before. They are rarely so agreeable."

She lifted a shoulder. "Perhaps your previous engagements simply lacked a chocolate blancmange."

His smile was genuine. "That they did."

The fire shifted, settling lower. A log broke in two, sending up a brief flare before subsiding. After a moment's contemplation, she said, "We are a formidable pair, are we not?"

Her husband's gaze held hers. "D'you doubt it?"

They were closer now, though she could not recall either of them having moved. Rebecca was acutely aware of her husband. The breadth of his shoulders. The way his loosened cravat exposed the column of his throat. The rough edge to his voice.

Five years before, she'd trusted him enough to marry him. She'd been intrigued by his sharp mind, assured by his quiet confidence and attracted to his pleasing form.

But he'd been a solution to a problem. A gentleman she could respect but did not expect to know.

Now she knew him. She knew the breadth of his shoulders came from laboring alongside his men. She knew the rough edge to his voice appeared only when he was tired or moved.

Her respect for her husband had become something far richer. And far more complicated.

Respect had turned to wanting.

He stood close enough that she could see the rasp of whiskers on his cheek and the lift of his dark hair where he'd disordered it with his hand.

Close enough that she must tilt her head back to meet his gaze. Her pulse quickened at the intensity she found there.

He lifted his hand and brushed a loose curl from her temple. Then, drawing his fingers along her cheek, he traced the line of her jaw. His touch was feather-light, but she felt it all the way to her toes.

"Rebecca."

The way he said her name stole her breath.

A moment later, his mouth found hers.

There was no hesitation in his kiss, no question or careful testing. His lips were warm and firm, his hand coming up to tangle in the curls at her nape. She gripped his coat, the wool bunching in her fists.

He tasted of chocolate and port. His other hand settled heavily at her waist, pressing her closer. The warmth of his palm burned through her layers of silk and stays. The fire popped as her pulse hammered against her ribs.

She leaned into him and returned his kiss.

He made a sound in his throat, and her stomach swooped. His hand loosened her hair, and when her pins hit the carpet, she thought her heart would leap from her chest, so quick was its pace.

The clock continued its steady rhythm, turning seconds into minutes. She didn't know how much time had passed when there was a shuffle at the door, then a faint gasp.

It took a moment for these new sounds to penetrate the blissful haze wrapping Rebecca's awareness. When they did, she drew back in her husband's arms, her breaths uneven.

Beyond his shoulder, she caught the flutter of grey skirts disappearing down the hall. The unmistakable figure of Mrs. Tilbury, whose senses had surely just received a considerable shock at finding her employers so engaged.

Rebecca looked back at Merryn. His breaths were as unsteady as her own, his eyes dark. His fingers remained tangled in her hair. Another pin slipped loose and fell.

A laugh bubbled up from deep in her chest, light and fizzy. She touched shaking fingers to her lips, where the imprint of her husband's kiss still lingered.

"We have been caught," she whispered.

"I cannot be sorry for it." His voice was rough enough to raise gooseflesh on her arms.

"Nor can I."

His hand slid from her hair to her cheek, his thumb inching along the line of her jaw as if he might measure and record the shape of her. She covered his calloused hand with her own smaller one, feeling heat seep from his skin into hers and marveling at how his touch did not reduce her to cinders.

CHAPTER 25

MERRYN WAITED BEHIND a pair of ladies at the post office, content to let his thoughts drift where they would. Truth be told, they had long since slipped their mooring, drifting with ease to the curve of Rebecca's mouth beneath his.

He had visited the pavilion at dawn to approve the final placement of His Majesty's dais. All the while, his mind had wandered back to his own parlor, to the firelight, to his wife's kiss.

It had been this way for the last three days. The final preparations for the King's visit had kept him out until the small hours these past nights. When he did find his bed, sleep eluded him.

The memory of Rebecca's fingers gripping his coat, of the soft sound she made when he drew her closer—to say nothing of the thought of her sleeping on the other side of his wall—all conspired to keep him awake. He'd stared at his ceiling until dawn's pale light crept through the curtains.

Once, he'd gone to the door between their rooms and listened. There was no light coming through, and no sounds beyond the wood. The knob turned beneath his hand. He opened the door to see she slept on her side, the dying fire catching copper in her hair. He'd stopped himself from crossing the threshold, but only just.

Aside from that, he'd seen little of his wife except in passing.

But all was in readiness for His Majesty's arrival. Soon the royal visit would be behind them. He and Rebecca could travel to London, meet with her cousin, and settle this threat to her inheritance once and for all. And then, with Gregory Pearce's challenge resolved, perhaps he might persuade his wife to return with him to Cornwall. A month ago, such a notion would have seemed impossible. Now he thought she might be agreeable to it.

There was still light left in the day. He might see if she would like to walk to the cliff again. Perhaps they might share another kiss as the sun sank into the sea.

"Merryn."

He blinked. The ladies were gone. Cadan stood at the counter with an inquiring expression and a letter in his hand. His cousin had said something, and Merryn was caught smiling at the wall.

He smoothed his expression and took the letter.

"I gather the chocolate met with your wife's approval." Cadan's tone was wry as Merryn paid his postage. "Shall I order more?"

Merryn paused. "Aye," he said lightly. "Bricks of it. Cases, even. I'll buy them all."

Cadan's eyebrows climbed. "Cases? 'Twas that good?"

A laugh escaped him. "Per'aps I'll build a house of the stuff."

His cousin shook his head, and though Merryn knew he sounded ridiculous, he could not care.

Outside, the afternoon sunlight filtered through patchy clouds, and the high street bustled with carts and foot traffic. He turned the letter in his hands, noting the familiar seal of Cross and Jones, Solicitors.

He had written to Nathaniel Cross as soon as Rebecca explained her purpose in Cornwall. The solicitor's opinion on Gregory Pearce's complaint had seemed worth seeking.

He broke the seal, unfolded the pages, and began to read.

His smile faded.

Cross enumerated the arguments Pearce's solicitors would likely make: separate residences, five years of living apart with the Channel between them, and the blasted Newford Inventory. The reasoning was compelling and rather elegantly stated. The man sounded more like counsel for the plaintiff than the defendant.

But it was Cross's closing paragraph that settled cold and heavy in his chest.

Pearce had not been expected to reach England for another fortnight at best, but he'd caught favorable winds. His ship had landed at the West India Docks on Monday. Pearce was back in England, and he'd renewed his inquiries.

The news was not good, but Merryn and Rebecca would manage it together. This new accord between them, whatever it was and whatever it might become, would surely persuade her cousin that his complaint was groundless.

He folded the letter and tucked it into his coat, then strode to where his horse waited. He must tell his wife.

Rebecca reached for another sheet of paper and found the drawer empty. She set down her pen with a soft noise of frustration. She had written again to her investment ladies, but now she must hunt for supplies if she would apprise her aunt of Merryn's dinner party. Tante Eugénie would delight to hear about the chocolate blancmange.

She rose and descended the stairs. Her husband was out attending to all the final details for the King's visit. She had watched him ride off before dawn, his broad shoulders straight and his seat on the horse as assured as everything else he did. It had been all she could do to keep a silly smile from her face these last days.

She paused at the threshold of his library. The room smelled of leather and wood polish and something fainter beneath, perhaps the soap he used. Books lined the walls in neat rows, and papers were stacked on his desk beside a worn leather portfolio. A case clock ticked softly in the corner.

She had no wish to invade her husband's private space, but if she could find his store of paper, she would be in and out in moments. She crossed to his desk and hesitated before pulling open the first drawer. Inside, she found ink, quills, and sealing wax, but no paper. She tried the second.

A bundle of letters lay on the top, tied with a string. She recognized her own handwriting, and her breath caught. Her replies. He had kept them.

She lifted the bundle. The string was slightly frayed at the ends, as if it had been untied and retied. The letters themselves showed similar signs of wear—the folds soft and creased. These were not letters tucked away and forgotten. They had been read, and often, judging by their condition.

Much as she'd taken to reading *his*. She replaced the letters, biting her lip against a smile.

Distracted from her purpose, she was too slow to catch a slim bank book when it slid from the bundle onto the floor. She lifted the book to replace it, but the name on the first entry caught her eye: *R Pearce*. Merryn had drawn a line through her surname and added *Kimbrell*.

R Kimbrell, deposit one thousand pounds. The date she recognized immediately—it was her wedding day. This was where he'd recorded his portion of their bargain.

She should not read further. She knew she should not. But just below that first line was another entry: *Wm Pearce*, deposit two thousand pounds. The date was the same. She blinked and read it again.

Two thousand. Twice what she'd given Merryn.

Her breath left her in a rush. Her husband had made a far better bargain than she had credited. All in all, he'd earned three thousand for the task of marrying her.

A sound at the door made her look up. Merryn stood in the doorway, still in his coat. He carried the post in one hand. His gaze dropped to the bank book she still held.

Heat flooded her face. She had been caught rifling his things. Rather than surrender to the shame of it, she lifted her chin. "I was looking for paper."

"Bottom drawer, right." His voice was even, betraying nothing.

She lifted the bank book. "You are a far shrewder negotiator than I credited." The words came out sharper than she intended, and she regretted them even as she spoke, for she knew Merryn. He was no fortune hunter.

But the evidence in her hands told a different story than the one she had believed.

"'Tis not as it seems," he said.

She strove for an easy tone, though her chest felt tight. "It is not so extraordinary. Many gentlemen marry for money."

"I did not."

His words were flat and final. She perceived pride in the set of his shoulders and the width of his stance.

"Truly." She softened her voice. "I do not think any less of you for it."

He made a noise in his throat, something between frustration and exasperation. "Did you note the balance?"

She frowned and looked down at the book. The initial deposits were there, and the quarterly interest, but the balance at the bottom—

She turned the page then another. The principal remained unchanged. He had not spent a farthing of it. She looked more closely at the entries. Quarterly interest had been added then immediately subtracted. The amounts were eerily similar to the drafts she had received from him each quarter. A pattern emerged, each entry confirming the last.

He had been sending her the interest. All of it. Every quarter for five years. Something melted inside her.

She had not needed the funds—certainly not as much as he might have made use of them. She'd tried returning his first payments, but he would not have them.

"You have been sending me the interest," she said softly. "All these years."

"Aye."

"And I have been investing it." His brows lifted, and she almost laughed at the absurdity of it. "The amount I sent for your royal project—"

He frowned. "'Twas from your trust, you said, and your investment ladies."

"A portion, yes, but the larger balance—it came from your own quarterly drafts."

Something shifted in his expression. "Let me be certain I understand," he said. "You took the funds I sent for your comfort and invested them in… me."

"Yes."

"I have been funding my own project."

"It would appear so."

He pinched the bridge of his nose on a sigh.

"Why?" he asked. "You could have invested in any number of ventures—shipping or textiles. Steam engines, even. Why mine? And none of this nonsense about respectable returns. The truth, this time, if you please."

She eyed him across the desk, weighing her words. Finally, she said simply, "Because you are my husband, and you needed it."

He stared at her, uncomprehending. She looked down at the book in her hands, equally amazed at their mutual stupidity. "You never spent any of it—neither my draft nor my uncle's."

He shook his head. "No."

"But why?" Her voice caught. "You could have grown your father's firm. It is what you wanted. You could be building in Truro by now, or Bath, even."

"My father's firm has grown without it. Slowly, but it has grown."

"But that was our arrangement—"

"Hang the blasted arrangement."

The soft vehemence in his voice startled her into silence.

He moved toward her, crossing the distance in three long strides. "I did not marry you for money. I came to London for capital, yes, but I was not desperate. I married you because I wanted to. I married you—stubborn, foolish woman—because I love you."

The air left her lungs. She stared at him with the bank book forgotten in her hands, unable to speak or move or do anything but stand there as his words reshaped everything she thought she knew.

Every letter he had written. Every quarterly draft. Every inquiry after her welfare—*I trust this letter finds you in good health*—all of it was transformed. What she had taken for duty, for the careful maintenance of their arrangement, had been something else entirely.

She had assumed his restraint came from obligation, from the terms of their agreement, from the practical nature of the man himself.

Now, looking at the fierce expression on his face, she understood. He had been holding his heart in check.

"Why did you never say anything?" Her voice came out barely above a whisper.

Something raw crossed his features before he mastered it. "Would it have made a difference? I saw the longing in you when you spoke of France, of joining your aunt and seeing a bit of the world." His voice roughened. "I would not stand in the way of your desires."

His words landed heavily. What would have happened five years ago if he had spoken? She knew the answer without giving it too much thought.

"I would have stayed, if you had asked."

He cut a sharp glance toward her. "But would you have been happy?"

Ah. She swallowed. His question cut to the very heart of things. "I think I could have been." Then, because honesty compelled her, she added, "For a time, at least."

He rubbed the back of his neck. When he spoke again, his voice was soft, though no less compelling. "And now? Has that changed?"

She stared at him. She knew what he wanted to hear, and part of her wanted desperately to give him the words. But another part held her back. The part that remembered her mother's unhappiness, the way she had grown smaller year by year in a house where she had no choices of her own.

"I do not know."

The expression that crossed his face made her chest ache. She had hurt him, and she could not bear it. She reached a hand toward him. "Merryn—"

But the fragile accord that had been growing between them these past days felt suddenly brittle, stretched too thin, as if it might shatter at the slightest touch. She ached to recall her words and to explain what she could not yet understand herself.

He lifted the letter he carried. His voice, when he spoke, was matter-of-fact, as if he discussed the price of lime and timber.

"Your cousin has arrived in England earlier than anticipated. I suggest you begin packing. We can leave for London as soon as His Majesty's visit is concluded. We will settle this matter with Pearce, and you may return to France." He paused before adding, "If that is your wish."

His words were quiet—Merryn was not one to rely on volume. He turned for the door, but before he could leave her, voices came from the hall. Mrs. Tilbury's familiar tones, and a gentleman's voice. It was vaguely familiar, though she could not place it.

Through the window, she saw a hired carriage on the drive. When had it arrived? How had they not heard it? Her stomach knotted. She had no wish to entertain anyone, and from the look of her husband, neither did he. His expression might have been carved from Cornish granite.

But whatever had passed between them moments ago would have to wait as Mrs. Tilbury appeared in the doorway, slightly breathless from the stairs. She held a calling card.

"Begging your pardon, but there is a gentleman below asking for Mrs. Kimbrell." She glanced at the card. "A Mr. Gregory Pearce."

CHAPTER 26

Rebecca's cousin had taken the most comfortable chair in the parlor. She sat across from him on the settee, the tea service arranged before her on the low table. Behind her, Merryn was at the window, looking out at the carriage on the drive.

He'd insisted on receiving Gregory with her, and despite the awkwardness between them, she thought it was better that they were two against her cousin.

Awkwardness. The word was inadequate. Less than an hour ago, her husband had declared himself, and she'd been unable to return the words. Now they must give the impression of a true marriage for the man who threatened to destroy it.

She studied her cousin as she lifted the teapot. He was tanned from his years abroad, his forehead smooth despite his five-and-thirty years. Though his coat was well-cut, the cuffs showed the faintest bit of wear at the edges. A man stretching his resources, she thought.

There was something of her uncle in the shape of his chin, but little else was familiar. She'd been eleven when Gregory had left his father's home and sailed for the West Indies. He was as much a stranger to her now as the groom walking the horses in the drive.

Why he had come all the way to Cornwall she couldn't fathom. Surely, Mr. Cross had relayed her plans to return to London. If Gregory had only waited another fortnight, he would have been spared the inconvenience of the journey.

He spoke, and she realized she'd missed some of his conversation. "I beg your pardon?"

"I said you're in fine looks, Cousin." He shifted in his chair, and his moustache twitched above his lip. "The Continent seems to agree with you."

His emphasis on her living arrangements was unmistakable. The performance must begin.

She smiled at him. "I do not imagine you can know what agrees with me, Cousin. I was only a girl when last we met. In point of fact, I find Cornwall very much to my liking."

Gregory's nose wrinkled. "Indeed?"

"Oh, yes." She kept her voice light. "Only the other day, my husband and I discussed the merits of Cornwall's wildflowers. Though perhaps you prefer your gardens more disciplined."

Merryn turned from the window at this reminder of their walk on the cliff, his eyes catching hers. He was unsmiling. Of course—he would believe her words were only part of the performance.

"Sugar?" she said, indicating the bowl.

Gregory cleared his throat. "No, I thank you."

He made a comment on the weather as he surveyed the room. His gaze moved from the furnishings to the curtains to the landscape above the mantel. He seemed to be searching for something and not finding it. His fingers drummed once against his knee before he stilled them.

"A pleasant house," he said, though his expression suggested he found it lacking.

"It suits us quite well, though I'm sure it's not as grand as the plantations in Jamaica."

"My home is well appointed," he said without a trace of modesty.

Rebecca turned them to other matters. "How do you find London after so many years abroad?"

"Damp." He paused, seeming to consider his curtness. "And rather changed. I feel a stranger in familiar streets."

Merryn stepped away from the window. "I confess, Pearce, your visit comes at an inconvenient time." It was the first he'd spoken since the introductions were made.

"Does it? Surely, family does not require an invitation."

"Family is always welcome," Rebecca said placatingly. "What my husband means is that you've caught us at sixes and sevens, preparing for His Majesty's arrival."

Gregory nodded. "This royal visit—it is all anyone talked about at the inn." He turned to Merryn. "I gather you've been instrumental in the preparations."

Merryn inclined his head but said nothing further.

"My husband is modest," Rebecca said, "but he has worked tirelessly these past months. The pavilion, the harbor improvements, the roads and bridges—all of it bears the mark of his skill. Newford is fortunate to have him."

She felt Merryn's gaze at this speech. She did not look over at him.

Gregory hummed an agreement, but the sound suggested he was not convinced. Rebecca reached for a second cup for her husband and hesitated. How did Merryn take his tea?

They had breakfasted together these past days. She'd noted his preference, but now the knowledge scattered. Sugar? Milk? She could not recall.

Gregory's gaze sharpened at her hesitation. "Is something the matter?"

"Not at all." Smiling, she added one lump of sugar from the bowl. Then another. She stirred and offered the cup to her husband.

His eyes met hers as he took a sip. There was a flicker of something there that only she could see — amusement, perhaps, or alarm. Now she remembered: milk, no sugar.

But he only smiled, doing nothing that might give away her error.

Rebecca clasped her hands to steady them, for Gregory watched her with a speculation she did not like. Merryn must have seen it too. He set his cup aside and addressed her cousin.

"You've traveled a long way, Pearce. What is your business in Cornwall?"

Rebecca exhaled her relief for her husband's directness. Perhaps now, they might get to the heart of the matter.

Gregory's countenance showed a flash of irritation before he hid it. "You are very plain-spoken, Kimbrell. But perhaps I am only accustomed to the slower pace of things in Kingston."

"There's much yet to address before His Majesty's arrival on the morrow," Merryn said. "If you've come with something to say to my wife, I suggest you go on with it."

Gregory set down his tea and crossed his legs. "Very well. I had hoped for a moment alone with my cousin. I've a matter of import to discuss with her."

"You may discuss your matter with the both of us or not at all," Merryn said.

Rebecca frowned, irritated by his presumption even while she was intrigued by his fierceness. Then she recalled their performance. Recovering her smile, she said to her cousin, "Please, won't you tell us why you have come?"

"Your husband's high-handed manner is rather the point of it. But if you insist, then very well: I have come to stand as your protector. As the only remaining male of your father's line, it falls to me to ensure you have not been ill-used."

Rebecca choked. "I beg your pardon?"

Gregory uncrossed his legs and stood, moving to examine the items on the mantelpiece. "I confess, Cousin, I always thought my uncle was rather close-fisted with you. A modest trust, my father said. Enough to keep you comfortable but nothing extraordinary." He paused, his hand resting on a small porcelain figurine. "When I learned the true sum…" He shook his head. "Ten thousand pounds. Certainly, you should not have been left unprotected."

Rebecca's stomach fell. Nathaniel Cross had been right. Whatever papers the solicitor had sent on to Gregory, they had brought her cousin back to England. Part of her had hoped they were wrong, that the last weeks had been much ado about nothing.

To Merryn, Gregory added, "I find the circumstances of your marriage to my cousin troubling, to say the least."

"Your father consented to the match."

Gregory turned from the mantel. "Did he? Or might a dying man, desperate and vulnerable and fearing for his ward, have been easily persuaded? I take no pleasure in suggesting it, but the circumstances demand scrutiny."

Rebecca was moved to protest. "You go too far!"

"On the contrary. I regret that I did not go far enough five years ago. I would have, had I known what was afoot. You were understandably grief-stricken over my father's illness and worried for your future, as any tender-hearted lady would be. This man"—he gestured to Merryn—"offered a solution. A marriage that would win your inheritance before it could be properly safeguarded. Without his intervention, I would have become your trustee. I would have protected you from fortune hunters."

"You were abroad," Merryn interjected. "You could hardly have served in such a role from the other side of the world."

"I would have returned." Gregory's smile was thin. "I assure you, Cousin, had I known of your situation, had my father or his solicitor written to me, I would have come to your aid much sooner."

Rebecca imagined that many would have crossed

oceans for ten thousand pounds. She now recognized Gregory's earlier scrutiny of her husband's parlor for what it was: a man searching for signs of extravagance and finding none.

Good. Let him see his error.

She knew his true aim now. He meant to paint himself as her indignant protector, the dutiful heir returned to right a wrong—all while positioning himself to control her trust.

She had wondered how he meant to couch his argument, for he couldn't simply claim his trustee duty without some pretense of proper concern. Only her marriage stood between him and her inheritance.

Rebecca lifted her chin. "You presume too much. I'm sorry you have come such a distance, but I have no need of your aid, I assure you."

Gregory reached into his coat and produced a folded news sheet. *The Newford Inventory*. "I know you think yourself well-protected by your marriage, but I regret to be the bearer of unsavory news: your husband has been putting himself about as a bachelor while you live alone in France."

"I have hardly been alone," she said. "I have enjoyed my aunt's home, but that is neither here nor there. Many couples live separately. They are no less married for it."

Gregory waved a hand to indicate Newford beyond the window. "I suppose it was funds from your inheritance that paid for all these improvements. When my father died, I should have guided you and seen you properly settled. Instead, my father, incapacitated by his illness and manipulated by false promises, consented to a sham marriage." He shook his head. "For that, I am truly sorry."

Merryn remained motionless at the window, but Rebecca could imagine the turmoil roiling inside of him, for she felt it herself.

"It was nothing like that," she said. "*Merryn* is nothing like that."

But by their own actions, they had created exactly the picture her cousin painted. The funds Merryn received through their marriage *had* paid for his royal project, though not in the way her cousin meant. Her husband had taken pains to avoid spending her money, but in a ridiculous irony, he'd done just that with her anonymous investment.

She stared at him, feeling helpless against her cousin's accusations.

But Gregory was not finished. He reached into a leather portfolio and produced a sheaf of papers.

"I have made this simple for you, Cousin."

He placed two identical documents on the table and slid one across. She did not pick it up, though she could read the words clearly enough: *Petition for Annulment*.

Something hot turned in her stomach. Her gaze shot to Merryn, whose expression was thunderous. He stood with his hands behind him, feet braced. She imagined the strength of will that kept him silent, but she had come to know her husband. He would want to hear the full extent of Gregory's argument so they might better defend against it.

Her cousin seemed only too willing to oblige.

"My solicitor has drawn up this petition," he said. "It argues lack of valid consent due to undue influence upon a dying man, and lack of genuine intent to form a marital union. I have taken the liberty of having two copies prepared—one for you, Cousin, and one for Mr. Kimbrell. Your signature here is all that's needed, though should you both sign, the matter would proceed all the more smoothly."

It was a long moment before Rebecca could speak. When she did, her voice was incredulous. "You cannot expect me to sign this."

"Cousin Rebecca. This marriage is a fraud. Sign the petition, and you will be free to pursue your happiness elsewhere."

"Free to become your dependent?" Merryn's voice was low.

"I would become her trustee, as I should have been these last five years. Naturally, I would receive a trustee's compensation—a modest sum, to be sure.

More importantly, I will ensure her funds are properly invested and protected." Gregory straightened. "I will guide her to a more suitable match, someone of her own station. Or she may remain unwed if that is her wish. It is barbaric in this age to expect a lady to endure an unwanted marriage simply for want of proper guidance. We live in more enlightened times."

Rebecca's hands fisted in her lap. Her eyes were hot with anger. "I am aware that you need money," she said. "Your holdings in Jamaica are failing, and it's rumored you have lost a rather large cargo these last months."

A ruddy flush stained her cousin's cheeks. He looked away briefly before meeting her eyes again. "My own ventures have no bearing on my concern for your welfare."

She flicked a glance at the papers on the table. "And if I do not sign?"

Gregory's face hardened. She could not tell if the shift was caused by fear or determination. Perhaps a little of both. The combination sent alarm winging through her.

"I should not like to do this," he said with a shake of his head. "I do not wish to see you suffer, but if you cannot see the danger of your position, I shall have no alternative but to make the circumstances of your situation—of Mr. Kimbrell's dishonorable actions—known."

The words hung in the silence before he added, unnecessarily, "The scandal of it would be considerable. I suspect His Majesty has little tolerance for such behavior, especially given his own marital troubles. Even should the scandal escape royal notice, I imagine the effect on Mr. Kimbrell's future prospects would be rather dampening."

A chill spread through Rebecca's limbs, settling in her fingers and toes. Gregory's threat was clear. Merryn's reputation, his livelihood, everything he had built, would be ruined.

Her husband stated his objection more plainly. "'Tis extortion."

"It is merely concern for my cousin's welfare. Sign the petition, and we can end this quietly."

"My husband and I are content in our marriage," Rebecca said evenly. "No one will believe your accusations."

Gregory's lips pressed thin. "Perhaps not. But they will certainly talk about them."

"My wife is not signing." Merryn's voice was quiet but absolute.

"Mr. Kimbrell, I am attempting to spare my cousin an unfortunate situation—"

"Of your making."

"Of *yours*!" Gregory drew a breath and regained mastery of his emotions. "You may have the night to think it over. I will await your answer in the morning."

Rebecca shook her head. "I need a week at the very least."

Merryn angled a glance at her, his brows pulled low. She had no intention of yielding to her cousin's demands, but they needed time to sort this. And with a week's delay, His Majesty would be halfway across Devon. Any discomfort caused by her cousin could not affect the royal visit.

Gregory considered this, his tongue poking at his upper lip before he shook his head. "A day. I will allow that much, but understand, if you have not signed by the King's ball, I must make my concerns known. I leave the choice in your hands, Cousin."

He rubbed his own hands together. "Now then, I shall require accommodation. I inquired at the Feather and Fin—"

"Fin and Feather," Rebecca corrected dully.

"—but they are quite full up."

Rebecca's stomach fell even further. They would have to house her cousin.

Gregory looked about as if gauging the size of the house. "Surely you've a room available? I could take lodgings in Truro, but the expense, you see... And how odd would it appear if Rebecca Pearce's relation does not stay in her husband's home?"

With what remaining grace she could muster, Rebecca stood. "I am Rebecca *Kimbrell*, Cousin. You would do well to remember it. But of course, I shall see that a guest chamber is readied."

He smiled. "I promise not to be any trouble."

Rebecca turned to Merryn. Her husband's arms had been crossed for so long she feared they might break if he unfolded them. "Perhaps you might summon Jem to assist my cousin with his trunks."

"He can manage his own trunks."

"Ah, that is quite all right," Gregory said. "What time do we dine?"

Across from her, Merryn's jaw worked as Rebecca's own irritation climbed. "We keep country hours," she said, resigned. "Dinner is at seven."

CHAPTER 27

MERRYN LIT ANOTHER branch of candles in his study as the first ones had all but gone out. He sat at his desk with Pearce's petition spread before him, reading the same paragraph for the fourth time. The grounds for annulment were false—he had *not* exerted influence, undue or otherwise, over a dying man. But the rest of what Pearce would say, the facts he would trumpet before anyone willing to listen, those were harder to dismiss.

It was true they had married to secure Rebecca's inheritance. At least in part. Immediately after, Rebecca had left for France, and he for Cornwall.

He had allowed his name to be listed in the blasted Inventory. The funds he'd gained through the marriage had been used for his royal project, however ironically.

All of these things were true. None of his actions were dishonorable in and of themselves, but combined, they presented a pattern that her cousin was only too willing to exploit. Pearce's petition might fail in court, but his accusations did not need to succeed to ruin them both.

But the worst of it, the fact that caused an unending tightness in his chest, was this: if Rebecca signed Pearce's petition, she would be precisely back where she had started. Until she reached thirty, her funds, and consequently her independence, would be at the mercy of a man who had no interest in preserving either. And with Pearce controlling her allowance, she would have no alternative but to marry again—or to wed Pearce himself, if Merryn's suspicions about her cousin's motives were even close to the mark.

She'd warned him of her cousin's return. He ought to have anticipated Pearce's scheme, but he'd allowed himself to become complacent. He'd been courting his wife when he should have been protecting her. His head ached, and Cook's fish pie sat heavy in his stomach.

The meal had been an exercise in forbearance with Pearce's none-too-subtle probing about their courtship, their wedding, their years apart, seeking any crack he might use to bolster his case. Rebecca had neatly turned his questions back on her cousin, inquiring about his time in Jamaica until the man's expression soured.

More than once, Merryn had been tempted to leave or throw the man out, but he'd been unable to do either without making matters worse. And so, he'd contributed terse answers when pressed, until slowly, he became grateful for the years of quarterly correspondence that had given them something to draw upon.

He and Rebecca knew more about one another's habits than he would have believed. She knew he had a weakness for his cousin's raspberry tarts. He knew cats made her sneeze.

And when conversation turned to books, he recalled she preferred plays to novels. Indeed, one of her favorite lines was from Julius Caesar: *The fault, dear Brutus, is not in our stars, but in ourselves.*

When she'd shared the line with him that night in her uncle's library, he'd felt both admiration and sadness for how perfectly it fit his wife and her determination to go off and make her own fate. It was the line by which she lived her life, and he was no less convinced of it now.

When he'd relayed her fondness for the theater to her cousin, she caught his eye across the table. Her expression softened, and he wondered if she, too, recalled their wedding night conversation. For a moment, Pearce had disappeared, and it was as if the two of them dined alone.

The clock on the mantel chimed eleven. Merryn

rubbed his eyes and turned to the next page of the petition. There must be a way through this.

Presently, he heard steps in the hall, and Rebecca appeared in the doorway. "May I join you?"

"Of course."

She closed the door softly behind her and came before his desk, nearly the same place she'd been mere hours ago. It seemed an age since he'd spoken of love. The memory brought a warmth to his neck for his candor, and her uncertain reply when he had pressed her. *I do not know.*

Neither of them mentioned it now.

"Dinner was…" she began.

"Excruciating."

The corner of her mouth lifted. "Abominable."

The room fell silent again, and he did not know how to fill it.

Rebecca licked her lips. "We should discuss what we mean to do."

He nodded at the papers on his desk. "I have been reviewing his petition."

"And?"

"The argument is thorough."

She lifted it from his desk, turning the pages. He watched her face as she read, saw the furrow deepen between her brows. He worried what she might be thinking, and when she gave a little sigh of resignation, his worry grew.

"If I sign this," she began.

"No."

"—it may be settled quietly. There would be talk, of course, but the scandal would be far less than if we allow my cousin to spread his tales."

"No," he repeated.

She set the papers down. "You could claim you were deceived as well. That it was *I* who used you to gain my inheritance rather than the other way round. That is far closer to the truth, though I hope you do not see it in such an unflattering light. But your reputation would be clear—"

He went around the desk to her. "And what of you? Your trust would fall to Pearce's management until your thirtieth birthday, at which time there may not be any of't left. He would be your guardian in deed, if not in fact. You would be under his will for all practical intents. Subject to his decisions about where you live, whether you marry. *Who* you marry."

"I know what it means."

"Then you know I cannot allow it."

She tilted her head back to meet his gaze, and he saw the spark in her dark eyes. "You speak as though I require your permission."

"Rebecca—"

"You cannot prevent me from signing it."

He tugged his cravat, loosening the knot that

seemed to grow ever tighter. "On the contrary. I am your *husband*, whether you desire it or not." He knew his mistake as soon as the words were out, but he could not stop them.

"And that is rather the point!" Her voice climbed. "You would forbid me from signing a paper that would free me of you—yet the moment I sign it, your claim over me ceases—which means it cannot exist to stop me."

"It ceases only if a court is persuaded to say so." His own voice rose to meet hers. He lowered it to a harsh whisper, conscious of the man upstairs who would not scruple to listen to every word.

She moved closer, her color high. "You cannot claim a power that would be undone by the very act you forbid."

"I claim the power the law presently grants me," he said. "You speak of what may come. I speak of what stands now. And *now*, we are married in the eyes of the church."

"But—"

"Rebecca." He closed his eyes and squeezed his temples. A part of him wished to continue their argument, if only to watch her sharp mind dissect his logic. Under different circumstances, he could debate with her until dawn and count it time well spent. But they had no such luxury.

"We can argue in circles all night," he said. "But

at the end of't, I will not allow you to deliver yourself into Pearce's hands. He won't be content as your trustee. He'll deny you what's yours until you have no choice but to marry him. Is that what you want?"

Her shoulders dropped a little. "No."

"Then do not sign it. Regardless of your feelings for me, I am the better choice."

Above them, the floorboards creaked as Pearce settled in his room. Neither of them moved until the sound faded.

"You are the *only* choice," she said at last.

He stilled, uncertain of her meaning. Her words could be taken to mean any number of things. That she had no other options available to her. That he was the lesser evil. That—

"But if I refuse to sign," she went on, "Pearce will ruin you. You'll lose your business, your family's investments. Everything."

"Then we must convince him—and anyone else—that his accusations are baseless."

"How?"

"Pearce argues the marriage lacked proper consent from the start. That I manipulated a dying man into consenting to the union."

She considered. "The elder Mr. Cross drew up the settlements. He witnessed our intentions and knew my uncle's mind." Her face fell. "But, of course, he has been dead these two years."

"Perhaps his son kept his papers—"

She shook her head. "What was not sent to my cousin in Jamaica was lost in a fire." She pressed her fingers to her temples before looking up. "What can we do in only a day?"

Merryn hated the note of dejection threading her voice. Behind him, the clock ticked and beyond the window, an owl called.

"We do what we planned from the start," he said. "When you first arrived in Cornwall."

"We play our parts."

"We show the world we are married," he corrected. "When His Majesty arrives, we stand together in the pavilion."

"It will not prove our intent five years ago."

"No. But it proves our intent now. If nothing else, 'twill weaken your cousin's accusations." He paused. "From Pearce's manner, his need seems rather urgent. If his accusations lose strength, perhaps he will know his efforts are futile."

"Do you think he will simply abandon this?"

"No. But I think he will negotiate."

"It does not sound like much of a plan."

He couldn't disagree, but it was all he'd been able to devise in the hours since Pearce's arrival. Tomorrow, he would meet with his cousins. Perhaps some of their inquiries into the man's dealings had borne fruit.

Another creak came from the room above. They fell silent, waiting until the footsteps stilled, then she turned to go.

"Rebecca."

She paused at the door and looked back.

"The two thousand pounds from your uncle—'twas never my expectation, never my intention to profit from our marriage beyond what you and I agreed to."

Her expression softened, and she shook her head. "I know."

Her words eased a bit of the tightness in him. Still, he needed to explain. "His draft came from Cross after I returned to Cornwall. He said your uncle wished there had been more time to draw up proper settlements. If I had known, I would have refused."

"Instead, you sat with it untouched, save for sending the interest to me."

He gave a short nod. There were many more things he wanted to say, but the words caught in his throat, trapped by his inability to solve this for her.

He said only, "We shall find a way, Rebecca. I will not let Pearce take what is yours."

"Husband," she said, "I fear you are far too honorable."

Then she slipped through the door and was gone.

CHAPTER 28

THE NEXT MORNING, Rebecca paced the rug in her room. Gregory's petition lay on the dressing table where she'd left it the night before, having read and re-read the thing until the words swam on the page. She suspected her husband had done much the same after she'd left him.

The document was unassuming in its brevity. Gregory's threat was not.

His ridiculous allegations painted her husband in the worst possible light when their marriage had been her notion from the start. Their separation, her doing. She did not think her cousin's claims would hold up under scrutiny, but it was the scrutiny that concerned her. Scrutiny that could ruin her husband, for gossip cared little for truth.

The night before, she'd confided her cousin's scheme to Sarah, who'd listened with wide eyes and a tight mouth.

But her governess-turned-companion, a woman who'd stood her mother for longer than Rebecca's own parent, had been able to offer little more than a willing ear and the comforting press of her hand.

This matter was for her to sort.

From Merryn's chamber came the creak of floorboards, the scrape of a wardrobe door. Rebecca listened to the familiar sounds of his morning, the heavy tread of his boots crossing the room, the splash of water. Since her arrival in his home, she had grown accustomed to his sounds.

His footsteps moved into the hall and descended the stairs. She listened to them cross the landing below, but they didn't go into the breakfast room as she expected. Instead, she heard the front door open and close.

Rebecca went to the window, drawing the curtain aside. Below, in the pale light of early morning, Merryn swung onto his horse and rode down the drive. She watched until he disappeared from view.

Of course he must go. The royal barge would arrive today. She could hardly expect him to tarry here when there must be a hundred details that required his attention. And yet, she felt his absence as if she'd removed a warm cloak on a winter's night. When had his presence become so essential to her comfort?

She let the curtain fall and sank onto the stool before her dressing table. Her reflection showed a woman still in her wrapper, face pale from a restless night.

She had made her hasty flight from England five years before to secure her independence, believing their arrangement would serve them both. She had built a life in Paris on that foundation. But now, faced with her cousin's threat, she saw the trap clearly.

If she did not sign Gregory's petition, then her husband would lose his reputation.

And if she did, she would most certainly lose her independence—and her marriage.

Both outcomes seemed impossible to bear. But what course was there if they were to emerge unscathed? It seemed the only way through was to persuade her cousin from his scheme—a daunting prospect, to say the least.

She folded the petition and tucked it into her dressing table. Unaccountably, her maid's words came back to her: *I am free so long as I think I am.*

Would that things could be so simple.

REBECCA ENTERED THE breakfast room with Sarah to find Gregory with a plate of eggs and squab pie before him. He'd taken her husband's place at the table, and—she sniffed—he was drinking her chocolate. He rose at their entrance.

"Good morning, Cousin. Miss Denning."

Rebecca checked her frown. Nothing could come of showing her frustration. If she meant to turn Gregory from his course, she would need patience—and a steadier hand than anger could provide.

"Good morning," she replied evenly. She moved to the sideboard with Sarah, grateful for the task of filling her plate. Toast, jam, chocolate—simple fare for an uncertain stomach.

They took their seats. For several minutes, the only sounds were the clink of cutlery until Gregory spoke. "Your husband departed early. I heard him in the passage."

"There's much to attend to before His Majesty's arrival." Rebecca put blackcurrant jam on her toast with more attention than the task required.

Gregory tucked into his pie with the same fervor with which he'd enjoyed his dinner the night before. It made her wonder what manner of accommodation he'd enjoyed on his travels.

"This project of his," he continued, "it is quite the undertaking for a man of his station."

Ah, the first volley. Sarah stilled, cup halfway to her lips as Rebecca set down her knife. This was how he meant to begin. Very well.

"My husband is an accomplished builder. His

achievements have gained the trust and respect of many."

Gregory nodded, chewing. He swallowed before speaking again, his tone almost casual. "My solicitor made inquiries into his affairs. I wished to know more of this man who married my cousin so precipitously."

Rebecca's hand stilled on her cup. "If you've made inquiries, then you must already be aware of my husband's sterling reputation."

His mouth twisted. "Do you wish to know what my solicitor found?" When she only answered him with a frown, he went on. "It is nothing so bad. Quite the opposite, in fact. Kimbrell has done well for himself. This royal project of his has enhanced his reputation beyond this backwater. I heard mention of possible commissions in Bath. London, even. Your husband has ambitions."

"There is no fault in that. Surely, you must have aims of your own."

He took a mouthful of egg, chewed and swallowed. "You mistake my point. I meant only that it would be a shame if such promising opportunities were suddenly closed to him."

His threat landed precisely as it was meant to do.

Sarah's cup clinked against her saucer, and Rebecca looked at her cousin properly now. The morning light coming through the windows revealed what shadows had concealed the day before: the deeper lines at the corners of his eyes, the slight tremor in his hand when he reached for his chocolate. His fashionable cravat was tied in the latest style, but the knot sat slightly off-center—understandable, as he'd brought no valet with him.

A man stretched thin, she thought again. That he had arrived in Cornwall without a valet was unusual for a gentleman of his standing. Neither her father nor her uncle had ever done without a man to assist them. Was Gregory's situation even more desperate than she'd imagined? Even without her funds, he would have had a substantial inheritance from his father. Surely, he had not lost all of it?

Vaguely, she recalled the occasion of his departure to the West Indies. She'd been too young at the time to fully understand what had driven her cousin from England. Creditors, she'd heard later, but now she had a glimpse of the young man who had sailed for Jamaica with his father's disappointment on his shoulders.

Something in her chest eased—not toward pity, exactly, but recognition.

"Your father cared for you," she said.

Whatever response Gregory had expected to his threat, it was not this. His hands stilled above his plate. "I beg your pardon?"

Rebecca set down her chocolate. "He spoke of

you, even after—" She stopped herself.

"Even after I disappointed him." Gregory's voice had lost its smooth edge.

For a moment, neither of them said anything. Sarah, who'd always had good timing and better discretion, rose and busied herself at the sideboard.

"You say my father spoke of me, and yet, he refused to lend his aid when I appealed to him. Instead, he gave two thousand pounds to a fortune hunter." He cut her a sideways glance. "Do you know of his payment to your husband?"

Rebecca hid a frown, aware that had her cousin come a day sooner, she would have been obliged to lie. "I do," she said, "though I am curious that you know of it."

"There was some mention in my father's papers from Cross," he said. His shoulders fell, and he returned his attention to his breakfast.

"My husband has not spent it, you know."

Gregory frowned, though he did not look up. "The more fool, him."

As he finished his pie, she chose her words. "I understand your situation at Jamaica is not what it once was," she said carefully. "What has happened?"

He would not meet her eyes. He swallowed, his voice rough as he answered. "Bad weather. Worse partners. Spanish privateers." His laugh held no humor. "Choose whichever you like. It doesn't really matter. The result is the same."

"It matters that you are family."

Something shifted in his expression. "Then help me, Rebecca." His voice dropped. "Sign the petition. We can both walk away from this. You'll have your portion when you reach thirty, and I—" He stopped, then continued more carefully. "Naturally, as your trustee, I would be entitled to reasonable fees for managing your affairs. Nothing extraordinary, but perhaps enough to discharge my more immediate obligations."

There was an eagerness in his eye, and she perceived what her cousin could not bring himself to admit. His need would not be satisfied with only his fees. If her inheritance were given to his control, he would use it to settle his debts, to chase some new venture that might restore his fortunes. And when the money ran out, when she had nothing left to her, then what? She could hardly count on him to support a penniless relation.

"I'm afraid I cannot do that, Cousin."

His expression closed like a heavy oak door. Gone was the vulnerability she'd glimpsed in him, replaced with a hardness she could not like.

"Then I hope you take pleasure in the day's festivities." He dabbed at his mouth with a serviette and rose. "They may be the last events your husband enjoys as a man of good standing."

Her own voice took on an edge as her ire climbed. "You know your claims are baseless," she said. "My husband is an honorable man, but you would see him ruined to save yourself?"

"Happily." He bowed, a mockery of courtesy. "If you will excuse me, I've a mind to see a bit of your high street before the King's address." He paused. "You will secure my admission to the pavilion, I trust, and your squire's ball? It would be rather awkward to be relegated to the onlookers with my cousin's husband so intimately involved."

She took a breath before answering. It was on the tip of her tongue to refuse, but she had no wish to antagonize him any further. "You shall have your admission, Cousin."

He left, and when the door closed behind him, the room felt suddenly larger. Sarah rejoined her at the table with a fresh cup of tea.

"My dear," she began then fell silent.

Rebecca managed a feeble smile, though her throat closed as she looked at Merryn's empty place. They sat for a long moment in the quiet that followed, neither speaking, the breakfast dishes growing cold as Sarah sipped her tea.

Rebecca's chest felt impossibly tight, as if her stays were laced with steel rather than satin. She had built a life in Paris that was her own, cultivating her investments like a garden, certain they were the soil in which her freedom would flourish.

But in her pursuit of her independence, she had failed to acknowledge what she'd left behind. Or who, rather.

She loved her husband.

The recognition was not new. It had begun five years before, driving her from England with haste and growing with each quarterly letter. But since her arrival in Cornwall, it had been gathering, like a storm on the horizon.

It was there in the way Merryn's sure presence steadied her, and her pride in watching him command a situation. In the delight she found debating with him and simply hearing about his day.

But sitting here now, with her cousin's petition upstairs and Merryn's absence filling the house, pretense was no longer possible. She had sought her freedom by marrying him and found herself bound all the same.

But what a contrary creature she was! To have kept her marriage at bay for so long, only to learn now, of all times, how desperately she wanted it.

"Sarah," she whispered, her breath catching. "I do not want to end my marriage."

Her companion's smile was far wider than the grim situation warranted. "Then you should not."

"But I cannot let Gregory ruin my husband's

prospects. Merryn has worked too hard, and he is too honorable to be subjected to my cousin's accusations—the irony of it is too much."

Sarah's hand covered Rebecca's. "You will find a way," she said. "You are not without resources."

Rebecca looked down, considering, then back to her companion. She had resources, Sarah was right about that. Her investments, her Paris accounts. Resources enough to solve this problem, if only she could see how.

But perhaps the question was not *how* to solve it, but *what* she was willing to surrender to protect her husband. The answer was surprisingly simple: anything.

Something loosened in her chest, and she felt, for the first time, Marie's words: *I am free so long as I think I am.*

CHAPTER 29

A CART RATTLED past on the high street beyond the window, and two more swiftly followed. Newford was awake and preparing for His Majesty's arrival.

"Pearce means to ruin me," Merryn said.

His cousins stilled as they took their places—James behind his desk, Gavin in his constable stance near the door, Jory at the bookshelf. The morning was still early enough that the bank's usual custom had not yet begun.

"He intends to accuse me of fraud and see my marriage annulled." He kept his voice even as he relayed Pearce's claim that Merryn had taken advantage of a dying man's worries to secure Rebecca's inheritance for himself.

His cousins' expressions shifted as he spoke, moving swiftly from confusion to incredulity to anger on his behalf. Though Merryn was grateful for their unquestioning loyalty, he couldn't forget that

Pearce's arguments were precisely what James had predicted.

"You were right," he said to James. "When I first told you of my marriage, you laid out your concerns. They were all sound."

"Would that they weren't," James muttered.

Merryn released a breath. He hoped his cousins' inquiries into Pearce's affairs had turned up something useful. "What have you learned?"

Gavin exchanged a glance with Jory. "We still have a number of inquiries out, but Jory and I spoke with a factor who does business with the Jamaica trade. He knew the Pearce name—said the father held title on a plantation near Kingston. It passed to his son on his death five years ago, but the property's been sold long since."

"Sold?" Merryn's attention sharpened.

"And not well, from what we gather. The factor heard rumors of debts—gambling, mostly. Said the younger Pearce tried to keep the place running, but…" Gavin shrugged. "The market for sugar—'tis not what it once was. Too much competition from the east now."

"Aye," Jory said, continuing their report. "The factor also said Pearce arrived in London on a merchant vessel. Paid his passage in coin—Spanish dollars. Not the usual way for a gentleman to travel."

"No letters of credit?" James asked.

"None," Jory confirmed.

"You said he arrived with only a single trunk?" James asked Merryn.

"Aye."

The room fell quiet as they absorbed this. A man with only one trunk had either gone in haste or had little left to carry.

Merryn pressed his boot against a board in the bank's oak floor—the same board he'd sent one of his men to repair some weeks before. He was pleased to see it held firm, though his mind remained fixed on what his cousins had discovered.

A plantation sold. Debts in Jamaica. Passage paid in coin rather than credit. One trunk.

"Pearce is desperate," he said aloud. He'd suspected as much the day before, but now he was certain.

"Then he's dangerous," James said quietly.

Merryn nodded and clasped his hands behind him, thinking. "He has been living a lie," he mused. "He's gone about as if he still has a plantation, as if he's a gentleman of means. But if others were to know the truth of his circumstances…"

Jory's brow lifted. "You mean to counter his threat with one of your own."

"If he persists in his scheme, I'll make it known he's angling for my wife's inheritance to save himself."

"It could work," Gavin said slowly. "A man in his position cannot afford to have his circumstances known. He'd lose what little standing he has left."

James tapped his pen against the ledger before him. "'Tis a gamble. What if he calls your bluff? What if he presses forward anyway, thinking scandal to you is worse than embarrassment to him?"

Merryn's jaw tightened. James was right. Who could say what lengths a desperate man might go?

Jory drummed his fingers on his elbow. "If threats don't move him, we could pay him."

"Pay him?" Gavin's voice held distaste.

"I cannot like it either," Jory said. "But if we offered enough that he could return to Jamaica or start fresh elsewhere—per'aps he'd take it and be gone."

James nodded. "Men in his position often act from desperation rather than malice. If his need is met…"

"He'd have no reason to persist with his scheme," Gavin finished, though his expression remained doubtful.

Their discomfort was plain. None of them liked the idea of rewarding such a man. Merryn's own stomach turned at the thought, but if it kept Rebecca safe, it was a course worth considering.

"How much would it take," Jory asked, "to satisfy a man like Pearce?"

"Two thousand, at the least," James said. "Three or four per'aps, depending on the extent of his debts."

"We'll gather what we can. I don't know that we've enough between us, but amongst our cousins—"

"No." Merryn's voice was firm. "I'll not take your money for this."

"You cannot manage so much on your own," Gavin protested.

"'Tisn't a question of managing it." Merryn drew in a breath. "If't comes to paying the man, I have the funds."

The silence that followed was profound. Jory straightened. Gavin's arms uncrossed, and James's quill, which had been scratching notes, went still.

"You have—" James began.

"Three thousand pounds," Merryn said. He hesitated before adding, "At Coutts in London."

"Coutts," James repeated. Something—hurt or irritation, perhaps—crossed his face before he mastered it.

Merryn grimaced. "I should have moved it," he admitted quietly. "But I never intended to use it—"

James waved a hand. "We can discuss later why you've been holding funds at another bank."

"Three thousand?" Jory's voice held the incredulity of a man who'd just learned his cousin had been hoarding a king's ransom.

Gavin shifted his stance. "I beg your pardon if 'tis an impertinent question, but how the devil did you come by three thousand pounds?"

Merryn could well understand his cousins' shock. The Kimbrell family was not pockets to let by any stretch—his grandfather had done well in the free trade until his sons legitimized their fortunes through honest work—but three thousand was a rather large number.

And so he told them of William Pearce's unexpected payment on top of the bargain he'd made with his wife.

"And you never touched it?" James asked. "*Any* of't?"

"'Course he never touched it," Gavin said.

James leaned forward. "But 'tis yours to spend as you wish."

Merryn sighed. How could he explain that spending Pearce's money, much less the portion from his wife, would have felt… wrong? That it had been pride, not right, that had kept him from it?

"It didn't seem… fitting."

"His wife left," Gavin said slowly.

"Ah," Jory's brow smoothed as understanding dawned. Both Gavin and Jory had some experience with this, though their wives had had the grace to depart *before* the marriage.

James, the bachelor among them and a man who traded money for his living, only stared. The room fell quiet. Outside, a dog barked and more carts moved past the window.

"So you're prepared to offer Pearce three thousand to withdraw his petition," Jory said finally. "As a last resort."

"Aye," Merryn said slowly. If he wasn't warming to the notion, he was at least coming round to it. "Pearce's need is urgent. I cannot think he'd refuse three thousand now on the hopes of more later. Not when it could take weeks—months, even—for a court to hear his petition for annulment, and then more time yet for him to gain control of my wife's funds."

They were quiet as they took this in. Finally, James nodded. "If you're certain…"

"I am."

"I'll arrange for a letter of credit. 'Twill take the better part of a day."

James made a note then set his pen aside. "But whether you threaten Pearce with exposure or offer him payment, you'll still be at his mercy. What's to stop him from returning in six months with new demands?"

The question landed heavily. It was precisely the question that gave Merryn pause. He'd been turning it over in his mind since last night, when the notion of buying Pearce's silence had first occurred to him. Such a man would not simply disappear because Merryn wished it.

"Nothing," he admitted. "Which is why neither option sits well with me."

Jory released an exasperated sound and turned to Gavin. "What this Pearce fellow is doing—the threats he's made—surely, it must be criminal. Can you not simply take him up?"

Gavin's jaw shifted. "'Tis extortion, simply put. Any other time, I'd bring him before the magistrate and let justice sort it."

But the magistrate was Squire Carew, whose mind was occupied with his royal ball and the supper to follow.

"Carew will not suffer any disruptions to his bid for royal favor," Jory said.

Merryn shook his head. "Not over a gentleman who claims a proper concern for his cousin's welfare."

"Even if you pressed it?" James asked Gavin.

"*Especially* if I pressed it."

Jory shifted. "We know his circumstances. But if we could draw him into revealing his scheme—to admit his concern is not for his cousin but for his own purse, 'twould weaken his position…"

"Aye, but how?" James said. "He'll hardly confess his scheme before witnesses."

Gavin's brow drew low. "A man speaks freely when he believes his words are private."

The words caught on Merryn's mind, and he stilled. *When he believes his words are private.* What *if* Pearce could be drawn into revealing himself? Threats and rumors could be denied, but a man's own words could not.

It was not a comfortable thought. Merryn preferred direct action—an honest day's work, a fair bargain struck between men of honor. But Pearce had shown himself to be neither honest nor honorable. The petition Merryn carried in his coat proved as much. And the intelligence his cousins had gathered on the man's circumstances only confirmed it: Pearce was a desperate man, and desperate men were prone to overreach. If Merryn did nothing, if he threatened exposure or offered payment and hoped for the best…

No. Pearce would only return with fresh demands, just as James suggested.

Which left Merryn with few options. He could not simply ignore the threat. He could not reason with a man motivated by greed or desperation. And he would not let Rebecca pay the price for his failure to act.

He considered the day ahead. There would be the King's arrival later that morning and the procession through Newford. A performance at the theater followed by the squire's ball at the Abbey.

If Merryn thought he could maneuver Pearce onto the theater's small stage—perhaps before the curtains were drawn—where he might be persuaded to reveal himself before a crowded theater... No, it was too uncertain.

There were the London actors to consider, and the timing... too many things could go wrong. Besides, he really had no wish to put his marriage on such a large stage.

The Abbey, though. The Abbey was different. It was a much more intimate setting. He need only get Pearce to reveal himself to the right ear...

The shape of a plan began to form. It was not the sort of plan Merryn favored, but desperation made strange allies of circumstance and opportunity.

He must have betrayed something in his expression because his cousins had gone silent and now watched him. Their faces were earnest, their jaws hard, and James's words came back to him: *We will stand with you.*

For too long, Merryn had kept his own counsel. He was quick to lend his aid whenever it was needed, and he didn't hesitate to make use of his cousins' intelligence, but rarely did he seek their advice.

But this problem was too great to trust to his own judgment alone. "Tell me," he began, "what d'you think of this?"

CHAPTER 30

THE PAVILION ABOVE the harbor gleamed white against a brilliant afternoon sky. Blue silk draped the dais where His Majesty would hold court. Merryn had made his final inspection an hour past, checking each gilded flourish and marble surface.

Satisfied that all was in readiness, he'd gone home to wash and change and now stood at the edge of the southern colonnade, dressed in his Sunday coat. His trousers bore creases so sharp from Mrs. Tilbury's iron that he was afraid to take a step for fear of injuring himself. His household would not let it be said that a Kimbrell dared to receive their King in wrinkles.

Rebecca, Mrs. Tilbury had said, was out. She would join him presently at the pavilion. If he'd been disappointed at not finding his wife at home, on this of all days, he thought he'd done a fair job of hiding the fact. But they'd agreed to greet the King together, to show all of Newford they were married. To play their parts, as Rebecca put it.

He looked for her as the crowd continued to gather along the road. Excited chatter carried up to him as men, women and children vied for the best view, mingling with the sharper calls of the militia officers keeping the lane clear. Gulls cried overhead, and an enterprising fellow shouted, "Ribbons for the King's visit!"

Squire Carew and his wife stood at the pavilion's entrance with Newford's mayor, both men perspiring beneath their hats. Mrs. Carew's feathered bonnet bobbed as she whispered instructions to the couple's grown daughter.

Behind them, Merryn's investors and their wives were taking their positions, with Trewyck assuming a place at the head of the line.

Merryn withdrew his watch to check the time. His wife would be late if she didn't—

A movement on the high street drew his attention to where Rebecca approached, dressed charmingly—and perhaps a bit boldly—in a gown of striped silk, her bonnet trimmed with ribbons that lifted on the afternoon breeze. Sarah walked beside her and behind them, like a shadow that would not be shaken, came Pearce.

Merryn's jaw tightened at the sight.

Rebecca paused to nod to acquaintances as she

passed, and even Mrs. Pentreath greeted her with the hint of a smile. As Rebecca and her companion drew near the pavilion, Merryn went down from his place to meet them on the steps.

Rebecca smiled, and her hand found his arm. The warmth of her fingers reached him through his layers of wool and linen. Conscious of the eyes of Newford upon them, he leaned close to whisper, "I thought per'aps you had changed your mind about coming."

"And miss the culmination of all your efforts? I think not." She bent her head toward his. "My cousin has insisted on joining us. I feared to refuse would be to risk an unnecessary scene, but I thought the less time he has to move among the company, the better."

Merryn followed her gaze to where Pearce had joined the investors and was even now speaking with Trewyck. Measuring the ground, most likely, for Merryn's future undoing. Given the sight, he couldn't fault his wife's tardiness.

"Aye," he agreed somewhat reluctantly. "Better to keep him close so we might know what he's about."

When his wife turned her gaze up to him, her cheeks were pink from the afternoon's warmth. Her eyes held his, steady and unflinching. Despite all that was yet to be resolved, despite her cousin's petition burning a hole in his coat, they were of one mind.

Let Pearce press his claim. He would find no division between them.

Merryn had not imagined their accord five years before, and he did not imagine it now. There was an unmistakable thread binding them to one another more surely than any marriage arrangement. It held them fast, despite her desire for independence—and despite the pride that had kept him from asking her to choose him instead.

But before he could do something unthinkable like close the distance between them and kiss his wife before all of Newford, a cheer went up from the crowd.

"The King!"

Merryn straightened and pressed Rebecca's hand. Ahead, the royal yacht rounded the headland with its naval escort, an impressive frigate of some thirty guns. Down below, the crowd rippled with excitement and a child squealed.

The frigate fired the first gun of its royal salute. Thunder rolled across the water to vibrate the ground at Merryn's feet. More cheers rose, and children clapped their hands over their ears.

A beat later came the answering volley from the small battery above Newford—two guns only, but they boomed bravely down the hillside, carrying the acrid scent of gunpowder toward the shore. A second cannon followed, then another until the salute was complete.

The King's yacht anchored and his ceremonial barge, a gleaming thing of polished brass and gilded trim, was lowered into the water. His Majesty's blue-coated oarsmen took their places. It was all very neatly done.

As the royal standard snapped smartly in the breeze, the Master of Ceremonies called commands from the stern.

Merryn watched the barge's smooth progress toward the quay he had built, bearing a King who would walk through a pavilion of his construction. He should have felt triumph. Instead, he felt the weight of the petition in his coat and the uncertainty of the hours ahead.

His gaze sought Pearce once more in the pavilion's crowd. Now he had found company with Alderton. As Merryn looked on, Pearce murmured something beneath his breath. Alderton responded with a nod and a glance in Merryn's direction. Whatever game Pearce played, he played it well.

Merryn pulled his attention from the man as the King's barge reached the quay. There was little he could do now anyway, and it would not serve to allow the distraction.

Down below, the harbor master stepped forward

to receive the mooring lines, and as one, the oarsmen shipped their oars.

"His Majesty the King!" the Master of Ceremonies called.

George IV rose from his cushioned seat. Even from a distance, he cut an impressive figure. The blue ribbon and star at his breast were bright against a coat that strained at the middle, and his dark hair lay carefully dressed above a florid face.

An equerry offered his arm, and the King stepped onto the quay. With a gracious nod, he acknowledged the harbor master's bow.

The royal equipages, sent ahead from His Majesty's previous landing in Devon, stood waiting. His Majesty settled onto the velvet seat of an open carriage, arranged his coat, then lifted a hand to acknowledge the crowd. The horses sprang forward, the King's guard closed the lane behind, and children were lifted onto shoulders. As the procession moved up the harbor road toward the pavilion, Merryn led Rebecca to their places.

It was some minutes before the carriages came to a stop at the pavilion entrance. The King alighted, and the remaining carriages were soon emptied of a dozen or more men and several ladies in fancy dress.

Newford's mayor stepped forward to give his formal address. The King listened with admirable patience, nodded at the appropriate moments, and responded so his reply might be heard by those on the road closest to the pavilion.

Carew followed the mayor's address with a deep bow before launching into his own elaborate speech about Cornish loyalty to the Crown and the honor of hosting His Majesty at Trevelyan Abbey.

Finally, at a gesture from the Lord Chamberlain, the company moved to the shade inside. Only once the royal party had arranged itself at the dais did the formal presentations begin.

Carew performed the honors, and presently Merryn and Rebecca advanced to the head of the company. "Your Majesty," Carew said, "Mr. Merryn Kimbrell, master builder, and his wife, Mrs. Kimbrell, lately of France."

They went forward and bowed. When Merryn straightened, the King's eyes were upon him, shrewd and assessing beneath heavy lids.

"Kimbrell. You are responsible for the improvements we see about us?"

"I had the honor of organizing the work, Your Majesty, but the skill and diligence belong to my men."

"We are curious to see the full extent of it all." He turned his attention then to Rebecca and inclined his head.

"Mrs. Kimbrell. You have been abroad?"

"I have, Your Majesty."

"And yet you returned to Cornwall for our visit. We are flattered."

The words seemed innocent enough, but Merryn's heart hammered. The King's own wife had lived abroad for years. Would His Majesty find the similarity an unwelcome reminder of his own unhappy situation?

Rebecca's answering smile held just the right amount of modest sophistication, being neither too coy nor too retiring. "I could not absent myself when my husband had the honor of greeting our King."

His Majesty smiled warmly in reply. "The sentiment does you credit. Your husband is fortunate in a wife both sensible and beautiful."

Relief loosened the knot in Merryn's chest as Rebecca curtsied once more. How could their monarch *not* be charmed by his wife? They moved aside and Pearce took their place. His presentation was brief and blessedly unremarkable. The King made a polite inquiry about Jamaica, his tone distantly courteous, but without the warmth he'd shown Rebecca.

Pearce moved on, but Merryn couldn't miss how easily he'd inserted himself into proceedings where he had no rightful place. His wife's cousin would have no trouble gaining an audience for his tale, if and when he sought it.

With the presentations completed, refreshments were brought out. As the King sipped sherry, he turned his attention to the pavilion itself, remarking the carving here or the shape of a polished stone there. When he tilted his head back to take in the sweep of sky-blue ceiling and gilded sunburst, Merryn held his breath. For a long moment, the King said nothing, and Merryn's pulse beat a heavy cadence in his ears.

"Curious," His Majesty said at last. "We are accustomed to more... elaborate tributes. Why this restraint?"

Before Merryn could answer, Carew stepped forward. "Your Majesty, I assure you, there was no slight intended—"

The King silenced him with a raised hand. "We would hear it from the builder."

Merryn pulled in a breath. "I have studied Your Majesty's commission at Brighton, which suits that town admirably. But here in Cornwall"—he nodded toward the prospect through the columns—"I judged a simpler treatment more fitting, that nothing should seek to rival what Brighton already achieves, and that the landscape itself might serve as tribute to Your Majesty."

The King's expression remained unreadable as he moved more fully beneath the dome. He looked out between the columns to the green hills and valleys above Newford, then to the other side, where a three-masted ship glided neatly on the sea.

Finally, the King lifted his chin. "Restraint in decoration shows confidence in structure. It is nicely done, Mr. Kimbrell. You have given us a frame worthy of the subject."

Merryn bowed his acknowledgement, not trusting his voice.

A footman relieved the King of his glass and the royal party moved back toward the entrance. The squire bowed deeply. "Your Majesty, all of Newford looks forward to welcoming you. We have arranged a performance at our theatre, followed by a grand ball at Trevelyan Abbey, with a midnight supper."

"And a special event to crown the evening," Mrs. Carew added somewhat breathlessly. "My husband has prepared something quite spectacular, for your viewing from a private box on the Abbey's terrace."

The King inclined his head. "We are intrigued by such a promise and pleased by your hospitality."

After everyone had gone, Merryn stood alone in the structure with his wife. The sounds of celebration had moved off with the crowd, leaving only the distant lap of waves in the harbor below, but Merryn's nerve endings were curiously alive—the King had viewed his pavilion and not found it wanting. Even with everything else weighting the day, that was a fine thing.

Rebecca turned to face him, her eyes bright. "You, Mr. Kimbrell, ought to be well pleased with yourself. His Majesty said your work shows 'confidence in structure.' That is high praise from the man who commissioned the Royal Pavilion."

Though Merryn tried to restrain his smile, his grin broke through. "'Tis high praise indeed."

Rebecca stood close, and a trace of her lavender perfume reached him. The setting sun caught the copper in her hair and gilded her fair skin. All about them, the air was quiet and expectant.

"I think we put on a rather convincing performance," she whispered.

Performance. He'd nearly forgotten their aim. They were meant to show Newford they were well and truly married. To play their parts and head off any tales Pearce might put about. But the crowds were gone now, as was Pearce.

Merryn followed his wife's gaze to where their fingers were twined together. He couldn't recall when her hand had left his sleeve and found his, or when he'd threaded his fingers through hers.

There was no one about to convince, and still she held his hand. He tugged her gently closer. She came easily, her skirts brushing his over-pressed trousers.

"I daresay we are quite persuasive," he agreed.

He could feel her breath on his cheek. Her lips

were close enough to kiss. He nearly yielded to the impulse, but there was still too much between them, and much to be done before the day was out.

With an inward sigh, he pressed a kiss to the back of her fingers then settled her hand on his sleeve once more. "We ought to ready ourselves for the evening ahead."

Rebecca blinked, and her smile faltered. If he didn't mistake the matter, his wife had been thinking of another kiss as well. The notion sent heat spiraling through him.

"Yes," she agreed brightly. "There is much to be done."

He led them to the pavilion steps. Whatever happened at the squire's ball tonight, whether he succeeded in thwarting her cousin or not, he would find a way to protect his wife. To give her the freedom she craved, whether that freedom led her back to France or somewhere else entirely.

He only hoped, when it was done, that she might choose to stay.

CHAPTER 31

THAT EVENING, GREGORY sat opposite Rebecca in the carriage, his face half in shadow as they rattled toward Trevelyan Abbey. She felt his gaze on her, assessing and calculating, but she could not think of anything to break the silence. Not with Merryn's shoulder pressed to hers, his leg warm against her own. Not with the words she wanted to say to her husband taking up much of her thoughts.

The carriage swayed, and Merryn's arm pressed hers more firmly. Her husband's tall form certainly took up his share of the space. He was well turned out for the squire's ball with a neatly brushed coat of dark cloth. His breeches were well fitted, his shoes well polished, and his white cravat simply but capably tied. He wore no jewelry beyond his watch chain and a modest gold pin in his tie.

As Rebecca had dressed, she'd rehearsed silently what she wished to say to her husband. She needed to tell him she did not wish to return to Paris. That she desired a true marriage, not an arrangement.

But before she could say anything of her wishes to Merryn, she must first address matters with Gregory. Every time she thought of her cousin's annulment petition, her stomach tightened. She could not speak of the future while her cousin's threat remained.

Twice today, she had sought a private moment with Gregory. Once at the theater as they'd taken their places for the London performance, but Gregory had been hailed by one of his new acquaintances and quickly left their side. And then again, moments before they left for the Abbey, until they were interrupted by her husband's arrival in the parlor.

The squire's ball was her last chance before their day was up. She would make her offer to her cousin and have done with it. Then she looked through the carriage window at the line of vehicles stretching before them, their torches ablaze in the evening air, and felt the futility of that hope. The ball would be a tremendous crush with half the parish in attendance. Amidst the dancing and music, and the squire's supper and fireworks display, there would be few opportunities for quiet conversation.

The carriage inched forward. Through the open windows came the sounds of laughter and conversation, the distant strains of music already spilling from the house. Gregory continued to watch her from the opposite bench, and Rebecca knew a childish urge to kick his shin. How she wished to attend the squire's ball with her handsome husband at her side and none of her cousin's nonsense hanging over them! One way or another, she would see an end to it.

At last the carriage reached the Abbey steps. Merryn descended first and turned to hand her down. His gloved fingers closed around hers, and she held his gaze, attempting to convey something of her thoughts and searching his blue eyes for her own reassurance. He gave her hand the slightest press before releasing it, a wordless reply that eased a bit of the tension in her.

Gregory followed, adjusting his cuffs and endeavoring to look bored, as if he attended such balls all the time in Jamaica. "A respectable gathering," he observed with an eye for the crowded entrance.

They were swept inside on a tide of guests. The Abbey's great hall shimmered with candlelight, hundreds of flames reflected in tall, polished mirrors. Music floated down from the gallery where the musicians played, and the air was thick with beeswax and perfume.

Squire Carew and his wife greeted the line of arrivals at the ballroom's entrance. Mrs. Carew's gown was a splendid confection of gold beads and embroidery over darker gold silk—likely something commissioned from London.

The squire bowed over Rebecca's hand. "Mrs. Kimbrell. A pleasure. I trust you've enjoyed the day's events?"

"Very much so, thank you."

Carew's eyes moved past her to Merryn. "Kimbrell. The pavilion was a triumph today. His Majesty was most complimentary of our efforts."

"Indeed, sir," Merryn replied.

They moved on, making way for the other guests behind them. In the ballroom, couples were already moving through the figures of a country dance.

Rebecca searched for Gregory, but she caught only a glimpse of his coat disappearing in the crowd before a group of ladies swept between them.

"Mrs. Kimbrell." Merryn's voice was low at her ear, and she shivered. "You're frowning."

"Am I?" She smoothed her expression. "I was looking for my cousin."

"Ah. A provoking endeavor, to be sure, but I'm afraid Pearce must wait." He nodded toward the entrance as a stir moved through the crowd. "The King has arrived."

Conversation about them dimmed, and heads turned. Momentarily, the announcement came.

"His Majesty the King."

The room sank into bows and curtsies as George IV entered. He was resplendent in his evening dress with a coat of dark velvet above white satin breeches. His party followed: a handful of courtiers, two bejeweled ladies with elaborate ostrich plumes adorning their hair, and an equerry who hovered at His Majesty's elbow.

The King went through the room, pausing here and there to acknowledge a familiar face or accept a bow. Finally, His Majesty reached their corner. Rebecca curtsied deeply as Merryn bowed beside her.

"Mrs. Kimbrell, we meet again." The King's voice held a note of warmth. "Cornwall has done well in reclaiming you from France. We are pleased to find such elegance gracing the countryside."

Rebecca's cheeks warmed. "Your Majesty is very kind."

The King angled his gaze toward Merryn before bringing it back to her. "Enjoy the evening, madam. We understand there's to be a fine show at midnight."

He moved on, making his way to a gilded chair opposite the gallery where he might observe the dancing. From a nearby alcove, Mrs. Pentreath's voice carried just enough for Rebecca to catch the words "marked attentions" before the noise of the crowd swallowed the rest.

Beside her, Merryn stood rigid and a touch too close for propriety.

"The King's attentions are rather warm," he muttered beneath his breath.

"He is only being gracious."

"He is being particular." There was an edge to his voice she could not quite interpret, but she did not mind it. She rather liked it when her husband was being gruff.

"Would you prefer he ignored me?" she said teasingly.

His jaw shifted before he admitted, "I would not." Around them, couples began arranging themselves on the floor. Her husband's expression brightened. "If I do not mistake the matter, a waltz is next."

She glanced at the card on her wrist and smiled. "So it is."

The waltz was still considered fast in some quarters of English society, though it had been commonplace on the Continent for years. Here in Cornwall, at a ball honoring the King and with her husband at her side, it seemed both appropriate and dangerous.

Merryn sketched a short bow. "May I have the honor?"

She placed her fingers in his, and her pulse quickened as his hand settled warmly at her waist. She rested her palm on his shoulder. His form was solid beneath his coat, and when she recalled the firm skin and smooth contours of that shoulder, her throat instantly warmed. Perhaps, if she'd had occasion to study her husband's form as she'd done her aunt's statues, she might not blush whenever such recollections entered her thoughts.

"Should I ask what has caused you to color so charmingly?" he said.

She pretended to consider the question before saying, "You should not."

He closed his eyes in a show of long-suffering resignation. "So long as I am not obliged to call out our monarch."

She was startled into a laugh, as much by her husband's words as by the unexpected note of teasing in his tone. "Never," she assured him.

The musicians struck up the first notes, and the steps carried them in a dizzying rotation across the squire's new parquet.

They had danced together in London, of course, but never the waltz. Their previous quadrilles and country dances had never brought them so close. She was acutely aware of every point where their bodies nearly touched, and of the space between them that propriety demanded.

"I daresay we are being rather scandalous," she murmured.

He lifted a brow. "Newford is not so backwards.

Our assemblies have had the waltz for some time now, though not without complaint from our staunchest residents."

"I do not mean the waltz," she clarified. "In Paris, few people dance with their own spouse."

His eyes met hers. "Ah, but this is not Paris."

His reminder hung between them, and there was a hint of challenge in his tone. A challenge she was finally prepared to meet.

"No," she agreed. "This is not Paris."

She wanted to say more, to tell him how she wished to make her life in Cornwall—with his hand at her waist, his shoulder beneath her palm, for this dance and many more after it. Soon, she would tell him.

She thought again of the offer she meant to give her cousin, and her hands grew cold despite her gloves.

"Rebecca." Merryn's voice was low, pitched for her ears alone. "What troubles you?"

"Aside from my cousin's threats, do you mean?" She managed a smile. "Nothing of any consequence."

His hand firmed at her waist. "You are a poor dissembler."

"And you are too observant."

The corner of his mouth lifted. "Shall I look away?"

"Would you, if I asked?"

"No," he admitted. "I cannot help looking at you."

And she couldn't help her smile when her practical husband said things like that.

The music swelled, carrying them through another turn until the final notes faded. They stood still for a breath too long before Merryn released her and offered his arm.

She needed to find her cousin. She must put an end to his ridiculous threats.

They reached the edge of the floor, and she took her hand from Merryn's arm. "I must go and find the retiring room."

He nodded, though something of suspicion flickered in his gaze. She slipped away before he could say anything further, and the crowd soon swallowed her. She pressed through, searching for Gregory.

There. He stood at the entrance to the gentlemen's card room, speaking with a man she did not recognize. As she watched, the pair of them went through.

She could not follow him without inviting comment, but neither could she wait for him to emerge. The crush in the ballroom was too great. She would never secure a private word with her cousin unless she contrived it.

A footman passed bearing a tray of champagne. Rebecca motioned to him. "Is there a writing desk nearby? I require paper and ink."

He inclined his head. "In the morning room, madam. Just through that door."

Rebecca followed his direction. The squire's morning room was blessedly empty, lit only by a single branch of candles. Rebecca crossed to the writing desk. The message she penned was brief: *Meet me at the garden temple. R.*

Returning to the corridor, she placed her note on the footman's tray. "Deliver this to Mr. Gregory Pearce, if you will. He has just entered the card room."

"Yes, madam."

She watched him go then returned to the ballroom. The crowd was even thicker now, if that were possible. She searched for Merryn's tall form, but he was not where she'd left him. Nor could she see him among the dancers. He must have gone in search of refreshment, or perhaps he'd taken a respite of his own in the gentlemen's withdrawing room.

It was just as well. She could slip away undetected, make her offer to her cousin, and return before her absence was noted. Beyond the terrace doors, several guests enjoyed the cooler air after the heat of the ballroom. Rebecca moved past them, down the stone steps and onto the garden path.

She knew the way from her previous visit when Merryn and Carew had shown her the Abbey grounds. Moonlight silvered the tops of the trees, and night sounds rose around her—crickets in the grass and the whisper of the wind through the rose bushes.

From ahead came voices. She slowed, peering around an ornamental shrub. Two gentlemen stood in conversation on the main path—Gavin and Jory, she realized.

She had no wish to encounter anyone who might wonder at her solitary walk, much less her husband's cousins. Before they could see her, she ducked onto a smaller path that curved through the shadows.

She passed the squire's conservatory and neared the King's private box. To her right lay the hedge maze and at its center, the garden temple. Her slippers whispered on the soft grass. She kept her head down, composing what she would say to her cousin.

She would offer him her inheritance. The funds that had bought her independence and built her life in Paris. They were surely enough to settle his debts, and with such a sum in his hands, he would have no reason to press for an annulment. He would have what he had come for, and far more besides.

If the notion of yielding to her cousin, of giving over her fortune to him, caused her palms to grow damp, it was nothing to the hot, twisty sensation that plagued her whenever she thought of the damage his distasteful accusations could do to her husband's reputation.

No one would care that they were false. No one would care that her uncle had *approved* of Merryn for her husband. They would hear only what her cousin wished them to—that Merryn had acted dishonorably to gain her inheritance.

She rounded the final turn of the hedge but stopped on finding the temple's entrance occupied. Merryn stood frowning at his watch. He looked up, and for one frozen moment they stared at one another.

MERRYN HAD GONE to the garden ahead of his appointment with Pearce to ensure their privacy, but he had not expected this. His wife, who'd left his side with a suspicious manner, now stood before him in her evening dress of silver tissue.

He'd been right to be suspicious. But then, had he not taken advantage of her absence to advance his own plan?

She was the first to speak. "Why are you here?"

"I might ask you the same question."

Her eyes dropped to the watch in his hand.

"You're meeting someone. My cousin, I presume?"

He took a step toward her. "Aye. You as well?"

Her nose wrinkled as she nodded. Then, voice dry, she said, "We seem to be working at cross-purposes."

He should have known. While he'd plotted with his cousins, he should have anticipated that his wife, who managed a fortune through her own cleverness, would not sit idle while Pearce threatened it all. Of course she would have her own scheme.

He kept his voice low to ask her, "What d'you mean to offer him?"

Her chin lifted. "What are *you* planning to offer?"

"Rebecca—"

"I know you will not have signed his petition, so I must assume you have come with something else to offer in its place."

He winced inwardly, aware of the petition folded in his coat. He said only, "I mean to persuade him to leave off his scheme. And if that does not succeed, then I will offer him three thousand pounds."

Her lips parted. In the dim light, he could not read her expression, but her voice softened. "You would do that?"

"To protect you from Pearce's schemes? How can you doubt it?"

She lifted one hand toward him. He thought, briefly, that she meant to touch his cheek, until her fingers fell away.

"But that money is yours," she said. "You ought to use it for new commissions, for the projects you wish to undertake."

"That money was never mine," he replied. "I have only been holding it for your protection and comfort. If spending it now keeps you safe from Pearce, then 'twill have served its purpose."

Before he could lose his courage, he reached into his coat and withdrew her cousin's petition. Whether he succeeded tonight or not, his wife should know she still had choices. He would not keep her bound to him simply because he could.

After a moment's study of the folded paper, he extended the petition to her. "'Tis for you."

Frowning, she took it and unfolded the pages. Her eyes went immediately to his signature.

"What have you done?" she whispered.

"I have signed it," he said, "for you to hold. Use it on your thirtieth birthday, when your cousin is no longer a threat. I understand 'tis an easier thing if both parties sign."

She studied the paper, and he studied her. Every muscle, every tendon in him, felt impossibly tight.

Finally, she tilted a wan smile at him. "Even if it had both of our signatures, I do not think it will stand if we go on living in the same house."

His hand went to his coat again. He removed the ticket he'd acquired that afternoon and tapped the edge against his palm. "'Tis why I have also secured passage for you to return to France, should you wish it."

She stared at him. "Is that your wish?" she said at last.

He rubbed a hand over his mouth. "An honorable man would say I wish only for your happiness. With this"—he nodded toward the petition in her hand—"you can be truly free for the first time, with neither trustee nor husband to bar your way. An honorable man would say these things, but I—"

He paused to collect himself. It was time to say what he should have said five years before, when she had stood before him in her traveling dress with her trunks packed.

"'Tis my most fervent wish that you will stay."

Rebecca pressed the fingers of one hand against her lips. The white silk of her gloves was stark in the shadows, and her eyes were bright.

"That is my wish as well," she whispered.

He went still, uncertain if he'd heard her right.

"I came to the garden," she continued, "to secure our freedom from Pearce. Not my freedom. *Ours*. I do not want to return to Paris. I want a life in Cornwall. I—" She drew a breath. "I desire a true marriage, not an arrangement."

He stood motionless, scarcely breathing, as her words settled. She wished to stay.

"You're certain?" His voice was rough, and he cleared his throat. "What of your life in Paris?"

She shook her head. "I have guarded my independence because I saw what marriage made of my mother. I vowed I would not yield to any man's authority." Her voice softened. "But you are not my father. From the first, you have given me a choice when you might have pressed your claim." Her eyes held his. "True freedom lies not in protecting my heart from fear, but in choosing where to place it. It is a lesson I have been slow to realize."

For a long moment he couldn't move. Couldn't speak. Five years of regretting his silence, of wondering about his wife and persuading himself he was a fool to imagine this day—

He closed the space between them and kissed her. His arms tightened around her, holding her against him as though she might vanish if he let her go. She made a small sound against his mouth, and something inside him—five years of wanting— broke loose. His heart soared when her hands gripped his coat, pulling him even closer.

When at last they drew apart, his heart sped behind his ribs. Her eyes were dazed, her lips reddened from their kiss. The corner of his mouth lifted. Soon he would be grinning like a fool.

"Rebecca."

"Why did you never tell anyone of our marriage?" she asked.

It was the question he'd braced himself for since her arrival in Cornwall—only not, he thought, in this moment, with the taste of her still on his mouth and the knowledge that Pearce might appear at any instant.

He swallowed then gave her the truth of it. "I was heart-sore."

Her brows dipped low, but before she could ask what he meant by that, he pushed on. "I had fallen in love with my wife, you see. So deeply, in fact, that I couldn't see my way out." He lifted his gaze to find her watching him, her lips parted.

"I had hopes of persuading you to stay, until I saw how much you wanted to go. What you didn't know—what I never told you—was that your uncle had already given his permission for me to court you properly. It was later that same day when he took ill. Then you came to me with your proposal, and I…" He paused to draw a breath. "I've spent five years regretting that I never asked you to stay. My heart has ached with it ever since."

He had never confessed the depth of his regret aloud. Now, to release it into the night, lifted an impossible weight from his chest.

A long beat passed before she said softly, "I was foolish to go."

His breath caught.

"I was even more foolish to stay away. I left so soon because I feared..." She paused, her lashes shadowing her cheeks until she lifted them again to meet his gaze. "I feared my feelings for you. I thought if I stayed—even to mourn my uncle properly—I would lose the very independence I meant to secure. I was wrong."

He shook his head. "It had to happen as it did," he said, and to his surprise, he believed it. Had he asked her to stay, had she remained behind, he did not think their hearts would have found one another as they had now.

Her fingers were cool as she laid them against his cheek, and it occurred to him that at some point she'd lost her glove. Had she removed it, or had he? He spied it on the ground at their feet and retrieved it for her.

As she took it from him, she leaned up and pressed another kiss to his mouth. It was quick and firm, and he didn't think he would ever tire of feeling her lips beneath his.

She withdrew and whispered in an unsteady voice, "We must still address the matter of my cousin."

Pearce. The King's box and the plan Merryn had

devised with his cousins. The time must be near. Then he recalled Rebecca's earlier confession that she'd come to the garden to secure their freedom. The blissful fog of their kisses began to fade as his uneasiness returned.

He drew back, though he kept hold of her hands. "What d'you mean to offer Pearce?" he asked her again.

She swallowed. "My inheritance."

His breath left him. "No."

"It is surely enough to settle his debts. I have already prepared a letter to Mr. Cross instructing him to transfer the funds to my cousin once I have Gregory's agreement to end this."

He shook his head. "You cannot."

"I must. Three thousand pounds is an impressive sum, but I cannot think it will be enough. He will return for more, and what will you do then? If he has my inheritance—if he has what he came for—there can be no question of his returning for more."

Merryn stepped away from her to pace the temple. "He will not return."

"You cannot know that."

"I mean to make sure of it."

She looked at him, her head tilted, considering. He realized his words carried a darker edge than he'd intended.

"I do not mean to do him bodily injury," he said,

though the idea was not without its appeal. "What time did you arrange to meet him?"

She frowned. "I did not give a time in my note. I thought he must be as eager to see an end to this as I am, but it seems the card room holds more appeal than I anticipated." Her expression shifted as she studied him, and something bright appeared in her eyes. "You have a plan."

Her wonder at this was not flattering.

"Aye." He checked his watch. "But if your cousin does not make his appearance soon, I cannot speak to its chances."

Even as he said this, footsteps sounded on the gravel path. Someone approached from the other side of the hedge. There was no time to explain further.

"D'you trust me?" he said in an urgent whisper.

"Of course."

"Enough to follow my lead?"

She hesitated only a moment before nodding. "Without reservation."

CHAPTER 32

PEARCE ROUNDED THE hedge and stopped. His gaze moved from Merryn to Rebecca and back again, and a satisfied smile crossed his features.

"Rebecca. Kimbrell." His tone was almost cordial. "I'm pleased you're both here. I trust you've had sufficient time to consider the petition."

When neither of them replied, a crease formed between Pearce's brows. His gaze flickered from Merryn to Rebecca and back again. "I received notes from the pair of you. You do wish an end to this unpleasantness, do you not?"

"Aye." Merryn kept his voice level. "We've come to resolve matters, though not in the way you expect."

Pearce's crease deepened into a frown. His shoulders were drawn back, his chin lifted. It was the posture of a man preparing for battle.

He turned his attention to Rebecca. "You do understand that if you persist in denying the truth of your husband's actions, I shall have no choice but to present my evidence publicly? The suspicious timing of your marriage only days before my father's death, and then five years spent apart. And that is to say nothing of *The Newford Inventory*, which has clearly put your husband out as a bachelor rather than a man already wedded."

Merryn tightened his hand on Rebecca's, willing her to continue to trust him. Her reply was a gentle press back.

Pearce's voice gained confidence as he continued addressing Rebecca. "Your husband will be exposed as a dishonorable opportunist. He will lose his commissions. His reputation, everything he has built, it will all be destroyed."

Rebecca shook her head. "You do not want to do this," she said softly.

"Of course, I don't *want* to do this." Pearce's tone shifted to something almost plaintive. "Truly. But you leave me no alternative."

Merryn released his wife's hand reluctantly and stepped toward Pearce.

"Are you quite finished?"

Pearce tucked his jaw. "I don't think you fully comprehend—"

"I comprehend." Merryn clasped his hands behind his back. "You're desperate. You require money. And you thought creating a scandal out of whole cloth would force my wife to capitulate."

"My aim is only to make the truth known. I cannot account for what others make of it."

"Shall we discuss the truth, Pearce?" Merryn let the question settle between them.

Pearce's expression cooled. "And what truth is that?"

"I've made inquiries," Merryn said. "I'm aware of your situation."

Merryn felt Rebecca's curious gaze on him as the color left Pearce's face. In the moonlight, his complexion took on a grey cast.

"You've not had a plantation for some years now." Merryn watched the words land. "My cousins discovered you sold it at a loss to cover your gambling debts, though the new owner has done rather well with it."

Pearce adjusted his cravat, his hand tightening the knot.

Rebecca spoke. "What of your inheritance from your father? Was it not enough to support you?"

"Spanish privateers—" Pearce began.

Merryn shook his head. "All fabrications—the sugar, the privateers. There was no ship, Pearce. No lost cargo. The vessel you named never sailed from Kingston."

Beside him, Rebecca gasped softly at this new information. Pearce tugged at his cuffs as his story fell apart, his eyes narrowing with the calculation of a man seeking a way out.

"You're grasping," he said, though his voice lacked its earlier certainty. "You know nothing of my situation."

"I know you left Jamaica owing vast sums to merchants, tavern keepers, and at least one money lender of questionable reputation." Merryn kept his tone even. There was no satisfaction in cornering a desperate man, only the necessity of doing what he must. "You've come here because you've nowhere else to go. Your creditors abroad have long memories, and passage back to England was far cheaper than what you owed."

Pearce's jaw worked. "These inquiries of yours... you had no right—"

"To protect my wife?" Merryn's voice hardened. "I have *every* right."

Rebecca tucked her fingers round his arm. "I'm sorry you find yourself in unfortunate circumstances," she said to Pearce, "but you cannot truly believe my marriage—or my husband—is anything less than honorable."

Pearce's eyes flashed. Anger warred with something else in his expression. Shame, perhaps, or the bitter recognition of his own failings.

He straightened his shoulders. "Fine. Do you

want the truth? I don't care whether your marriage was fraudulent or not. The *appearance* of impropriety is sufficient for my purposes, and you know it as well as I. The fact remains: you still have no proof your marriage was not made by manipulating a man in his dying hours."

Merryn could scarcely credit the man's persistence. Even now, faced with the exposure of his own lies, Pearce refused to release his grip on this last desperate hope.

"You can make your accusations," Merryn said. "And I will make certain everyone knows why a man like yourself would trouble himself over a union that was properly made five years before." He let that settle before adding, "I needn't rely on the *appearance* of impropriety when the truth is so readily apparent. No tradesman will take the credit of a man who flees his obligations."

Pearce went very still, and Merryn's certainty rose. He and Rebecca would prevail; Pearce couldn't argue the facts before him. The man knew he was as good as ruined. Merryn couldn't like it—he felt little more than pity for the man—but Pearce had brought it on himself.

Then Merryn glanced at his wife. Her face was pale, her hand tense on his arm as she came to the same understanding. Her eyes met his, and what he saw there was his undoing. There was pity for her cousin's plight, but also something softer.

That she had no wish to see him ruined so thoroughly was clear. Reluctantly, Merryn admitted to himself that were it not for Pearce's desperation, his wife might never have sought him out again. That, alone, was worth a scrap of compassion for the man.

"Do you think…?" Rebecca began in a whisper.

She didn't need to finish her thought before Merryn heard himself agree. To Pearce, he said, "Per'aps there is another way."

Pearce's expression was wary as Merryn withdrew his letter of credit from his coat. Even the crickets had fallen silent in the hedges, as if they were intent on the drama being played on their night stage.

Merryn had long thought himself a fool for holding on to the funds his marriage had brought him. Now, he *knew* he was a fool for giving them up. But Pearce was Rebecca's family. If aiding him gave her some measure of peace, it was well worth it.

"Three thousand," he said, "and passage to France, should you desire more distance between yourself and your creditors."

Pearce's brows shot toward his hairline. Merryn could see the calculation behind his eyes—three thousand pounds was a boon for a man under the hatches, though it was far less than the ten thousand Pearce had wagered on.

"'Tis all you will have," Merryn said. "I suggest you invest it wisely rather than wager on *vingt-et-un*. The cards have not been your friend."

Pearce's gaze remained fixed on the papers, his body tense.

"But your marriage—" he began.

"Will not be annulled!" Rebecca said with irritation.

"Take the money and leave Cornwall," Merryn urged. "Cease with your accusations, else I begin with mine."

Pearce's shoulders sagged. "Why do you offer this?" His confusion was understandable. Even he must have realized how thin his argument had become.

Rebecca answered for them. "Because I think you are not a cruel man, only a desperate one. And because your father would have wanted better for you than this."

Pearce's face tightened at the mention of his parent. The bluster and calculation fell away, leaving only a man who had made a muddle of his chances and knew it. "Three thousand," he said quietly.

"I have some knowledge of investments," Rebecca offered. "I can advise you, if you will allow it."

"You?" Her cousin's frown deepened, and his tone bordered the offensive side of surprised.

Merryn had no wish for Rebecca to have any

more to do with her troublesome cousin. Her offer was more generous than Pearce deserved, but neither could he deny the man's chances of success without it were slim.

"'Tis true," he admitted. "My wife has a head for figures and such. Heed her guidance and your funds will prosper. The choice is yours, but either way, there will be no more money for you. You'll have no further claim on my wife's inheritance."

Pearce finally took the papers from Merryn and turned, but a motion drew his gaze upward. On the terrace above the garden, in the gilded royal viewing box, stood George IV.

———

MERRYN DROPPED INTO a bow at once, Rebecca following with a deep curtsy beside him. Pearce stiffened, then spun to make his own obeisance to the King. His bow was deep but hurried, his voice tight.

"Your Majesty."

The King's voice carried easily down to them, much as Merryn knew their conversation must have carried *up*.

"We have come to view the gardens. Your squire has been waxing enthusiastic about his private box." His Majesty's dry tone suggested this enthusiasm had not been entirely welcome. "We did not expect such diverting entertainment, but we venture to say it has surpassed even today's theatrical."

He inclined his head, lips twitching in amusement. "For a time, we supposed this to be the special event Mrs. Carew promised, but our courtier informs us it is only a prelude to the fireworks."

Pearce's face drained of what little color remained as the King's words—and their implication—settled. Merryn could practically see the man's thoughts as he searched them frantically, trying to determine how much the King might have overheard.

His Majesty's gaze was sharp as he turned it on Pearce. "Your situation, sir, does you no credit. You have brought with you accusations of fraud, and yet we have heard you admit your own inventions. A plantation that is no longer yours. Cargo that never sailed."

Pearce opened his mouth then closed it again.

"We do not appreciate," the King continued, his voice hardening, "men who prey upon family connections to advance false accusations. Particularly in the midst of our royal progress."

Pearce bowed lower. "Your Majesty, I only sought to protect my cousin—"

"You sought to profit from her inheritance."

The King's attention shifted then to Merryn. "Mr. Kimbrell. You have confessed to keeping your marriage secret out of an excess of feeling."

The linen knot at Merryn's throat felt too tight. His Majesty had been listening far longer than he would have liked, but he could only acknowledge what the King already knew. "I have, Your Majesty."

"We know something of matrimonial difficulties." The King's words were measured. "Of marriages made for duty versus those built on genuine regard."

His gaze moved to Rebecca. "And Mrs. Kimbrell. Now that you have had your time abroad, do you return your husband's sentiment?"

Rebecca's voice remained clear and steady. "I do, Your Majesty. With all my heart."

There was a long pause as the King looked between the three of them, his gaze piercing and direct. Two courtiers stood behind him, along with the ostrich-plumed ladies. The royal party remained silent, awaiting the King's speech.

"We have witnessed many marriages," he finally said. "Unions of convenience, of fortune, of duty. We have rarely witnessed such evidence of genuine feeling."

"Your marriage is your own concern. Heaven knows there are plenty of men who would offer their opinion whether you wish it or not, but we have seen enough this evening to be satisfied of its merit." He paused, and when he spoke again, his voice carried the weight of a royal pronouncement.

"We have had quite enough of scandal," he continued. "Of courts and petitions and accusations. Henceforth, no petition challenging your union shall find favor with any court. We shall not suffer a scandal to be contrived where none exists."

The King's gaze returned to Pearce, and his expression cooled.

"You may go, Mr. Pearce. We suggest you do so with all haste."

Pearce straightened from his bow. "Your Majesty..."

"That was a dismissal."

Pearce bowed again, deeper this time. Then he turned and hurried for the garden path. His footsteps faded quickly through the hedge until only silence remained.

Merryn and Rebecca remained frozen in place, bound by protocol until the King released them. Presently, His Majesty inclined his head. "Enjoy the fireworks. We understand they begin shortly."

With that, he and his party withdrew into the shadows of the box.

Neither Merryn nor Rebecca spoke for a long moment. Finally, Merryn released his breath. The tension fell from his shoulders, leaving him feeling hollow and light. After years of secrecy and weeks of threats and schemes, it was finished. Not with scandal or ruin, but with a royal blessing he could not have anticipated.

"'Tis done," he said, and his voice sounded strange to his own ears.

Rebecca did not respond immediately. She looked at the place where Pearce had disappeared beyond the hedge, then up at the King's empty box.

"The King has blessed our marriage," she said with no small amount of wonder.

Merryn took his wife's hand and drew her into the shadows at the temple's edge, where they could speak behind the columns without being overheard.

"Aye." He turned to face her fully. "Even should Pearce fail to make something of his new fortune, he will have none of yours. No one in England would dare lend credence to his tales now."

A whistle pierced the air. They both looked up as a rocket climbed the sky and burst into a shower of amber light, briefly illuminating the temple. The first of the squire's fireworks.

Rebecca tilted her head to study him, her features outlined in reds and golds. "You knew," she said.

He gave her a questioning glance.

"You knew the King would hear. The placement of the royal box, and this temple… the sound carries dreadfully, I believe you said."

Merryn allowed himself a rueful smile. "I did not know he would hear, and certainly not so much of our private conversation."

Her eyes widened, and a smile touched her lips. She must have realized, as he had, that the King had witnessed their kisses. That had certainly *not* been a part of his plan. *Genuine affection*, indeed.

"I had hopes," Merryn said, "that he might hear something of Pearce's scheme. The squire has long planned that His Majesty would view the gardens before the fireworks, and I thought…" He shrugged. "I thought it worth the attempt, though I could not have done it were it not for my cousins keeping the other guests from entering the garden."

She laughed. "That was remarkably clever."

His brows rose. "Your surprise is hardly flattering. I see I must endeavor to raise myself in your esteem."

"I shall look forward to the effort." A smile played at her lips before she turned her attention to the fireworks.

Blue and silver burst across the sky, painting the stone columns in cool light. The hedge walls muffled the appreciative cries from the crowd now gathering on the terrace above. As his wife watched the display, Merryn watched her.

For the first time since Rebecca had come to Cornwall, he could imagine a future for them. A future where they might begin. *Truly* begin.

When she looked back at him, her eyes reflected the light from the fireworks.

"We ought to return to the terrace." Her voice was soft. "People will have noticed our absence."

She was right, of course, but neither of them moved to go. Rebecca's hand found his in the shadows. Her fingers were cool from the night air, but they warmed quickly against his palm.

Under the cover of another fiery burst overhead, he bent his head once more. "We are married," he whispered against her lips. "Let them notice."

CHAPTER 33

A THUMP ON the stairs stilled Rebecca's hand. She sat at her dressing table, one earring halfway to the jewelry case before her. She heard the scrape of something heavy being maneuvered down the passage, and the muffled exchange of voices she couldn't quite make out. They moved toward the house's entrance with another thump.

Gregory's trunk.

She knew it even before she crossed to the window and drew aside the curtain.

Below, the carriage waited in the drive, its lamps casting twin pools of light across the gravel. She watched as Merryn emerged from the house with the groom, Jem, her cousin's trunk hoisted between them. They loaded it onto the carriage with remarkable efficiency.

Gregory followed a moment later, his figure dark against the lamplight as he toted his valise. He strode to the carriage without looking back, and the vehicle bounced as Merryn shut the door on him.

She allowed the curtain to fall. She and Merryn had won. Her cousin had schemed to take what was not his through accusations he knew to be false. The King himself had witnessed his confession. There would be no scandal now, no accusations to threaten Merryn's reputation or his commissions.

She knew an inordinate relief for it, but beneath that lay a strange thread of pity for her uncle's son. Gregory had certainly not earned it, but she couldn't help but feel it. Like her, Gregory had sought some measure of security in an uncertain world. Unlike her, he had not the head for money, nor the patience to build something lasting. Now he must begin again in France.

She had been surprised by her husband's generosity toward him, though she should not have been. Merryn's grace—to offer her cousin not only his own funds but the means to begin anew—was simply who he was.

He would claim giving Gregory passage to France was the practical course—an expedient means of removing her cousin from Cornwall. And perhaps there was something of practicality in his decision, but beneath it lay the honor of a gentleman who would not see a defeated opponent crushed so thoroughly.

But whatever her cousin's failings, were it not for Gregory's scheme, she might never have come to Cornwall. The thought was a sobering one.

She turned so Marie could undo the fastenings of her ball dress. With the gown removed and her stays unlaced, she drew a full breath for the first time in hours.

The cool air of her chamber was a welcome relief. She bathed as Marie put the wardrobe to rights. Then, dressed in her nightclothes, she drew the cool silk of her wrapper about her shoulders. She watched the maid in the mirror as Marie collected her discarded garments over one arm.

I am free so long as I think I am. If it had taken Gregory's scheme to bring Rebecca to Cornwall, it had taken Marie's remark to bring her to her senses. For someone who prided herself on her independence, Rebecca owed much of her current happiness to others.

"How did you come to be so wise, Marie?"

The maid straightened. "Madame?"

"You told me once, *I am free so long as I think I am*. How did you come to such a profound conclusion?"

"Oh, I did not come to it, Madame. It came to me. The French women, we know how to be content with our lot, yet still hold a little freedom for ourselves. It is our own little rebellion." She paused in straightening the brushes on the dressing table.

"And, too, my father served Monsieur Rousseau."

"Jean-Jacques Rousseau—the philosopher?"

"*Oui*, Madame."

Rebecca laughed. "Marie, you are a treasure. I am granting you an increase in your wages. If you wish to remain in my employ, that is. Of course, if you would like to return to France instead, I will see to it."

"I am content, Madame. Shall I take down your hair?"

"No, that is all. Go and find your bed."

The maid bobbed a curtsy and slipped from the room. The hour was late, but rather than exhaustion, Rebecca felt a curious energy humming within her. She returned to her dressing table and seated herself before the glass. Her cheeks were still flushed from the evening, her hair beginning to slip from its arrangement.

She withdrew the remaining pins, setting them in the case with her earrings. Taking up her brush, she pulled it through her hair. Tonight, she would become a wife in truth. The thought sent heat along her throat.

Somewhere below, a door opened and closed. Then, footsteps on the stairs. A tread she had come to know these past weeks. Merryn.

She listened as his footsteps reached the landing then continued down the passage. They paused, and she heard the creak of hinges when he reached his chamber. The house settled, and through the door between their rooms, she heard movement. The scrape of a chair. Water splashing in the basin.

Presently, the sounds ceased. Thin light still seeped beneath the door, proof that her husband had not yet put out his candles.

She crossed the room, her bare feet silent on the carpet. At the door, she paused with her hand against the wood, just long enough to gather her courage. Then she knocked.

The door swung open—too quickly for her husband to have been anywhere but just the other side of it. He had removed his coat and waistcoat. Gone also was his cravat, his shirt loose at the collar.

He took in her silk nightclothes. There was appreciation in his gaze before he brought his eyes to hers. Never before had she appreciated her fine French modiste quite so much.

His dark hair was rumpled, as though he had run his fingers through it, and his eyes, shadowed by the late hour, were the deep blue of the sea at twilight. She was struck by how handsome he appeared, though it was far more than his looks that held her heart.

It was his strength. His selflessness that had led him to offer her freedom even when he wished for more for himself. These were not qualities he proclaimed or paraded. They were simply a part of him.

He opened the door wider, and when he extended his hand, she took it. The press of his large palm against her own was both firm and gentle. He drew her forward, his touch warm and steady and electrifying.

His chamber was lit by a low fire and candles on the bedside table. She looked about her, taking in the space and the small, intimate details of his life: the bed with its linen turned down, his coat draped over the chair by the window, his boots beside the wardrobe. He'd left a book on the table by the bed, and she recalled he preferred tomes on building techniques to novels. The air held the faint scent of his cologne and something else that was simply him.

Entering his room felt like coming home. Not to a place, not to this house, but to a person. To the man who still held her hand, who watched her with an intensity that made her pulse quicken.

She turned to face him fully.

"Rebecca." His voice was low and rough as he lifted a hand to her cheek. She leaned into his touch, feeling the line of his thumb along her jaw.

She placed her own hand against his chest. Through the fine linen came the steady beat of his heart.

He lowered his head, his kiss certain and unhurried. His lips were smooth against hers, his breastbone firm beneath her touch. There was no hesitation in him, and she responded in kind. Her fingers curled into the fabric of his shirt, drawing him closer.

It struck her sharply that they had a lifetime ahead for this: mornings and evenings, quiet conversations and shared silences, touches and kisses. A lifetime to learn one another, to build something that was theirs alone. A lifetime to make a family, perhaps.

His hand settled at her hip, deliciously warm and insistent, pulling her still closer. With his foot, he eased the door closed behind them. The latch clicked softly as he bent for another kiss.

EPILOGUE

OAK HILL, CHRISTMAS EVE

"A BIT HIGHER on the left." Rebecca complied with Anna's direction, and Jory's wife stepped back to consider the mantelpiece. The great hall at Oak Hill smelled of fir, and beyond the windows, the winter afternoon was already softening toward evening. A sharp draught carried the chill of December through the stone hall as male voices and laughter rose from deeper in the house, punctuated by the occasional bark from one of the dogs.

For several days, the Kimbrell ladies had been at work, arranging greenery throughout the hall. Now they put the finishing touches on the decorations as the gentlemen prepared to fetch the Yule log. Wynne and Kate strung the last of the berry garlands, while Mari and Eliza pressed cloves into oranges that would scent Oak Hill's rooms for the season.

Anna nodded her approval, and Rebecca stepped down from her ladder.

"Anna has a fine eye for such things," Keren observed from the sideboard where she fussed with a bit of ivy. "Your decorations look very festive, though I cannot say the same for this poor display."

Bronwyn shifted on the settee, drawing her shawl more tightly about the swell beneath her dress. Her confinement was imminent. "What sort of decorations were you accustomed to having in Paris?" she asked. "I imagine they must have been very elegant."

Rebecca considered. "They were beautiful, certainly. My aunt favors gilt ornaments and French ribbon work. Everything is very fashionable, although it's been some time since I've had a hand in it. My aunt's servants manage it all."

There was a moment of silence before Wynne, who'd been threading tiny holly berries onto a string this last hour, murmured. "You poor dear." Then she promptly passed the berries to Rebecca.

"Indeed," Rebecca said wryly as she accepted the bowl.

Glancing around at the cheerful chaos, Rebecca couldn't deny that Oak Hill was a festive place with nearly all the Kimbrells in attendance. Even Merryn's cousin Ben, who'd been away in London these last months, had returned with his wife Kate for the holiday.

Only Sarah was missing. Rebecca's companion had departed for Taunton in October, having earned enough from her investment in Newford's improvements to set up a neat cottage near her sister as she'd always wanted. Rebecca missed her steady presence at times, and she would always be grateful for her aunt in Paris. But here, among the Kimbrells, she had found the life where she belonged — surrounded by people whose warmth and care made a home of every ordinary moment.

Underfoot, the youngest Kimbrells raced about. Leo, Wynne's lad from the Feather, had claimed a length of ribbon, trailing it behind him like a banner and delighting Anna's toddling daughter Tamsyn, who gave a gleeful chase.

Rebecca's attention went to the center of the hall, where she'd been watching her mother-in-law with some amusement the past hour. Mrs. Kimbrell was not ordinarily given to fussing, but she had adjusted the same arrangement of ivy no fewer than three times. Now she stood beneath the kissing bough, tweaking the ribbons with a distracted energy.

"Mama," Bronwyn called out, "if you pull at those ribbons any harder, you shall have them off entirely."

Mrs. Kimbrell startled and dropped her hands. "I was merely ensuring they drape properly."

"They have draped properly since Tuesday."

The older woman pressed her lips together, but her eyes were bright, and a flush had risen in her cheeks. She looked, Rebecca thought, rather like a kettle on the verge of boiling. Rebecca could hardly fault her, for the news they both carried was precisely the sort that demanded release, though Merryn would not like the fuss.

Rebecca went to her mother-in-law. Reaching up, she twitched one of the ribbons back into place. "You've done an admirable job holding your tongue," she whispered.

Mrs. Kimbrell's expression turned rueful. "Am I so obvious?"

"Only to another who must keep the same secret." She gave the ribbon a final twitch. "Though I confess, I'm not certain how much longer you can manage it. You've rearranged the ivy above the mirror three times in the past hour alone."

"Three? Surely not—" Mrs. Kimbrell caught herself and laughed. "Very well. Perhaps I do not appear as indifferent as I would like to believe."

"Merryn will share his news when he is ready," Rebecca said gently. "You know how he is about such things."

"Too modest by half. But this is his *family*. 'Tisn't

as if I expect him to post an announcement in Eliza's newspaper."

Rebecca patted her hand. "Of course not."

Mrs. Kimbrell sighed. "But you're right, of course. I shall endeavor to contain myself, though I make no promises. A mother has her limits."

Rebecca smiled. "I would expect nothing less."

Her mother-in-law squeezed her fingers before releasing them. "Merryn deserves so much happiness, and now he has it. I am glad you're here." Her words carried weight beyond the day's celebration—a recognition of how far they'd come since their first awkward meeting in Merryn's parlor.

"As am I," Rebecca said.

"What are you whispering about?" Bronwyn said from the settee.

"Nothing," Mrs. Kimbrell replied a little too brightly. Rebecca pressed her lips against a smile, not entirely convinced her mother-in-law could hold her husband's secret.

As Mrs. Kimbrell attacked an arrangement on the pianoforte, Rebecca moved to where a maid had set out a tray of saffron buns on the sideboard. She selected one and bit into it, and the familiar sweetness spread blissfully across her tongue. Of all things Cornish, saffron buns had to be her favorite, and Oak Hill's cook had a particular gift for the things.

"You look well," Eliza said, joining her at the sideboard. "I would dare to say your marriage agrees with you."

"As yours does with you." Rebecca glanced at Eliza's hand resting against her still-flat belly. "You are certain?"

A smile tugged at the other woman's mouth. "Alfie doesn't know yet. I mean to tell him tonight. He will be insufferable with his mothering, of course, but I cannot mind it."

"I am glad for you," Rebecca said. And she was.

In the last months, she had come to count Eliza among her dearest friends. Their shared interests in unconventional pursuits had formed the foundation of their acquaintance, but something deeper had built the rest. In Eliza, she'd found a kindred soul, a woman as at ease with her marriage as she was with her independence. It was the sort of friendship Rebecca had never thought to have, but one she couldn't imagine doing without.

Eliza touched her arm. "With the baby's future to consider, I would like your advice on financial matters once more. I know Alfie has relied on your counsel for the cidery, and I should like us to plan ahead."

"Of course." Rebecca considered. "A modest sum set aside each month would serve you well. By the time the child comes of age, you could have a tidy amount—safe investments, nothing too speculative. The Navy Fives, I should think, would do nicely."

"That is precisely what I hoped you would say." Eliza pressed her arm. "Thank you."

Anna had abandoned the holly on the mantel and was now examining the straw stars in the windows with a critical eye. "Only you two would discuss funds on Christmas Eve," she said, though her tone carried no censure.

Keren laughed. "I wish I understood them half so well as Rebecca does."

"I am content in my ignorance," Anna replied.

"They are not so complicated as gentlemen would have us believe," Rebecca said. "A bit of study is all that's needed—"

A shout of laughter from the terrace cut her words short, and a moment later the doors opened. The men spilled into the room, bringing with them a sweep of wintry air.

At their center, Jory and Gryffyn bore the heavy Yule log between them.

"Make way," Jory called out with a nod toward the cold hearth. "This thing weighs more than it appears. Marsh insisted on the largest tree on the farthest edge of Penhale."

"It needed removing anyway," Bronwyn's husband said.

"'Twould help if you carried your share," Gryffyn said to Jory.

The log was maneuvered into the great hearth amid much discussion of weight and counterweight and the proper "distribution of the load." When it was settled to everyone's satisfaction, Merryn's grandfather came forward, leaning on his cane.

Alan Kimbrell ran his free hand along the bark with a satisfied expression. "'Tis a good Mock," he said, using the old Cornish name. "'Twill burn well through Twelfth Night. We'll light it after dinner."

Some of the older children went to inspect the log as two footmen cleared the carpet of leaves left behind by the men's passage. Rebecca moved aside and Merryn joined her.

His hand found hers, and their fingers tangled. She didn't think she would ever tire of his touch.

"Your mother," she murmured, keeping her voice low. "I believe she will expire soon if she cannot share your news."

Merryn's jaw shifted. "Aye. She nearly blurted it to Parsons when he came round with the sherry. The old man was nearly undone by her enthusiasm. I daresay he suspects she's already been tippling."

Rebecca held a smile. "Do you not think you ought to remove the temptation?"

He rubbed his mouth with a sigh. "Per'aps."

Before he could go on though, a discordant note

was struck on the pianoforte. His mother's face was alight with barely contained excitement as she pressed another chord to gain everyone's attention.

"Mother—" Merryn began.

She spun from the instrument, hands clasped before her. "I cannot bear it another moment." Her voice carried across the room. "I have held my tongue, Merryn, but if I must wait through dinner as well, then I shall go quite mad."

The room fell silent. Even the children paused in their inspection of the log to look up at the commotion.

"Mother," Merryn tried again, but his parent was not to be deterred.

"The King," she announced, "has seen fit to honor my son."

A beat of silence.

"Honor him how?" Bronwyn demanded, struggling upright on the settee.

Mrs. Kimbrell's smile broadened. "Merryn is to have a knighthood. For his service to the Crown and Cornwall during the royal progress."

The room erupted.

Rebecca turned to find her husband's face flushed, his jaw set in that particular way that suggested he wished to be anywhere else. He caught her eye, his expression rueful.

"I did try to warn you," she said.

They were soon surrounded, and James clapped Merryn on the shoulder. "'Tis well earned," he said. "Your father would have been proud."

Gavin offered his hand. Bronwyn extracted herself from the cushions to embrace her brother with the sort of sisterly enthusiasm that threatened to knock him from his feet.

"I shall have to remember to bow," Jory said.

"You shall do no such thing," Merryn said.

"Per'aps only a small genuflection?" Alfie suggested, his eyes dancing. "Just the one knee?"

"Alfie—"

"We shall have to address you properly at dinner. 'Sir Merryn, will you pass the salt?' 'Sir Merryn, might I trouble you for the fish?'"

"If you persist with such foolishness, I will throw the fish at your head."

His threat only broadened Alfie's grin.

"We ought to commission a portrait," Gryffyn said.

Gavin considered this, stroking his chin with mock solemnity. "Aye, Merryn in ceremonial robes. Per'aps astride his horse."

Merryn tossed a scowl at his cousins.

Through it all, Rebecca watched her husband. He bore the teasing with the resignation of a man who knew resistance would be wasted, but beneath his protests, there was a contented expression in his eyes. He had never sought recognition for its own sake, but to be valued by his family, and now to have his work acknowledged—she suspected that mattered to him more than any title.

Presently, his grandfather's cane tapped the floor, and the room quieted. Alan Kimbrell rose from where he'd taken a chair away from the cold windows.

"A toast," he said. A footman appeared with glasses, and soon everyone had wine in hand.

Alan lifted his glass. "To my grandson, whose work has brought honor not only to himself but to the Kimbrell name." He paused and blinked, his eyes bright. "My son Pedrek would have been proud to see *his* son today. Pedrek built his business with honor and integrity, and Merryn has carried that legacy forward with distinction." His voice roughened. "And your grandmother, God rest her, would have delighted to see the family prospering so, and serving Newford as we do."

Merryn had grown rather stiff at so much praise, but he yielded enough to nod at his grandfather.

"A knighthood is a fine thing," Alan continued. "But I have always known my grandson's worth is not in titles or honors. 'Tis in the buildings that will stand for a hundred years or more. In the families his work provides for. In the wife at his side and the future they will build together." He raised his glass higher. "To Merryn. And to Rebecca. And to all the years and all the Kimbrells ahead."

As the room echoed Alan Kimbrell's toast, Alfie gestured broadly at the infants across the room then at Bronwyn's enormous belly. "I'd say the next generation is well on its way, Grandfather."

Amid the laughter that followed, Rebecca met Eliza's gaze across the room, and they shared a private look of amusement. The other woman hid a smile as her husband, oblivious to his wife's secret, raised his glass with cheerful enthusiasm. "To many more Kimbrells to come," he declared.

Before the toast had ended, Bronwyn cornered her brother again, this time to demand details. When had he learned of the honor? Why had he not told her immediately? Did he realize the matrons would make quite a fuss at the next assembly?

"I thought to say something of't in the new year," Merryn said, casting a wry look at their mother. "I had hoped for a quieter Christmas."

Mrs. Kimbrell had the grace to look slightly abashed, though not enough to dim her smile.

Parsons appeared in the doorway to announce dinner. As the company began drifting toward the dining room, Rebecca felt the gentle pressure of Merryn's hand at the small of her back. He guided her not toward the door but toward the center of the room, where the kissing bough hung from the chandelier in its bower of ribbons and greenery.

The noise of the gathering faded as he drew her beneath it. Through the windows, the winter sky had deepened to indigo.

"Your mother stood longer than I expected," Rebecca said. "You should count it a victory."

His mouth curved. "A hollow one, per'aps."

She studied his face—the strong line of his nose, the deep blue eyes that had first caught her attention in London.

"Sir Merryn Kimbrell," she said, testing the sound of it. "It suits you."

"I would rather be simply Merryn Kimbrell. Husband. Builder." He paused. "Father, per'aps."

Heat stole up her neck, for they'd done their level best to bring *that* about. And, if her suspicions were correct, she would have her own secret to share with him soon. But for now, she said only, "I should like that."

His hand rose to cup her cheek, his palm warm against her skin. Beyond them, the family gathered in the dining room. She could hear Bronwyn's laughter, and Alfie's teasing voice, and the babble of children eager for their Christmas pudding.

This was what she had gained by staying. Not just a husband, but a family. Not just a home, but a place where she belonged.

"The knighthood," she said. "It truly does not matter to you?"

"It matters." He was honest, as he always was. "But not as much as them." He gestured toward the door where his family waited. "And you."

She smiled. "Now that you have me, you shall not be rid of me."

"I shall deal," he said with a wry twist of his mouth before his expression turned serious. "I would have you every day, for all the days we are given."

And then he kissed her beneath the kissing bough as the Christmas stars began to show themselves through the windows.

When he drew back, his eyes held hers. "Happy Christmas, Rebecca."

She smiled and tucked her hand through his arm. "Happy Christmas, husband."

THE END

A MUSICAL LOVE LETTER TO NEWFORD

I hope you've enjoyed this series! Writers are notorious for finding creative ways to procrastinate, so when the idea for a song around the cousins' husband lessons popped into my head, I was only too happy to follow it down a musical rabbit trail.

The result: a playlist of three original songs inspired by *Regarding Rebecca*. Subscribe to hear them all at klynsmithauthor.com:

- *Five Years Gone* – Merryn's dark country ballad
- *On My Terms* – Rebecca's bluesy anthem of independence and love
- *Husband Lessons* – The cousins as you've never heard them before (sea shanty edition!)

The Kimbrells have found a special corner of my heart, and as we close the book on the Hearts of Cornwall series, this musical tribute is my love letter to Newford—a celebration of family, laughter, and the bonds that made these books such a joy to write.

Subscribers receive access to exclusive bonus content like this, insight into my research and writing process, and early updates on new releases. I hope you'll join us!

Dha weles hwath—goodbye until later,

K. Lyn

AUTHOR'S NOTE

This book sent me down some delightful research rabbit holes. Below are a handful of historical notes and small inspirations that shaped the story—and a few Easter eggs for those who've followed the Kimbrells from the beginning.

SPOILERS AHEAD

Ladies & Wealth. The Regency era was a surprisingly sophisticated age of investment in ways that often escape our modern assumptions—particularly where women were concerned.

I was surprised to learn how much early industry was financed by women's investments. In one Essex village, for example, the vestry raised funds to build a school by selling annuities—fully one-third of which were purchased by women.

Jane Austen herself invested the proceeds of her novels in the "Navy Fives," government annuities that provided a steady income.

Most women investors were unmarried or widowed, as married women faced the added difficulty of preserving both their own social standing and that of their families. As a result, those who did invest often did so quietly, and at a distance.

George IV & Queen Caroline. George IV's coronation was shaped as much by personal scandal as by politics. His marriage to Caroline of Brunswick had long since collapsed into mutual hostility, and by the time he ascended the throne in 1820, she had been living abroad for some years. He was determined to exclude her from all royal ceremony. The months that followed were marked by parliamentary inquiries into the King's attempt to dissolve the marriage, political maneuvering, and popular sympathy for Caroline, all of which delayed preparations and heightened scrutiny of the King's conduct. By the time the coronation finally took place in 1821, it was as much an assertion of royal authority as a spectacle.

George IV's Royal Passage. Following the coronation, George IV undertook a series of public appearances and progresses intended to reassert the dignity and visibility of the Crown. Such royal passages were carefully orchestrated events, combining civic pride, local improvement, and political display. Towns selected for a royal visit invested heavily in temporary structures, decorations, and entertainments, seeing the King's presence as both an honor and an opportunity—one that could elevate local reputations and secure future favor long after the royal party had departed. Newford, of course, lives only in my head, but I imagine George IV would have seen in it a small reflection of England itself—steadfast, industrious, and deeply rooted in home and kin.

Jilting Jory Symmetry. I love symmetry, so knowing this was to be the last book in this series, I wanted to include a nod to the first. In *Jilting Jory*, when Anna first arrives at the Fin and Feather Inn, Wynne leaps to the mistaken assumption that she and Jory are secretly married. I loved turning that on its head for this story by having Merryn and Rebecca *actually* secretly married, although Wynne (and the rest of the Kimbrell clan) have no clue.

Mrs. Matthews. The widow Bronwyn mentions in Chapter 6 ("I thought the widow who came through last year might have succeeded where others have failed") was Mrs. Matthews from *Kissing Kate*.

This is a perfect example of how authors can paint themselves into sticky corners: *Kissing Kate* was originally supposed to pair Kate Parker with Merryn, not Ben. Their chemistry wasn't right, though, so then I thought I would set Merryn up with a widow.

When I finally got to his story, though, too much time had passed in Newford to resurrect Mrs. Matthews. Alas.

Room Twelve. Rebecca's room at the Feather was the same room Anna enjoyed in *Jilting Jory* (her second, much improved room) as well as Mrs. Kingsley's room in *Saving Miss Swan*. A lot has happened in room 12!

Mood Board. I create a mood board of the visual references I use when writing. If you would like to see my inspiration for Merryn, Rebecca and Newford, be sure to check out my Pinterest board at https://www.pinterest.com/klynsmithauthor/regarding-rebecca/.

BOOKS BY K. LYN SMITH

Something Wonderful
The Astronomer's Obsession
The Artist's Redemption
The Physician's Dilemma

Hearts of Cornwall
Discovering Wynne (Prequel Novella)
Jilting Jory
Matching Miss Moon
Driving Miss Darling
Kissing Kate
Saving Miss Swan
Charming the Captain
Engaging Miss Enderby*
Regarding Rebecca

Love's Journey
Star of Wonder
Light of a Nile Moon
Stars of Twilight Fair
Beneath a Brighton Sun

* Cadan's story appears in the
Hearts in Bloom Regency Anthology.
Visit klynsmithauthor.com for the most
up-to-date list of titles.

ABOUT THE AUTHOR

K. Lyn Smith writes sweet historical romance about ordinary people finding extraordinary love. Her debut novel, The Astronomer's Obsession, was a finalist for the National Excellence in Romantic Fiction Award, and many of her other titles have been shortlisted for honors such as the American Writing Award, the Carolyn Reader's Choice Award, the HOLT Medallion and the Maggie Award.

When she's not lost in the pages of a book, you can find her with family, traveling to far-off places and binging period dramas. And space documentaries. Weird, right?

Visit www.klynsmithauthor.com, where you can subscribe for new release updates and access to exclusive bonus content.

www.ingramcontent.com/pod-product-compliance
Lightning Source LLC
LaVergne TN
LVHW091657070526
838199LV00050B/2185